# Praise for
# Jenny Colgan

"She is very, very funny."
—*Express*

"A delicious comedy."
—*Red*

"Fast-paced, funny, poignant and well-observed."
—*Daily Mail*

"Had us eating up every page."
—*Cosmopolitan*

"A smart, funny story laced with irresistible charm."
—*Closer*

"Chick-lit with an ethical kick."
—*Mirror*

"Full of laugh-out-loud observations . . .
utterly unputdownable."
—*Woman*

"A chick-lit writer with a difference . . . never scared to
try something different, Colgan always pulls it off."
—*Image*

"A Colgan novel is like listening to your best pal,
souped up on vino, spilling the latest gossip—
entertaining, dramatic and frequently hilarious."
—*Daily Record*

# WEST END GIRLS

# WEST END GIRLS

*A Novel*

# Jenny Colgan

**WILLIAM MORROW**
*An Imprint of* HarperCollins*Publishers*

WEST END GIRLS. Copyright © 2006 by Jenny Colgan. All rights reserved. Printed in the United States of America. No part of this book may be used or reproduced in any manner whatsoever without written permission except in the case of brief quotations embodied in critical articles and reviews. For information, address HarperCollins Publishers, 195 Broadway, New York, NY 10007.

HarperCollins books may be purchased for educational, business, or sales promotional use. For information, please email the Special Markets Department at SPsales@harpercollins.com.

Originally published as *West End Girls* in the United Kingdom in 2006 by Time Warner Books.

FIRST U.S. EDITION

Library of Congress Cataloging-in-Publication Data has been applied for.

ISBN 978-0-06-286962-3

21 22 23 24 25   LSC   10 9 8 7 6 5 4 3 2 1

In memory of my beloved papa,
who taught me how to swear

# WEST END GIRLS

## Chapter One

Lizzie squinted at the old LED alarm clock she'd had since she was at school. 03:39. She had to get up in three and a half hours, which was a slightly comforting thought in itself—that was *ages* away, so that wasn't why she'd woken with a start.

There was a stumbling noise. Lizzie's heart stopped. Someone was in the room. Someone was definitely there. It was a burglar. A murdering, raping burglar. There were loads of them around here, everyone knew it. God, if only she kept a gun under her bed. She had never seen, touched, or learned how to work a real gun, and disagreed with them in principle, but . . . she wanted a gun, goddamn it!

"Oh, *tittin'* hell," came a familiar voice.

Penny. Lizzie's longing for a gun lasted for a couple of seconds longer than it ought to have.

In drunkenness, Lizzie noticed, and at 3:39 in the morning, Penny's Essex accent rang out even stronger than usual.

"What the *effin' eff* was that?"

Lizzie sat upright and turned on the bedside light, from which Penny recoiled, hissing crossly.

"*That* is my shoe," said Lizzie, trying not to shout and so wake their mother down the hall, although the walls were so thin she could hear her snoring from here.

"What's it doing in my bloody room?" Penny squinted. "And what are you doing in my bloody bed?"

For a second, Lizzie double-checked just in case it *was* Penny's room. "This is my room, you idiot."

Penny looked dumbfounded. "I know my own bloody room."

"You'd think."

Penny looked around her. "Oh. Bugger it."

Lizzie sat up. "It doesn't matter," she said. "I'm awake now."

This room had belonged to both of them when they'd had to share and their mother had had Sarcastic Alex, the lodger. When he'd moved out Penny had taken the smaller room, claiming it didn't matter, she'd be moving out practically any day to get married and live in London and only occasionally come to visit them in a really big car. Well, that was six years ago now, and it was the last unselfish act on her part Lizzie could remember.

"How was it?" said Lizzie, passing Penny her water glass. She could feel the waistband of her pajamas dig in as she did so. Oh, God. She wasn't going up another size, she absolutely wasn't, 16 was bad enough, 18, no way.

"What time is it?" said Penny, ignoring her question.

"It's an inbetween-y kind of time: between a good night out and a really, really bad one. So?"

Penny took a long gulp of water, then shrugged. "Hmm."

"Terrible?"

"Hmm."

"Did he lavish you with compliments and jewels?"

"Hmm," said Penny, squinting at the water glass. "You know, I'm beginning to wonder if this lavishing-with-jewels type really exists."

"My God," said Lizzie. "You can't stop searching now. That'd be like a nun renouncing Jesus on her deathbed."

"Shut up," said Penny.

There was a break in the snoring from down the hall.

"You shut up," said Lizzie. "And go to bed."

Penny sighed theatrically. "We *did* go to Gordon Ramsay's restaurant. He wasn't there though."

"That's good. That's very good. I'm very pleased for you. I thought restaurants shut at twelve, but we'll just draw a veil over that."

"And he spent the entire time complaining about the cost of his divorce. And the chateaubriand, as it happens."

"I don't know what that is," said Lizzie.

"Never mind, darling," said Penny patronizingly.

Don't think about the gun, thought Lizzie. "What is it then?"

Penny sniffed.

"So? What have you been doing? Taking cocktails at the Ritz? Dancing under umbrellas in the rain? Ice skating in Central Park?"

"Night bus."

Lizzie winced in sympathy. "Who'd you get?"

"One bung-eye, three general lunatics, and one wanker."

"Only one wanker on a night bus? That sounds amazing. There's usually hordes of them putting traffic cones on their heads."

"No, just one literal wanker. One man having a wank. There were thirty-five with traffic cones on their heads."

Lizzie tutted.

"And I had to change at Seven Sisters."

"Seven Sisters is far too *dangerous* for girls! What kind of man is he?"

"*Not* one who sends a nice girl home in a cab."

"What about a slightly sluttish girl?"

"Shut up."

"Get out of my bedroom then."

Penny heaved a big sigh. "Oh, it's *so* boring."

"Going to the Ritz for cocktails and out to fancy dinner. Well, it does sound boring. Mum and I watched *Property Ladder* and ate potato waffles."

"I had to hear about his terrible divorce and how that witch kept the house and how he's terrified of gold diggers getting hold of what's left of his money and did I mind getting my half of the bill."

Lizzie flinched. This was not something, she knew from previous vicarious evenings, that could be tolerated. Although Penny's minimum-wage waitress job was supposedly supplemented by tips, in reality her attitude, and the fact that a lot of men tried to ask her out, failed, and got aggressive, made the tip-giving side of things fairly erratic.

"Oh, my God! What did you do?"

Penny glanced in the mirror above the cheap dresser crammed in the corner of the tiny room. Despite the hour, Lizzie noticed, she still looked wonderful—her makeup had dribbled down under her eyes, but she looked sexy and a bit dangerous, not like Lizzie would: fat and a bit dirty.

4

"Legged it out the bathroom window."

"You *didn't*."

"No, of course I didn't, you idiot." She paused. "I told him I'd forgotten my purse."

"That's all right then."

"I'd have legged it out the bathroom window *next* though."

Penny rubbed her pretty face blearily. "Anyway it went a bit downhill after that."

Lizzie tried to smile sympathetically—she was going to have to listen anyway—but this wasn't exactly the first time she'd been woken up in the early hours. Penny was a cad magnet, but, as she pointed out (none too kindly), she was the only one with a hope in hell of getting them out of this shithole.

"Go to bed," said Lizzie.

"I mean, I didn't know the bloody brandy was a hundred quid a glass, did I?"

"No," said Lizzie calmly.

"I'm not the one saying, 'Hey, how's about a brandy?' while eyeing up my fishnets." She glanced down. There was a huge ladder up the left leg. "Shit. Shit, shit, shit."

"Say it's punk."

"'How's about a brandy? Chilled? You know, my ex-wife was really chilly in bed. Makes a man feel, you know . . . so lonely.'"

"Lonely and poor."

"Poor my arse," said Penny dramatically. "My three ninety-nine ripped tights cause me a lot more pain than spending bloody six hundred pounds on bloody brandy does him."

"*Six hundred pounds*," said Lizzie. How on earth could people do something like that? Lizzie lived as she ate: hand to mouth.

"Should have read the menu, the dick, instead of yelping 'Two glasses of your finest brandy' over and over again. No wonder the waiter was smiling."

"Did he tip?"

"Did he fuck. They were still screaming at each other when I ran out of the door."

"Finish the water," said Lizzie. It might not get Penny to work on time, but it might get her to work.

Penny took a long slug. "Ah," she said. "Like finest brandy on my lips."

"You're a bad, bad girl," said Lizzie. "Go to bed or I'm telling Mum."

Six hundred pounds kept running through Lizzie's head the next morning as she made her way to the bus stop. Six hundred pounds. That was unbelievable. Who could, did, spend money like that? Even by accident. Penny was still in bed; she didn't start her job, as Brandford's most glamorous and also grumpiest waitress, until later.

Nonidentical twins can have a head start on the knowledge, usually learned by children through a procession of tedious and time-consuming upsets, that life isn't always fair.

"Twins? *Really?*"

That was one of Lizzie's earliest memories; people disbelieving their mother as to their provenance. Along with, "Look at the size of you!" and, Lizzie's personal favorite, "So, is Lizzie *terribly* clever, then?"

Being dressed alike only made matters worse, so they both started having tantrums about it from as early an age as possible. After all, it wasn't Lizzie's fault that she stayed short and plump while Penny shot up. It might have been her fault that while

Penny made sure her dolls were immaculately dressed for their tea party, Lizzie scoffed all the scones. And while Penny smiled politely and learned to simper at adults from an early age, in case they had a spare pound coin in their pockets, Lizzie preferred to stay in the background before anyone had the chance to say, "Good eater, are we?"

"They're so different, aren't they?" their mother's friends would say, smiling meanly in a very unconvincing fashion.

"Out! Out! Out!" Lizzie would say to herself quietly in the kitchen. "Goodbye, visitors, time to go!" And once they'd gone, her mum would come in and give her a special hug and a biscuit, just for her plain little daughter.

And here the twins still were, twenty-seven years old and in the same tiny council house in Parkend Close, Brandford. Lizzie sometimes felt as if there should be a bus to take them off to real life, but if there ever was she knew she'd miss it, staying indoors and reading *TV Quick*.

Maybe the bus *had* come, she thought occasionally, as she spent yet another Friday night sharing a big box of Celebrations with her work friend Grainne and her mother in front of *Easties*, while Penny was off, weighed down by lip gloss, in borderline dangerous nightclubs, chatting up prosperous idiots who left their expensive shirts untucked and reeked of Hugo Boss. Maybe their dad had caught it instead.

Penny woke at eleven, screwed up her eyes, and groaned. OK. Another day, another minimum wage. That stupid bloody man from last night. She thought for a second and realized she could only just remember his name, and that it would probably be gone in a couple of days. Excellent.

She blinked in the cheap bathroom mirror. The whole place needed grouting, it was incredibly dingy. But their mother worked far too hard, Lizzie inexplicably was refusing to do it by herself, and Penny had paid a lot of money for these nails so she couldn't be expected to under the circumstances. They seemed to have reached something of an impasse.

She threw on her Tesco ultra-skinny jeans and diamanté top, and got to work on her makeup. OK, she was only going to work, but you didn't know who you were going to meet on the way, and by the time she'd changed into her uniform she'd look so awful anyway she'd be lucky to get a second glance from anyone half decent.

Penny rarely dwelled on her genetic luck, seeing it mostly as a means to an end, and preferring instead to wonder if she should get her boobs done and whether it really was worth applying for one of those loans she saw on television. So far, Lizzie's shocked expression had just about held her off, but if she had bigger knockers she'd definitely pull a better class of bloke, and would be able to pay it back anyway. But even in her work uniform she stood out. Pale hair—when she didn't go overboard with the highlighter, which she usually did—glowed over a small, heart-shaped face with a high forehead and full lips. Her eyes were long, like a cat's, which she made even longer with liberal amounts of eyeliner in daily changing shades, and she had the figure that only comes to someone who has spent too much time watching what really goes on at a deep-fat fryer.

Lizzie accused her occasionally of anorexia, but it was pretty much sour grapes. Penny knew she had to be thin—preferably with big knockers—and didn't think about food terribly often, unlike Lizzie, who turned to the biscuit barrel in times of joy, sadness, stress, tiredness, boredom, and random television.

Penny hated Brandford. She hated its estates, its graffiti. The underpass, the horrid cheap corner shops with plastic mop buckets, and cheap sweets being guzzled by fat grubby babies. She hated the stoved-in cars, the fact that practically her entire class had gotten pregnant at sixteen. She didn't feel like she was made for this. Was it so wrong to want more? Really? Just a nice car? Clothes that didn't come from a supermarket? So, school hadn't worked out so well. It was a shit school. There was nothing wrong with liking nice things, was there? Even—Penny bit her lip as she applied the white layer of her mascara—someone to fall in love with one day, though she'd never have admitted that to Lizzie in a million years. Lizzie was such a drip when it came to romance, and everything else. She'd seen *Dirty Dancing* nine million times, snottering into her extra-large popcorn all the while. Penny and her friends had scoffed. Penny's favorite film was *Pretty Woman*, closely followed by *The Thomas Crown Affair*.

Penny took the bus—God, she hated the bus—out to the junction of the motorway where the big shops were, at the entrance to London and the M11. In the vast fields of hypermarkets and massive, elongated versions of ordinary high street shops, there were mega-restaurants, huge places seating hundreds for birthday parties, hen nights, reunions, and kiddies' parties. Penny's was called the All-American New York Diner. There was a bucking bronco at the back, where girls would get on and shimmy their bosoms, and men would pretend they were having a laugh while taking it all incredibly seriously; the food was entirely brown and came in huge portions, and the cocktails were gigantic and sticky.

Penny hated it, but it had one major advantage: everyone went there eventually. Whether a works' night out, or a divorcing couple meeting for a child handover, all sorts of people ended up prodding uselessly at the Death by Chocolate with triple-brownie fudge ice cream and chocolate sauce supreme. And she could spot them a mile away; they'd look slightly perturbed about walking in, wouldn't know what to do with the sparklers in their drink, ask if she had fizzy water or salad ("There's our bacon-bit surprise, sir," she would say insouciantly), and she'd check out their shoes, or their watch, then play the comely wench a bit more. There weren't many well-off single men in Brandford—one or two footballers in nearby Saffron Walden, but the competition for them tended to be intense and exhausting—but serving four hundred covers a night very often yielded results, as well as occasionally spectacular tips, which made Lizzie green, particularly as she had an indoor job, in an office and everything.

"I'm off," shouted Penny, heading for the door. Her mother was at home again today. She'd been having horrible problems with her varicose veins—standing up doling out big scoops of cabbage, and nowadays chicken twizzlers, to ungrateful schoolchildren for nearly thirty years had pretty much done for her legs. Making it through to Friday tended to be a bit on the tricky side.

"Penny?" shouted her mother as Penny slunk past the sitting-room door. Fat and florid, she lay with her feet higher than her head, and an enormous flask of tea—made by Lizzie—by her side. "Where were you last night?"

"Why?" said Penny sulkily. For goodness' sake, she was

twenty-seven, not fourteen. "I went to Paris to visit Kylie Minogue."

"Well, could you let me know when you're going to be so late? I worry about you, you know."

"Well, you should stop, I pay housekeeping, don't I?"

"Not very bloody much," said her mother. "Wouldn't keep a mouse in cheese."

Penny rolled her eyes. "I'm running my own life, OK?"

"Just a bit of consideration, darling. That's all I ask for."

Penny heaved a sigh. She and her mother had been having this argument for ten years. "What are you watching?"

"The 1979 RSC *Macbeth*," said her mum. "Ian McKellen and Judi Dench. One of the best ever."

"Right. God, that crap is so boring. Do you want me to bring you back some salad?"

Her mother's face brightened. "Oh, go on then, sweetheart. And what about some potato wedges? And some of the fried chicken?"

"Mum! It's horrible! I've told you where it's from! It's not even all real chicken! And the doctor told you to lose weight."

"I know," said her mother, looking slightly ashamed. "But it tastes so good."

Penny tutted, and left the house.

Lizzie marched into work in an even worse mood than usual for a wet Thursday morning.

Stamp importing wasn't quite what she'd had in mind when, after a school career of almost total mediocrity spent entirely in the shadow of her misbehaving sibling, she'd landed a proper office job in Brandford—and she hadn't planned to be there for ten years either, but it was undemanding as jobs go—processing stamp orders from overseas. She'd made a friend, Grainne, who controlled reception and the import desk.

Grainne's hobbies were cats and crisps. It was an undemanding friendship. But it was nice, for once, not to be the shy one, especially when she'd been the one with a boyfriend for a change too. Felix had been tall and slim and handsome, and Lizzie couldn't believe her luck when she pulled him at an awful party Penny had dragged her to one night. It had taken her six months to realize he was actually as dumb as a stone box full of rocks. Lizzie had thought he was just amenable. His constant mumbled "Whatever you like" to films, TV, and sex had eventually grown tiring, even for Lizzie, for whom the novelty of a real live boyfriend was something that took a while to wear off. And she missed having something to talk to Grainne about; now they were back to pussies and Pringles.

"Nice evening?" said Grainne as she walked in.

"Uh, yeah."

"Why haven't you washed your hair? Were you out with a new man?" Grainne lived in fear of Lizzie getting a boyfriend and leaving her.

Lizzie slung her bag in the corner of her desk. It had taken her ages to get back to sleep again when Penny had bowled off to bed, and she felt fuzzy and out of focus.

"No," said Lizzie. "How's your cat? Bought her any new outfits?"

"Miss Friss is fine, thanks," said Grainne. "And she likes getting herself dressed up, don't you, sweetie?" She was addressing this to one of the photos.

"Are you sure it isn't a bit cruel to put animals in hats?"

"Oh, I think they're adorable," said Grainne. "And Miss Friss loves her little bonnet. She told me."

The reception phone rang.

"That's her now," said Lizzie. "All the mice are laughing at her and she wants to know what to do." On seeing Grainne's face she immediately regretted it.

"Actually, it's Mr. Boakle," said Grainne. "He wants to see you."

Lizzie flinched. Why was the boss asking to see her? She had a horror of getting into trouble; she'd spent so much time trailing after Penny into the headteacher's office. "You've got to look after your sister." She could hear her mother's voice again. "We're all she's got."

Lizzie sidled into the back office, which was dark, chilly, and piled up with files of colorful stamp samples from around the world.

Mr. Boakle looked at her. "Ah. Yes. Ah, Lizzie, isn't it?"

Given that she'd worked there for ten years, maybe it would have been nice if he occasionally remembered her name. No matter. She blushed anyway. Lizzie hated her tendency to blush, especially at times like this when really someone else should be embarrassed, surely.

"Take a seat. You may have noticed that it's been pretty quiet around here recently."

"Uh." Actually, it always seemed quiet, but now she thought about it, yes, for the past few months Grainne really had been spending a lot of time knitting Miss Friss a Santa Claws outfit.

"People just aren't using too many stamps anymore," said Mr. Boakle sadly. "So they don't collect them, see. There's some new invention—can't quite figure it out myself—called EU mail."

"EU mail?"

"Yes, you know. Something to do with joining the Common Market, probably."

"You mean email," Lizzie ventured. "The thing that's been around for years."

"Something like that. Anyway, whatever the bloody thing is called, it's cutting down on people writing letters something terrible. Sounds like a dreadful thing."

"How it works is, you type in a letter, then you send it for free and the other person receives it instantaneously. For free," said Lizzie.

Mr. Boakle paused. "*Really?* That sounds fantastic."

"It is," said Lizzie.

"Hmm," said Mr. Boakle. "Hmm. That's not good at all. Do you get many letters?"

"Do council tax summonses count?"

"Those damned franking machines," said Mr. Boakle, his face going red. "Worst invention ever."

"Until email," said Lizzie meekly.

"Well. Anyway, that doesn't matter because frankly the world of post has gone to hell in a handbasket and as a result I've got to lose a member of staff."

Lizzie suddenly had a horrible vision of herself in a dinner ladies' uniform and closed her eyes tightly to get rid of it. She couldn't lose this job. Please no.

"Oh, please," she said. She'd always thought being quiet and dependable, they wouldn't mind her staying there . . . but now. What would she do? Well, she hadn't thought that far ahead. But she couldn't do what Penny did, shouting at drunks and hollering across hen parties asking who'd ordered the double portion of ribs. But without any qualifications . . .

"Elizabeth," said Mr. Boakle. Briefly, Lizzie felt like she was in *The Apprentice* and wondered if he was going to point a big finger at her like Alan Sugar did, and growl, "You're FIRED!" like a big grizzly bear, but he didn't.

"I'm going to have to let you go. I'm really, really sorry."

"But . . . but . . ."

"You're young," said Mr. Boakle. "There's a big wide world out there. You should go and see some of it."

"And how would I pay for that?" said Lizzie, feeling a huge lump in her throat.

Back in Brandford, their mother groaned a little and lifted up her legs again. They really were killing her. Oh well. She thought about her girls. She worried about them so much, she really did. Penny was out and about all over the place, never stopping, never eating a proper meal, and she didn't even want to think about the kind of people she was hanging out with. Penny reminded her so much of Stephen it wasn't funny. She was her father's daughter all right.

And Lizzie was quite the opposite, seemed entirely happy to spend the evening with her old mum, eating choccy and catching up on the soaps. That didn't seem right either. She'd wanted so much . . . well, wanting didn't help anything, did it? It felt like such a long time ago, before she'd had them, when she'd met Stephen and everything had felt exciting and full of promise, and she'd been a young girl about town. He'd been so handsome and different from the boys she'd known at school. She'd grown up in

Brandford, and headed to London as soon as she could, finding a job in Chelsea Girl, sharing a tiny, freezing flat in Bermondsey with four other girls. She'd loved it. They'd all shared clothes and spent all their money going up to town and having a laugh. She'd even had dreams of taking up acting. Best time of her life.

And Stephen. He'd swept her off her feet without a second thought. And she'd fallen for it too, completely. Upmarket boy like him, bit of Essex trash like her. Why had she thought it could work? But she'd thought it would be fine, that love would pull them through.

She remembered, after five whirlwind months, the mixture of terror and excitement she'd felt on finding herself in the pudding club. Her mother would have a fit. But he'd do the right thing—Stephen Willis was a proper, well-brought-up boy, not like the drunken wife beaters from around her area. She hadn't known it was bab*ies* then, not till the doctor said he thought he heard two heartbeats.

In a pub in Chelsea, on a really lovely sunny autumn day, around the corner from his mum's cluttered flat, he'd had a port and lemon (she was paying), and she'd had a Bacardi and lime (they weren't so hot on not drinking during pregnancy in those days), and she'd broken the news. He'd just stared into his glass.

"Darling," he'd said. "You daft cow. You stupid cow. That's no good, is it?"

And his handsome face—Penny looked just like him—had twisted up into a mean look, and his eyes had turned cold on her, just like that.

She'd managed, of course. Well, she'd had to. Oh, the neighbors had been awful; that Eilish Berry, thinking she was better than them, taking herself off to London, and back less than a year later with a bun in the oven. Two buns, actually. Her mother had been furious to begin with, and softened, inevitably, when the babies came. They'd got their own council house and they'd all been there ever since, even though the estate just got worse and worse. She'd liked working at the school when the girls were little, she could walk there with them and home again at night and be off at holiday times. Until they got to about ten, of course, when Penny disowned her completely through embarrassment, which she didn't seem to have shaken off now, seventeen years later. Eilish sighed.

She hadn't seen Stephen much after that; he'd practically disappeared off the radar altogether. His mother, though, had tried—sent her some money and some ludicrously impractical knitted outfits, itchy and full of buttons. She'd taken the girls over there a few times when they were small, but Stephen's mother's place was a terrible mess, a huge old apartment in Chelsea that she'd filled with junk since his father had died. Mrs. Willis was a bit like one of these shut-ins, with piles of newspapers all over the place. It wasn't hygienic, and it took four hours to get there and back and the girls screamed so hard that, after a while, they just stopped and got on with their own lives. She'd watched the girls. It wasn't as if having no dad was particularly unusual in their part of the world. He'd visited for a while, every now and again, turning up with toys. Whenever he left, Lizzie would sit by the doorway for the next two days in case he came back. Penny would bite everyone in their nursery. She didn't think they'd remember; they were three when he stopped.

Then they'd seemed all right, until they'd hit their teens. Lizzie had gained puppy fat she couldn't grow out of. She never mentioned it, just gradually became more and more introverted till now, in her twenties, she barely went out at all. There'd been hardly any boyfriends—that last chap was a plank of wood—but she seemed happy to sit at home and watch life pass her by.

Penny on the other hand turned wild. She couldn't get out of the house fast enough, up to all sorts of trouble. She'd done her best, thought Eilish. She'd tried to get Lizzie to be more sociable, while at the same time keep Penny in check. Forcing them together only made Lizzie more painfully shy and Penny more outrageous than ever, but she was glad they were still together.

"Look out for Penny," she said to Lizzie all the time, till Lizzie worried sick. "She's not sensible like you. She could do something stupid in a heartbeat."

And she would have told Penny to look after Lizzie too, if Penny would listen to her, or stop for just a second. But she didn't.

Probably for the best their dad never appeared again. But she still had her lovely girls.

"Oi! You! Wanker!" Penny was shouting at the back of a departing fat man, part of a group of blowhard salesmen who'd come in for lunch to celebrate some bonus, then acted like they were city millionaires, ordering ridiculous cocktails and not drinking them, making her run around, asking if they could order "off menu," to which Penny had retorted that they'd cook one of their heads if they could fit it in the deep-fat fryer. They'd guffawed lustily and asked her if this was one of those American theme bars where the women wore bikinis, and she'd said no, it was one of those American theme bars where everyone tipped 20 percent.

Whereupon they'd got up to go, leaving a catastrophe of thrown food, knocked-over glasses, and ripped-up paper napkins, and they'd left her . . . a pound.

She held it up in the air.

The fat man turned around. He had grease from his surf and turf platter spattered all down his Crazy Frog tie.

"What?" he said.

She held the pound coin out to him.

"You left this behind."

His Neanderthal brow furrowed in incomprehension.

"That's for you, darlin'," he said.

"You'd have got more if you'd have given us a quick flash," said a weaselly-faced man next to him. He looked at his watch. "There's still time!"

"Why don't you take it," said Penny, advancing and handing it to the fat man. "Buy yourself a magnifying glass so you can see your own dick one of these days."

Eilish was falling asleep. She got so tired these days. The phone rang, starkly, shaking her out of her dream. Her television program had finished, and some house show was on. Eilish loved house shows. She would pretend she was the one who had to choose between the town house, the modern bungalow, the apartment in the stately home. Very rarely were the customers offered two-up two-downs on a council estate.

The phone rang again and, grunting a little as she moved her legs, she leaned over to pick it up, listening in silence, until finally, "Oh my God," she said. "Oh my God."

*

Lizzie looked at the phone. Mum. How was she going to tell her she'd been let go? Just shucked off, not needed. After all the work . . .

"How's Mr. Boakle?" said Grainne.

"Sorry," said Lizzie, making her mind up. "I have to take this call."

She sank to her desk, steeling herself not to cry. But her mother didn't even ask her how she was, just poured it all out in a rush. After asking her to slow down and repeat herself several times, Lizzie just blew her ratty fringe out of her eyes, and pushed back her chair from the desk.

"Oh my God," she said.

Penny was staring at Ravi, who was staring at the floor.

"You can't talk to customers like that!" Ravi was saying. He was about sixteen years old, and on a management training scheme that somehow made him her boss even though he hadn't started shaving yet. Disciplining people obviously made him unbelievably unhappy.

"OK," she said. "I won't do it again. But they were disgusting losers."

"They were *customers*, Penny," said Ravi.

"I know, I know," said Penny. "Most of our customers are disgusting losers, right, what can you do . . ."

"No," said Ravi miserably. "I mean, it says in the handbook . . ."

The handbook was a huge color-coordinated folder that laid out every single piece of information required to run the All-American New York Diner, including how many umbrellas per pina colada (2), how many napkins per rib rack (7), and how strong a word you could use against a customer before you were in serious trouble (meanie). Penny could get around Ravi, but nobody could get around the handbook. She sighed. Her phone rang, again.

"Oh, answer it," said Ravi, trying to put off the inevitable. Why hadn't he gone in for musical theater like he'd always dreamed of? He could be living in the real New York by now. He stared out of the window, looking at the 1,500-space car park and the way the clouds looked like they were touching the top of the gray corrugated-iron Bowl-o-rama.

"Mum?" said Penny. "What is it?" She listened intently.

And, finally, "Oh my God!"

She ripped off her employee badge, which said, "Hi. My name is Penny and I want y'all to have a nice day now, d'you hear?," threw it on the floor, and stamped on it.

"Ravi," she said. "You are a nice man. And not a very big one. So, it's going to be a bit painful to do what I'm about to suggest next. But I really do insist that you take this"—she lifted up the heavy handbook—"and turn to the color-coded section where it explains *exactly* how to get it up your arse."

## Chapter Two

The three of them crammed into the small front room at Parkend Close. This in itself was unusual. Penny was always just passing through.

"So, explain again slowly," said Penny. Lizzie had come in with a tray holding three cups of tea, the strongest thing they had in the house, and a new packet of chocolate digestives.

"Your gran . . . not Nana, but your dad's mum. Well, she's not well. She's had to go into a home."

"What's wrong with her?" said Penny impatiently.

"I don't know," said their mum. "Just old. Not dementia, just an 'episode' they think."

"You mean, crazy," said Penny with a shudder. "Remember you used to take us there. Brr. There were tins of dog food everywhere."

"And she didn't even have a dog," said Lizzie and Penny at the same time.

"Yes, well, she's not crazy," said their mum, "just a bit mixed up, that's all."

"There were cobwebs. And spiders," continued Lizzie, suddenly sounding exactly like her six-year-old self.

"But she wants to—" Penny shook her head. It didn't feel quite real.

"She wants you to move in there, yes," said their mum. "According to the nurse, she thinks somebody's going to nick her fifty years' worth of back copies of the *Radio Times*."

"But why us?" said Lizzie.

"You," said their mum. "Not me, of course, oh no. But you two apparently are the only family she's got left, or at any rate the only family she kept mentioning to the nurses."

"But we don't know her," said Penny.

"Well, blame your useless bloody vanishing dad for that, love." Their mother reconsidered. "And it's my fault, too. She did want to see you, but it was always such a long way in, and you two hated going so much, and she never offered to help pay the fares, or buy you anything. She lives in that big place in Chelsea and she never helped us out at all. I think she gave it all to your dad. I expect that flat's all that's left."

"Big place in Chelsea," breathed Penny, as if saying, "the magical land of Oz." "We're moving to Chelsea."

"For a bit," said their mum. "Just till she gets well enough to go home."

"But she's really old and mad and stuff," argued Penny. "I mean, she's not likely to be—"

"Penny!" said their mother sharply. "Have a little decorum for once."

"I don't see why I should," said Penny. "She owes us, doesn't she? We haven't had so much as a Christmas card from her for over twenty years, and as for . . ."

"Did she . . . I mean, doesn't she know where Dad is?" asked Lizzie timidly. Although their mother almost never talked about their dad, saying only it had been short, occasionally sweet, and that she'd been delighted with the results, i.e., them, she had never quite gotten over her childhood fantasy that it might all have been a mistake, that he might have been hit on the head by a brick and suffered terrible amnesia, and didn't even know he had twins.

Her mother shrugged. "Well, obviously not. Good-for-nothing." Her face clouded briefly. "And his mother obviously thinks she owes you for that. So, I think you should take advantage of your good fortune."

"Deffo!" said Penny, her eyes shining. "Oh God. I'm going to live up West."

She tried on a ridiculous accent. "Haylo! My name is Penelope Berry and I live in Chelsea. I have a terribly rich luff-er end I only shop at Christian Dior." She clapped her hands in glee. "Oh God. At last. I knew something good was going to happen. I just knew it."

"Well, an old lady is in a home," said their mother.

"Yeah. But an evil one, though," said Penny. "Honestly, until you tell me that she really encouraged *Stephen*"—Penny always referred to their father as Stephen, never as Dad—"to even phone us once, ever, I'm having real trouble dredging up the sympathy."

"I'm not sure about living in London," said Lizzie. "I need to find a new job, and it's really dangerous and expensive and busy and I don't know anyone . . ."

"But that's what makes it *great*," said Penny. "Honestly, you're such an old maid."

"Shut up."

"OK. Don't. Fine. I'm perfectly happy to move into a huge Chelsea apartment for free on my own. See you at my Chelsea registry office wedding, suckers."

"Stop it, you two," said their mum. "Lizzie, pet. You know, it really is time you thought about getting a place of your own. And now you've lost that job . . . it's a great opportunity for you, darling. You don't want life to pass you by."

"I don't mind," said Lizzie.

Their mother smiled. "Well, maybe I do. Just, you know, try not to get knocked up with twins in two months or anything."

Lizzie had a month's salary in hand, and Penny had raided the tips jar on her way out, so together they would have enough to afford a taxi to take them into town.

"And I'm never coming back," said Penny. "Well, only in a gigantic big car. Not a limo, you can get those for twenty quid an hour down at Rumours. A Rolls-Royce or something. It can come and get me in my wedding dress on my way to Westminster Abbey."

"Who are you marrying?" said Lizzie. "Prince William?"

"Or I'll have found some fabulous job. PA to a celebrity or something. And they'll pay me masses of money."

Lizzie stared out of their little bedroom window. Four ten-year-olds were jumping on top of a burned-out car.

"I'm not sure I'd know what to do if I had any money."

It was true, she mused, staring at the gray paint factory under the gray sky. She and Grainne had talked it over a lot, what they'd do if they won the lottery. For a start, she'd *have* to lose the weight. And, she thought, I'd get a horrid stick-thin personal trainer with an aggressive Australian accent who'd shout harshly at me in the park and act absolutely stunned when she found out how many Pot Noodles I get through in a week, and talk about how, once you're used to it, mung beans and broccoli are actually nicer than cake and hot buttered toast. Or it'd be some perfectly proportioned bloke with a wide-boy smile, and I'll end up getting a terrible crush on him because he's being a cheeky charming chappie and I won't realize that's how he speaks to all his "ladies" because it helps them to stay motivated, and he'll have to kindly explain this to me after I've been fantasizing madly about him for weeks and have convinced myself he's falling for my inner beauty. Then he'll be really kind and explain that actually he's seeing this Australian personal trainer girl whom he really thinks is the one.

"Don't be stupid," said Penny, interrupting her reverie. "You could buy something you've always wanted."

"A horse, maybe," said Lizzie, throwing her cheap market knickers into a holdall.

"What would you do with a horse?" said Penny. "Eat sugar cubes together?"

"Well, maybe," said Lizzie, making a face at Penny's narrow back. "*Maybe* we'd have a special bond nobody else could understand, and no one else could tame him and he'd have beautiful black hair and . . ."

"Ah, see what you've done?" said Penny. "You've confused a horse with Colin Farrell again, haven't you?"

Lizzie sighed and went back to throwing knickers in a pile. It was all right for Penny. She was good-looking and everyone liked paying attention to her. It wasn't quite as much fun when you were trailing along behind carrying the bags.

Their mother had been acting strange all week. Lizzie had tried to believe it was because she was sad they were leaving, but she seemed happy and excited.

"Well," Lizzie said finally, just as the taxi was drawing up outside the house on Sunday morning. It was a proper black cab and everything; Penny knew lots of the neighbors would be coming out to see the "little twins" head off to London, and wanted to do it in style. "I guess we're off."

"Oh, it's only London," said their mother. "I'll see you all the time."

"We're moving away from home!" said Lizzie.

"Yeah," said Penny. "That's how it works in *EastEnders*, isn't it? They go up West and they're never heard from again."

"And it's a good thing for you," said their mum. She leaned over and gave Lizzie a big hug.

"What are you going to do, then, Ma?" said Penny. She didn't really like being enveloped in her mother's big beefy arms.

"Well, get a couple of lodgers in, won't I?" said their mum. "I've had some good news too. The school's going to give me early retirement."

"Oh, that's brill," said Lizzie. "So you really will be able to put your feet up!"

"Oh, I don't think so," said their mum. "I've got a bit put away, after all these years. I was keeping it for you two, when you moved out to find your own feet, but you won't be needing that now, so . . ."

"So what?"

"So I'm going."

"Where?"

"Bingo?" said Penny.

"To the RADA, of course!" said their mother. Her face suddenly creased into a big smile.

"To the what now?" Lizzie had no idea what she was talking about.

"To the RADA, of course! I hope they've kept my place."

"Have you suddenly caught whatever Gran has?" said Penny.

"No, no, no," said their mother. "I've got a place at the RADA. The Royal Academy of Dramatic Arts. I'm going to be an actress, darlings."

"How can that be?" said Penny.

"Well," said their mother patiently, "I auditioned and I got in. It's really difficult."

"Yes, I know that . . . when?"

"Uh, let me see . . . how old are you two now?"

"Twenty-seven."

"Must have been twenty-eight years ago, then," said their mum. "Fell pregnant with you guys, couldn't take up my place. They said they'd defer it for me, though."

The children were silent.

"For twenty-eight years?" asked Penny finally. "You think they'd keep your deferred place for twenty-eight years?"

"I don't see why not," said their mother huffily. "It's my place."

Lizzie put her suitcase down and headed toward her mother. "Why did you never tell us?" she said.

"I didn't want you to feel sorry for me for missing all my opportunities by having children and ruining my life."

"We wouldn't have thought we'd ruined your life," said Lizzie. "Oh. Oh, did we ruin your life?"

There was a long pause.

"Uh, no, of course not!" said their mum finally. "But, you know, I am a dinner lady. Usually though I pretend I'm really heavily into method acting and playing a part in which someone is required to work as a dinner lady for thirty years."

"That sounds like the kind of movie I'd like to see," said Penny.

"Then she becomes embroiled in a conspiracy to defraud school funds and is the only one who can solve the crime."

The twins nodded.

"And she has to have a torrid affair with one of the children's fathers who turns out to be a spy. Only he's working for the other side." Their mother had started to go slightly pink.

"Oh, Mum," said Lizzie, giving her another hug. "That's fantastic! That's brilliant! It's so great!" The taxi honked noisily outside.

"And we really have to go," said Penny.

"Course you do," said their mum. "See you at my first West End opening!"

"And I thought it was only Stephen's side of the family who were completely crazy," said Penny, hoisting up her suitcase and leaving through the yellow-paneled front door.

# Chapter Three

Neither of the girls spoke much on the way into London. Penny was too excited. Lizzie was upset at leaving home, even though she was twenty-seven and thus it was patently ridiculous to feel that way. She wished her mother had come with them. Coming into London from the east the sun bounced off Canary Wharf, and even Lizzie felt a jump in her heart.

The cabbie muttered something about the congestion charge as they came down in through the city, past the Gherkin and the large white buildings of the Stock Exchange. Of course they'd been here a million times, up in town to shop or, very occasionally for Lizzie, to go out, but now . . .

"In for a holiday, are youse?" asked the cabbie.

"No," said Penny, in what almost sounded like a drawl. "We live here."

Lizzie suppressed a smile, and tried to stop looking at the meter. They were arriving in style, that was all. And it was stylish.

Lizzie felt her heart leap. And their mother too! RADA! What if she became one of those famous old lady actresses? They couldn't keep casting Judi Dench forever, could they?

They whizzed around past Big Ben and along the Embankment. Chelsea Bridge was pink and looked as if it was made of spun sugar, little lights popping along its length. The cabbie turned right and they were in Chelsea proper, heading down the King's Road. Tantalizingly, every street off it was filled with little pink and blue cottages, or large mansions, or big glass-covered apartment blocks. Neither of the twins could remember anything about the flat from the outside, except that it had seemed big to them when they were little, and dark and dusty. Both felt a definite thrill of anticipation.

"I suppose it will look really small to us now," said Lizzie.

"What, smaller than the shoebox rooms we have now?" said Penny. "That'll be interesting, given that I can touch all four walls at once."

"What if there's only one bedroom?"

"She brought Stephen up there, didn't she?"

The cab slowed, and turned left, as the twins stared out of the window.

Redmond Street connected the King's Road to the river. It was lined on both sides with high white-stuccoed houses, like a long wedding cake. There weren't ordinary street-lights—covered in graffiti and dog crap and with the lights blown out—like the girls were used to; instead, elaborately carved lampposts held up little clusters of bulbs. Black polished railings lined the small front gardens, all immaculate, behind which were painted and polished huge heavy doors in dark green, black, navy, and red.

The cabbie stopped outside their gran's flat. This door was navy blue, with a black knocker, and a large round brass door-knob inexplicably placed in the middle. The girls got out and stood, simply staring.

"OK, loves," he said, and named the price for their journey, which made Lizzie want to be physically sick. Penny, however, handed it over blithely, adding a fat tip on top.

"Come on," she said, at Lizzie's aghast expression after he'd driven away. "It's the high life now. You've got to fake it to make it."

"Fake it to make it ... all the way to debtors' prison," said Lizzie crossly, picking up the bag with the broken strap. "You do remember we're both unemployed."

"Yeah, yeah," said Penny, looking around the perfect street. It looked as if the cast of *Mary Poppins* might hop out and start dancing at any moment.

At last. She was where she belonged. She pulled out the heavy keys that had arrived for them, and fitted one into a large old lock. She pushed the door open tentatively.

Inside there was a large hallway with parquet flooring and a staircase with an elaborate balustrade and pale rose-covered carpet; Lizzie wondered how it was ever kept clean. To the right of the door was a shelf with neat piles of interesting-looking mail, and a huge mirror with a gold frame. A little white door indicated the first flat, but they went on up to the second floor.

On the landing, two flights up, it was a little darker, with only one window at the end of the hallway letting in light, along with a small electric candelabra set above another large gilt-edged mirror. Penny, fumbling with the keys, opened the door.

"Ready?" she said.

"Mmm," said Lizzie.

"One . . . two . . . three . . ." Penny attempted to flamboyantly throw open the door. But she failed immediately when it scraped and jammed.

"OK," said Penny. She put her shoulder to it and shoved again. "Three . . ."

And this time, with a grind and a twisting of paper, they were in.

The girls stood there, stunned, looking around.

"Well," said Penny eventually, "you can't say it's not big."

"No," said Lizzie. They had stepped directly into the main sitting room. It was vast, opening out on their right to a huge bay window. On the left, over by the windows at the back, was a kitchen. Straight ahead—although it seemed miles away—was a fireplace, and beyond that, a passageway with three doors leading off it.

Every single bit of surface, every single possible spot, was completely and utterly obscured by junk. The entire room inside was gray, despite the brightness of the day outside. The windows were utterly encrusted with grime. There was a table, placed in the bay, with five or six chairs around it, all mismatched and looking mostly broken, with legs and bits of wood on the floor. Everywhere else there was rubbish of the most spectacular fashion. There were broken children's toys; huge piles of dusty, ancient magazines; odd bits of knitting and macramé; a whole crate full of empty medicine bottles; boxes full of who-knows-what; piles of dresses and skirts; trolleys full of bric-a-brac of every description. Books, old dusty hardbacks giving off a terribly musty smell, were untidily scattered over every available surface and piles of newspapers lined the corridor leading off the back of the room.

The kitchen was full of plates, chipped and mismatched, more than one person could use in a lifetime. Hundreds of pots were chaotically stacked up, along with at least a hundred washed-out milk bottles. Lizzie breathed a huge sigh of relief when she noticed that someone had cleaned out the fridge and left the door open. She didn't think she could have managed that.

"So," said Penny after a time. "We're not supposed to move anything, right?"

"Right."

"Fuck that. I'm off to choose a bedroom."

And she started to pick her way across the rubbish.

The two bedrooms proved just as bad even though they were a wonderful size, with near perfect views if you squinted through the murk of the filthy panes, over the rooftops and Mary Poppins chimney pots of Chelsea. They were piled high with old shoes, and each had three wardrobes. The bathroom, with its old-fashioned claw-foot bath, was full of old perfume bottles and an odd collection of wooden-handled toothbrushes.

"You have to say," said Penny, "she's a site-specific crazy old bat."

Lizzie was too overcome to speak. She wondered how long the old lady had sat here, surrounded in rubbish, all alone. How they'd found her . . . and who. Despite realizing it wasn't her fault—she didn't exactly owe this woman much—her eyes cast over a huge box of old photographs, and she felt sad, culpable, and guilty.

Lizzie knew her mum didn't think she could remember their

dad, but she could. He used to bring sweets and he was incredibly handsome. Penny used to shriek all the time. Lizzie used to think that was why he didn't come back, and practiced being quiet. If they hadn't been twins . . . if she hadn't been so dumpy and useless, maybe they'd all still have been a family and they'd have been coming to Chelsea for years.

"Right," said Penny, "let's dump our stuff in this shithole and head out."

"You are joking?" said Lizzie. "Nobody is going anywhere until . . ." and she handed Penny a pair of rubber gloves.

"Oh for God's sake."

"House and jobs first. Fun later," said Lizzie. "Please, Penny. Please, let's not fall out quite yet."

Penny rolled her eyes.

"Plus, we've spent all the money on the cab," said Lizzie. "Plus, what if you want to get up for the toilet in the middle of the night and fall over and get smothered and die?"

Penny pouted.

By the end of the day, it looked a little better, but not much. You could make toast in the kitchen without immediately contracting salmonella, and even risk a bath, but Lizzie was conscious of her grandmother's strict orders not to move anything, and even if she wanted to, where would it go? Every square inch of the property was already stuffed full. She didn't know, it might even be valuable, though she doubted it very much, looking at the empty milk bottles. She'd done most of the scrubbing and Penny had sat around grumbling about it, but now, as they sat down with their Pot Noodle in front of the ancient television, she wondered if it had even been worth it.

"Ah. Pot Noodle in front of the TV," said Penny, casting a glance out of the window. "This is almost as good as being at home."

"You go out if you want," said Lizzie. "I'm tired."

Penny wobbled a bit. "I will," she said. "I'll go out there. Take it by storm. And all that."

"Yes," said Lizzie.

"Maybe a job first."

Lizzie nodded, a little surprised, but not much. Penny might have a veneer of hardness, but underneath there was a bit of mush only her twin got to see. Which was why, she thought glumly, she'd had to stick by her for so bloody long.

"But then," said Penny, "hold us back."

"Get up, get up!" shouted Penny the next morning, forcing her way into Lizzie's room. Four filing cabinets filled with leaves were piled in front of Lizzie's window. Lizzie had woken up a lot in the night, dreaming she was being buried alive. But now, as she woke, she realized where she was, and her heart leapt.

"It's a Chelsea morning! And we're going on a job hunt!"

"Aren't we lovely privileged ladies living in Chelsea?" said Lizzie, sleepily rolling over. "I don't have to go on a job hunt. I'm going out in my four-by-four to buy expensive belts and luxury wallpaper."

"No you're not," said Penny. "You're pulling yourself together and you're going to put food on the table."

"You don't eat food," said Lizzie. "And we don't have a table. We have six tea chests stuffed with identical copies of the 1967 Cheltenham telephone directory."

36

"That's detail," said Penny. "We're here now, and we're getting out there. We are going to find jobs and then meet men. Who will buy us Range Rovers and think our penchant for luxurious soft furnishings is simply hilarious."

"Why don't you just walk up and down the King's Road in a negligee winking suggestively?"

"Tried it. Up!"

"What kind of job am I going to find anyway?"

"Some crazy stamp-collecting one? I don't know. It's a new world out there."

"It's a scary world in here. What's for breakfast?"

"Water," said Penny. "But when we start making some money we'll get a juicer and juice up fresh fruits and vegetables in the morning and have them with sunflower seeds and grass and things."

"Water?" said Lizzie. "Are you sure? Is there nothing else?"

Penny rubbed the corner of her mouth. "Well . . ."

"Are those *crumbs*?" said Lizzie. "What have you got? You're holding out on me! Stop it!"

Penny shrugged. "Well, maybe . . ."

Lizzie leapt out of bed and into the kitchen.

"Jaffa Cakes!"

"And they're not even store brand," said Penny.

"Nothing like a good breakfast to set you up for a busy day," said Lizzie, munching happily.

"But we're going to get that juicer," said Penny with a warning glint in her eye.

"Yeah," said Lizzie sadly. "You maybe. I think I'll stick to a biscuit-based morning."

"OK," said Penny. "Clothes next! What are you going to wear?"

Lizzie's face turned down. "Well, I was thinking of black . . . with a further helping of black."

Penny nodded thoughtfully. "Well, maybe you could think of it as artfully chic."

"The trousers have an elasticated waistband."

"Don't eat any more Jaffa Cakes then."

"I won't," said Lizzie.

"Good."

"I've finished them."

"Oh. They were meant to last us until teatime."

"Do you think the smashing orangey bit counts as one of my five portions of fruit and veg?"

Ignoring her, Penny picked her way through the mess. "I'm going to wear my Dolce and Gabbana top."

"It's so obviously fake," said Lizzie. "You totally so obviously picked it up in Wellings market."

"It's not," said Penny. She picked up the corset thing from her suitcase and slipped it on over her tank top.

"Penny, it says 'Dolce e Banana' on the front."

"Oh, who'd notice that?"

"Only anyone leaning over to get a look at your tits, which as you stick them out all the time means absolutely everyone."

Penny sniffed. "We'll just see, shall we?"

"See what?"

"Who gets a job the fastest."

"What do you mean?"

"Have a little competition, shall we?"

"No," said Lizzie. "We don't need a competition. You'll get a job the fastest. You've got blond hair and perky tits and you smile nicely and look like you might conceivably be up for it. I wear elasticated trousers. Can we not have a competition, please?"

"You know, all you have to do is just drop a few pounds and you'd be really attractive, Elizabeth," said Penny, looking serious.

"Oh, and could we definitely not have the 'all you have to do is drop a few pounds' conversation," said Lizzie. "It's not as much fun for me as you seem to think, given how often you bring it up."

Penny stuck out her bottom lip. "Well. We're in a borough with no unemployment whatsoever and a definite need for what us Essex girls do best."

"Drink Bacardi Breezers?" said Lizzie.

"No."

"Go to Lakeside?"

"No."

"Do the shitty jobs nobody else wants to do?"

"No . . . uh, yes. Yup, that's us."

Chelsea looked shinier in the morning. Lizzie wondered if the people here just spat out their chewing gum less than people in Brandford. But then she saw the massive street-cleaning machine purring up and down. So everyone who lived here just got more good things even though they had more to start with. That didn't seem fair.

But it was so lovely. It was early and clear and bright and the pavements were being polished. What was it Penny had said? "Remember: we're looking for posh jobs in nice places where we meet nice men and you don't have to get salad-bar bits in your hair."

She crossed the King's Road, shivering slightly at the sight of the smart clothes shops. She certainly wasn't going to start in there; if she was too scared to shop in them, she certainly wasn't going to put herself through the humiliation of asking for a job there. Plus she feared that, for example, part of the interview might be having to get herself into an outfit they stocked, then all the other staff would come out and have a good laugh at her and she'd break the zip and be unable to get out of it and she'd end up three hundred quid down.

No, not the clothes shops.

Pondering whether to spend her last few pounds on a coffee so she had something to cling to as she pounded the streets, she wandered up past the rows of perfect, huge, white-stuccoed buildings—just like hers, she thought happily—interspersed with red mansion blocks. She wondered who lived in these, how there were so many rich people all living so close to one another. What did they all do? They couldn't all be rock stars and bankers, could they? Maybe they could.

Out of a large building with pillars on either side of the huge front door came a young family with a baby in a pushchair. The baby was snortling contentedly, and the couple, her with a lovely figure and long blond hair, him looking successful and well dressed, were laughing together at some little joke. Lizzie looked at them and found her teeth grinding slightly. She told herself they must be really unhappy underneath, or really nasty and were laughing horribly because they'd just ritually disembowled the underpaid foreign help. The idea that you could be rich, attractive, live here, and be happy . . . Well, Lizzie thought, she lived here now. She could be like that too. She was broke, chubby, squatting, jobless, and single, but apart from that they shared a postcode so they were the same really.

The little family got into a beautiful shiny black car just as it started to rain. Probably on their way to the divorce lawyers, thought Lizzie, as she trudged on, getting wet.

The Fulham Road was next up. It was full of rare book shops; incredibly expensive florists with about three carefully selected perfect blossoms on display; furniture showrooms that looked like they'd just been flown over from Versailles, and old-fashioned pubs quietly being scrubbed down, with beer being brought in and the doors and windows thrown open to get some fresh air. Lizzie wondered about a bar job. She could be the friendly, busty heart-of-gold barmaid cheerily serving foaming pints of frothy ale to the local squire's son . . .

Hmm. One of the bar staff threw a bowlful of soapy water out across the pavement, just missing her legs. She skipped out the way, and shot him a dirty look before she could help herself. Whoops. Maybe not apply there, then.

Right, no clothes shop, no street cleaning, no bar work . . . this was getting ridiculous. Either they were going to starve to death or she was going to have to go in and ask someone about a job. The next shop she saw . . .

The next shop was a smart-looking antiques shop. Nothing in the window had a price on it. She pushed on the door, before noticing there was a little bell she had to press before she could get in. Quickly she pressed it before she could change her mind.

After an age, an old man wearing a bow tie came to the door.

"How can I help you?" he said, looking at her somewhat distrustfully.

"I was going to buy your entire shop but now I see your unpleasant face I've decided against it," Lizzie wanted to say; but restrained herself.

41

"Uh, hello there." She took out her CV nervously. "My name's Elizabeth Berry and I'm particularly interested in working in the field of antiques. So if you have a vacancy . . ."

The man squinted at her.

"Vacancy? What do you mean, if I die or something?"

"No," said Lizzie slowly, "I mean, if you need an assistant or something."

The man looked behind him into the empty shop.

"Well, I suppose we could do with someone to manage the enormous queues in the mornings."

"There you go, then," said Lizzie. "And I'm sure you'd need someone at lunchtime?"

The man sighed. "OK. What's your opinion of that piece there?"

He pointed to an old earthenware vase. It looked like the kind of thing you could pick up at a furniture shop for about a tenner, and was entirely featureless.

"It's a vase," said Lizzie. "Uh, and . . . very suitable for all sorts of places in the home. Indoors, outdoors . . ."

"Well, well, well, it's a classical historian," said the old man. "Sorry, could you get off my step? I need to dust it for the hordes that come down here straight after queuing all night at Ikea. Oh, and it's Abyssinian and worth thirty thousand pounds."

"That's exactly what I was going to say next," said Lizzie, but it was too late. She trudged across the road to the pub. The man who'd sent the water along the pavement was still out there, looking at her.

"So, you're really an antiques dealer but you want to work in a pub?" he said when she approached him, CV in hand.

"No, I just want to work generally."

"Sorry, love," he said. "We're looking for people who really love pubs, you know, love the customers and all that."

Lizzie tried to think of a pub she'd been in where the bar staff had really loved her, but failed. She tried to smile, realizing as she did so that a) she seemed to be taking quite a lot of shit she didn't really deserve, and b) she would never be able to go in that pub, or possibly any pub in the street ever again as long as she lived, and headed farther up the road.

Everywhere it was the same. Skinny girls working in art galleries looked at her blankly and indicated that they thought she was trying to physically throw them onto the streets so she could have their jobs. Shop managers sniffed and, mentioning high interest rates and credit card debt, said they weren't hiring staff, which made Lizzie shuffle uncomfortably. Specialist shops wanted to know if she was specially qualified, which seemed a bit unfair. There weren't any stamp shops, she'd checked, and anyway, she didn't want to go back to that. And why did everyone have to be so *rude*? She only wanted a job, not ten pence for a cup of tea. She'd now been sneered at by girls who looked twelve, pinched-nosed women in Chanel suits with foreign accents, fat men wearing waistcoats and polka-dot ties, and bar and restaurant staff from every country in the *entire world*. What had happened to low unemployment?

Now she was getting too wet to be anywhere near presentable enough to go job hunting. Chelsea, soaking now, with shiny red postboxes and shiny red pensioners, no longer looked as if it was about to provide a backdrop to an Austin Powers spectacular. It looked hostile and hard and closed up. And she was hungry. Extremely hungry. Feeling in her purse she found a two-pound coin at the bottom. Right, that was it. Thank goodness she hadn't had that coffee. She was going to find something to eat and . . . reappraise her options.

She slunk into a little café on the corner, painted bright yellow on the outside, with cheerful hanging baskets. Inside it was dark and cozy, with wooden walls and tiles on the floor. Food was hung all around; large sausages and cooked meats from the ceiling, fresh fruit on the counter, and sweet-smelling herbs over the doorway. It all looked rather nice. Lizzie swallowed manfully and sat down, glancing around for a menu. What if it was one of these really expensive places that Penny went to with dubious men, places that charged a tenner for a piece of asparagus floating in olive oil?

"Yes. What you want?" shouted the man behind the counter. Lizzie winced. She didn't know what she wanted, but she'd quite like it to cost less than four pounds fifty.

"Uh . . . have you got a menu?" she said quietly.

"What's that?"

Oh, for goodness' sake. It was entirely reasonable to go into a café and ask for a menu. He was just pretending not to understand her because her face didn't fit around this stupid part of the world, and didn't everyone like to make her know it.

All the frustration of the morning—of being rejected and looked down on by every Tom, Dick, and Harry in the entire damn postcode—welled up in her suddenly, and she felt her face redden as she stood up.

"Nothing," she said. "Don't bloody bother yourself. I'm fine, obviously. I'll just go outside and lick the bloody McDonald's boxes in the gutter, shall I? In fact, maybe I should look for a job there. After all it wouldn't matter if I was all covered in grease and shit, would it? And I'd hate for anyone around here to *trouble* themselves."

She grabbed her handbag and headed for the door, shaking with humiliation and fury. The rain hadn't let up in the slightest.

"What? Hang on," shouted the man, but Lizzie pushed at the door. Of course, it was a pull door. As she stood there, fuming, she grabbed it again just as a great big hand came out and stopped it.

"Sorry. What is this babbling about? Are you OK?"

Lizzie turned around. "I came in to eat and you were incredibly rude to me and everyone has spent the entire morning being incredibly rude to me and I'm just sick of it, OK? You can all take your Chelsea attitude and stick it up your arse."

"Wait, what . . ."

The man stood back. He was dark and round, and Lizzie saw now his hands were covered in water and one was holding a huge, angry-looking langoustine. He also had a concerned look on his face.

"Sorry . . . you came in and I have fish brains on my hands, I miss you. Bad fish brains, no?" He smiled at her apologetically. "We have no people today. Well, only me, as you can see."

His accent was difficult to place. She looked around.

"Well, you're not exactly busy, are you?"

"You are very grumpy lady. Eleven o'clock is not the big time lunch rush."

He wiped his hands on a tea towel that was hanging out of the tie of the apron enclosing his capacious belly. "OK. You want lunch or you want to have big temper fit once again?"

Lizzie attempted a half smile. "Well, I don't know, do I? That's why I need to see a menu."

"I do not have a menu."

"You're too exclusive and smart to have a menu?"

"I make whatever is good and fresh on the day. You do not like the sound of that?"

"How much is it?" said Lizzie.

The man looked her up and down, taking in her cheap shoes and elasticated waistband.

"You are the first customer of the day and guinea pig, so you get a discount."

"How much of a discount?"

The man screwed up his face.

"I can do you some lunch for . . . two pounds. That's my absolute low price of the day for angry wet girls."

"Hurrah," said Lizzie, then remembering herself, said, "Uh, that sounds nice. Thank you."

She sat down again as the fat bloke went to work behind his counter, chopping and stirring things up. She found herself watching him, engrossed in his work. Although short, he was large all over; his hairy forearms were like the hams hanging over his head, his stomach was massive; even his features were big. Mediterranean she would have thought, but his eyes weren't black but a heavily fringed blue.

"You want something to drink?" came the voice.

"Tap water, please," she replied.

The man smiled to himself, then brought her a small glass filled with something light and golden and fizzy and delicious.

"Here," he said. "On me. As I am such a terrible host. And you have had such a terrible morning."

Lizzie accepted, feeling slightly giddy. Well, her day may have started horribly, but now a large stranger was giving her drinks and it was only eleven-thirty in the morning.

"That's delicious," she said.

"Prosecco. Better than champagne," said the man.

"Oh, yes," said Lizzie. "Champagne gets terribly boring as the morning drink of choice."

The man laughed. "So why are you so sad, wet girl?"

"I wasn't miserable, I'm job hunting. Do you have any jobs free? No, you're looking for someone with ten to fifty years' café management experience, I do understand."

"Hmm," said the man. "Job hunting is difficult. What's your speciality?"

"Stamp collecting."

"This is a popular job in England?"

"Not as much as you'd think."

"Why are you looking in Chelsea? The people don't collect stamps here. They work in American banks and make their tiny dogs wear clothes."

"I know," said Lizzie. "But we just moved here . . ."

"We?" said the man. Lizzie's heart jumped. Oh, my goodness, was he hitting on her? Why would he ask if she was a "we?" Hang on, she thought, was she going to be some kind of unbelievably easy lay for a dodgy waiter type? But on the other hand, she thought with some remorse, her life was so barren these days a dodgy waiter type marked a blinding improvement in her love life. Boy, was that depressing.

"Me and my sister," she explained. "We're looking after my gran's flat."

"That sounds nice," he said.

"It does, doesn't it?" said Lizzie. "It *sounds* nice."

"But it is not?"

"Well, it's tricky getting started. It's not the friendliest of areas."

The man nodded. "Well, let me say hello. I'm Georges."

"Hello, Georges. I'm Lizzie."

"What do you think, Lizzie?"

He placed a plate in front of her with a sizzling hot langoustine on a bed of linguine with olives, chilies, and little red roasted tomatoes that burst their flavors onto her tongue.

"Oh, my goodness!" exclaimed Lizzie, trying it before it had even had a chance to cool down. "This is absolutely delicious."

"You like, huh?" Georges said. "I like a woman who enjoys her food."

Lizzie swallowed abruptly. "Are you saying I'm fat?"

"I'm saying nothing, very grumpy girl!" said Georges, looking offended. "I'm saying you look like you're enjoying the food I cooked for you!"

"I am," said Lizzie.

"Now me, I am very fat," said Georges, but he didn't sound too sad about it. In fact he sounded quite jolly.

"No you're not," said Lizzie, who had a lifetime's experience of telling Penny she didn't look fat and was therefore convincing under all circumstances.

"But yes, of course I am, can't you see this?" he said, extending his large wobbly belly. "What is this, then? Am I having a baby?"

"It would eat very well if it was a baby," said Lizzie, wiping up the last of her sauce with bread. "That was amazing."

The man smiled. "I'm glad you liked it. And now . . . I must get back."

The clock on the wall struck twelve, and almost immediately people started coming through the door. Georges greeted them cheerily, many by name, and started dishing up great tongsful of pasta into polystyrene boxes. A small chap appeared behind him and started dashing about at a hundred miles per hour, dishing up teas and sandwiches and filtering through as many people as possible as they yelled out requests and grabbed their white paper bags. It was engrossing to watch and, having nothing better to do, Lizzie sat and enjoyed the atmosphere. Steam rose and mingled to form condensation that ran down the inside of the windows, making the place feel even cozier and protected from the damp and hostile world outside. Slender blond girls ordered salads, or the langoustine without the pasta; local workmen just asked for "Whatever, Georgie;" businessmen signaled what they wanted without looking up from their telephones. Occasionally, Georges would glance over at Lizzie and give her a wink, and she'd try not to smile and feel all pleased.

Suddenly the view from the window was totally blocked, and the entire sky went dark. Lizzie leaned over to see what on earth it was. It turned out to be a huge holiday coach, too wide for the road, the type prone to knocking off cyclists while a sleep-deprived driver on the left-hand side tries to decipher a Hungarian road map from 1964. It appeared wedged on the pavement of the narrow street.

Everyone looked around as a small bus driver walked through the door.

"Ah, I have a coach here," he said, looking almost apologetic, "they're all very hungry . . . do you think you could do some takeaway for them?"

Georges looked around at his already bustling café.

"I'm not sure," he said. "I'm very busy . . . how many?"

"Sixty?" said the man. Georges looked disappointed. "Oh. Then I don't think . . ."

Lizzie leapt up so fast she nearly knocked the table over. Here was her chance! She could help! OK, it wasn't stamps but surely she could dish stuff up—she'd watched Georges for nearly twenty minutes now and it certainly looked easy. She could show how useful she could be, then she could work here, and Georges seemed nice and . . .

Oh. She had indeed knocked the table over. A large glass sugar pourer smashed onto the floor into a thousand shards. Lots of ladies yelped and lifted their elegant ankles out of the way of the smashed glass.

Both Georges and the bus driver turned their heads toward her, Georges with a flash of irritation.

"Uh, sorry," said Lizzie.

"It's all right," said Georges. "Benoit!"

The younger boy dashed over with a dustpan and brush.

"We're too busy," said Georges to the bus driver. "I'm sorry. It's impossible."

"What if I help?" said Lizzie desperately.

Georges's smile was strained.

"You would probably help best by not standing up."

"I could help!" said Lizzie indignantly. "I'll pass things out and you can take the money."

"But when you drop things on the floor I'm afraid I lose money," said Georges.

"Well, I won't do that," said Lizzie. "I promise. And if you turn down this coach party, you'll lose a lot of money."

Georges sighed. "Can you heat things up and make sandwiches?"

"Do you lick the back of them and stick them in a book?"

He pointed her toward the back of the shop.

"Put an apron on. And wash your hands. Benoit will show you what to do."

For the next two hours Lizzie cut bread, dunked pasta, wrapped things (not terribly well), got drinks out of the fridge, ran up and down to the tiny cellar for more tomatoes, and was generally run ragged. As soon as she'd finished one thing there were plates and pots to wash in the tiny sink out the back. Georges shouted instructions overhead and handled the money, Benoit flitted to and fro like an extremely helpful mouse, and Lizzie kept her head down and got on with things. It was exhausting but slightly exhilarating too, the way it never stopped.

By two-thirty the rush had begun to die down and Lizzie finished washing up the last big pot. Exhausted, she took a cloth to wipe the surfaces with and headed back into the café.

Georges was standing behind the counter with a big smile on his face.

"We are done! We have sold everything in the shop! We even used that catering margarine." He frowned. "Which I said I would never, ever use. Ah, well."

Benoit dashed around picking up every coffee cup he could find.

"Benoit! Coffee for the lady, please," shouted Georges. Then he straightened up and looked at Lizzie properly. Lizzie smiled hopefully at him, but his face, briefly, looked concerned.

Lizzie knew exactly why. Her carefully applied job-hunting makeup of that morning was, she could feel now, halfway down her face. She wiped under one eye and it was black with melted mascara. Her hair, which had taken ages to tame into submission with Penny's ridiculous straighteners, was now bouncing around her head like a crunchy straw helmet. Beads of sweat prickled on her upper lip and she remembered she hadn't gotten around to bleaching her moustache . . . oh, fucking hell. This is why she hated going out.

Lizzie wiped her forehead with the back of her hand. "I must look terrible," she said.

"Not at all," said Georges. "You look . . . you look like you've been working very hard."

With a mouse-like squeak Benoit delivered a tiny cup of dark espresso. It didn't taste like the Nescafé Lizzie was used to but she sipped it nonetheless, feeling enervated.

"So, uh . . ." said Georges, looking at her from the table where he was sitting. He looked a little nervous and shy, for the first time.

"Yes?"

"I wondered if maybe you'd like to . . ."

Ridiculously, her heart suddenly thumped in her chest. Was he going to ask her out? Maybe he'd think she was an amazing woman with nice child-bearing hips who didn't mind a bit of hard work, i.e., exactly the opposite of everyone else he'd meet around here.

". . . take a job here."

Oh, of course. A job. Exactly what she was after, of course.

"Oh, now I realize," said Georges, noticing her slightly disappointed-looking face. "You are looking for places that can more fully satisfy your stamp-sorting requirements."

"Doing stuff like I did today?" she said.

"Yes," said Georges. "Apart from knocking over the sugar

thing. Benoit wants to leave. He is aiming to become a rugby international."

Lizzie glanced at Benoit, who couldn't have weighed more than eight stone soaking wet. He gave her the thumbs-up.

"OK," said Lizzie, nodding slowly. "OK."

It was only as she was leaving the café that she caught sight of herself in the glass door and realized she hadn't calmed down her hair or reapplied her lipstick. She was amazed Georges had given her the job at all in her customer-frightening state. But it wasn't as if he was looking at her like that, of course. Men didn't, on the whole.

Penny knew she looked good the moment she stepped out of the house, a good hour or so after Lizzie. She was wearing her red PVC raincoat and her high boots that put a strut in her stride. She jangled the big key—oh, the bliss of having a big key—so that anyone walking past would know this was hers, her house, her part of the world, and be outrageously jealous.

Penny hated working. She remembered a documentary she'd seen once about It girls. How they spent their mornings getting waxed and manicured and going to the gym, had lunch, then spent their afternoons shopping and their evenings going to the millions of parties they'd been invited to. So they had the time to look much better than everyone else, plus they'd meet lots of people at parties, therefore they had a much better chance of meeting a bloke who'd like to keep them living like that. It seemed entirely unfair, but a completely perfect arrangement.

She looked down the King's Road. No more waitressing. It hadn't gotten her anywhere in all the years she'd been doing it. And no shops. She'd hate working in a shop too, all that folding and turning up on time. What did that leave for someone without much of a CV and no qualifications?

Wandering in no particular direction, Penny fell into Barnes Street. Even smarter and more exclusive than the rest, it was lined with trees shading small exquisite shops selling art and furniture. It was a beautiful scene. Or rather, it would have been except that outside one of the galleries there was something of a commotion. Penny liked commotions, and slowed down.

A beautiful, extremely tall and slender blond girl in a fawn skirt and opaque tights was yelling.

"He pinched my arse," she shouted, in a very loud clipped voice.

"Maud, Maud, Maud," came a grizzled-sounding voice. "He was demonstrating Giotto's interpretation of the beauty of the female form."

"He pinged my thong!"

"Oh, come on, he's not that bad. He's ninety anyway. What was he going to do after that, ask you to take him to the toilet?"

"Right, that's it. I'm off. And you'll be hearing from Daddy."

The girl stalked off down the street like a disgruntled giraffe. The man looked around vaguely, as if trying to pretend he'd just come out to take the air. Penny thought about it for two seconds, then sashayed forward.

"That sounds uptight."

The man eyed her suspiciously.

"What, not liking getting your knickers pinged? Bit early for trade, isn't it, love?"

Penny puffed up her chest. "Ex*cuse* me?"

The man looked at her more carefully.

"Oh, sorry, I've got the wrong glasses on. Or something."

Penny looked at him. He wasn't wearing glasses. "I am looking for a job though."

"Really," said the man, retreating into his shop.

"Yes." Penny followed him. "What did Maud do?"

"She sat in here and looked pretty."

Looking around, Penny realized she was in an art gallery, or, she supposed, shop. She'd never been in one before. It looked warm, dry, and quiet. She liked it already. The owner himself was a long, skinny, cadaverous-looking chap, with sunken eyes and cheekbones. He was wearing a three-piece suit in a Rupert Bear check.

"I could do that."

The man looked at her again. "Hmm," he said.

"What?"

"Oh, no, you are very pretty. I wonder . . . a girl like you."

"What do you mean?"

"I mean, you wouldn't mind a bit of, uh. Well, some of our clients, they're a bit old-fashioned in their ways, and . . ."

"They'll want to pinch my arse."

The man waggled his head. "Not hard or anything."

"It's OK," said Penny. She was used to it. A huge number of men she met in her life tried to pinch her arse, including her PE teacher. "I wouldn't mind."

"You know," said the man, "sit on that chair there."

She sat behind the desk.

"You just might work," he said. "All the girls down here are exactly the same. Boring-looking really. Whereas you . . ."

"Great," said Penny. "Can I start today?"

"I think," said the man, "we should have a little lunch to get acquainted. I'm a great believer in the art of lunch. Gordon Ramsay?"

"Not there again," said Penny, shivering.

The man raised his eyebrows approvingly.


"So, I will see you at eight tomorrow?" Georges was saying. He reached out and pulled open the door for her.

"Yup!" said Lizzie. "Bye, Benoit! Good luck!"

"Eep," said Benoit.

As she emerged she nearly bumped into a tall blond girl who was with a tall man. They were both laughing hysterically.

"Excuse *me*," said Lizzie.

"Whoops!" said the blonde tipsily, just at the instant Lizzie realized it was Penny.

"What the hell are you doing?"

Penny whizzed around.

"Darling! It's so good to see you! This is my twin," she said to her companion, in a strange accent that sounded like posh socialite Tara Palmer-Tomkinson wrestling with a mouthful of chewing gum.

The tall, thin man looked at Lizzie, then Georges, who stood in the doorway behind her, up and down.

"How charming," said the man. "Which one?"

"Oh, Sloan," squealed Penny, "you are awful."

"This is my twin, Penny," said Lizzie to Georges. "And 'Sloan.' They're both awful, apparently."

"I see," said Georges, wiping his hand on his apron and holding it out. Penny affected to ignore it.

"Darling, I have to tell you. I've got the most wonderful job! In Sloan's art gallery! The first place I tried! Isn't that utterly fabulous! We had to go to lunch to celebrate."

"Well, it's not every day an angel from heaven drops in to improve your life," said Sloan elaborately.

Georges sniffed loudly.

"She's so unbelievably foxy," said Sloan. "She'll attract all the old codgers with cash. She flashes that grin and that little arse and we'll be quids in."

"That sounds like a great job," said Lizzie.

"Oh, I know it's difficult for you, darling. Maybe Sloan knows of some more openings . . ."

There was a silence during which Sloan examined the particularly intricate pocket watch he had tucked into the breast pocket of his Rupert Bear yellow-checked waistcoat.

"I've got a job too," said Lizzie finally.

"Congratulations! Oh, you should have called me. You could have come celebrating with us! Where is it? Ooh, please can it be somewhere hip where we can get into after hours. Or a private club! That'd be great, now I'm going to be moving in the art world."

"Actually, it's here," said Lizzie, indicating the little café behind her. "Great, eh? You can come and have your lunch and . . . things."

"Oh my God, carb central!" said Sloan. "Imagine."

Lizzie decided the safest thing to do with Sloan would be to ignore him.

"And this is my new boss, Georges."

Georges went to put his hand out, then decided against it.

"Hello," he said.

"Hello, Georgie Porgie," said Penny, giggling drunkenly. "Is this a pie shop?"

Lizzie's face was truly flaming now. She looked apologetically at Georges, who appeared to be politely biting his lip.

"Uh, I'll see you tomorrow," she said.

"Mmm," said Georges. Lizzie scarpered before he could reconsider the job offer.

"Right. Cocktails," said Sloan. "It's after three. Let's go to the Collection."

"I don't know what that means," said Penny, "but I'm up for it anyway."

"I think I'll just go home," said Lizzie, and she turned back down the Fulham Road, as Penny waltzed up it.

*"Owwwwoww."* Penny was roaming the flat like a very slim bear with a very sore head. *"Owoowwowow."* She'd had such a good day, she didn't deserve this. She was going to be a proper Chelsea girl, she was on the way up, and she was sure Chelsea girls didn't get nasty headaches as a result of overdoing the celebrations with the new boss, Sloan.

"Drinking in the afternoon?" said Lizzie. "How classy of you. Is that what people in Chelsea do now?"

"Shut up," said Penny, gulping back an Alka-Seltzer. She'd got back about four and immediately fallen asleep for two hours.

"This is going to either  work or make me really sick. Kill or cure." She paused for five seconds. "Excellent. It's down."

"So you got a new job and immediately went and got pissed up with your boss? Are you sure that's wise?"

"Are you joking? Sloan is incredibly influential in the London art world. It's going to be fabulous for me."

"How do you know that? Have you been keeping up with the art world, or did he tell you? And what kind of name is Sloan anyway?"

"A joke one," said Penny seriously. "I asked him. All posh people have joke names. Maybe I should get one."

"What about Pissed-Face?"

"Oh God, this place is depressing." Penny looked around her, her gaze settling on the pile of Victorian photographs Lizzie had tidied out of her room and put up on a shelf. "Every single person in these photographs is dead, dead, dead. Dead, dead, dead, dead buried and gone. Dead. Doesn't that depress you?"

"Well, when you put it like that . . ."

"And that noise."

From the apartment below was coming the deep bass of Duran Duran being played extremely loudly.

"It's doing my head in," said Penny. "I think I'm going to go and talk to them."

"Don't," said Lizzie. "It's been a long day. Have you ever been confronted with an angry Duran Duran fan? I'm telling you, it's not pretty. They slap you with bleached denim and spray Sun In in your eyes."

"I don't care," said Penny. "My head is spinning, and I've got to go to work tomorrow."

"With someone whose head will also be spinning," argued Lizzie, "and don't forget, it's only seven-thirty in the evening. You can hardly accuse them of keeping antisocial hours."

Penny rolled her eyes. "Well, anyway, I want to meet our neighbors. They might . . . be nice."

"They might be minted, you mean," said Lizzie. "You were

never very interested in meeting our neighbors in Parkend Close."

"That's because I could hear them screaming, 'Wayne! You're a fucking wanker that slept with Shelley-Marie' all night, every night, and I think I knew them about as well as I needed to."

"Do you remember when Shelley-Marie turned up?"

"Do I? 'I'm going to cut you, Wayne, cut you with this knife.'" They were both silent for a moment.

Penny shivered. "And now I'm working in a Chelsea art gallery and I'm making lots of nice new West End friends. Fantastic."

"Do you think telling our neighbors to turn the music down is the best way to make new friends?"

Penny shrugged. "You never know. There might be a nice man down there."

"Listening to maximum-volume Duran Duran?"

"Maybe he's a wild boy," said Penny, heading out and slamming the door.

Forty minutes later, Lizzie was getting slightly worried. Maybe there was a New Romantic psycho downstairs, locked up listening to "Fade to Gray" and planning terrible tortures and murders. Oh no! She left her bedroom, where she'd been looking at the clothes she'd brought with her. They were almost uniformly black, with a couple of cheap suits she used to wear in the office. They wouldn't be much use now, if she was going to get covered in grease every day. She really needed to wash her hair too, but was scared of that big bath. If she slipped in it she might never get out again.

Suddenly, she noticed Penny had left her mobile on the only bit of work surface not covered in antique cups and saucers. Oh, crap. She couldn't even phone her to see if she was all right. By now, she had undoubtedly been tied up with leg warmers and dumped in a cupboard.

Carefully she crept into the hallway. It smelled of polish and fresh flowers, and much nicer than their flat.

She went downstairs and listened outside the door. The music was still going as loudly as ever. Maybe she should go and get a weapon. No, that was just stupid. Nothing was wrong with her sister. But just in case, kick in the crotch. The crotch.

She knocked on the door. "Hello?"

Nothing.

"Hello?"

No one. Taking a deep breath, she reached for the doorknob. It turned in her hand.

"Hello?"

She pushed the door harder and, slowly, it started to open.

Lizzie stood in the doorway and stared. The huge sitting room was spread out in front of her, an exact replica of upstairs. But this room was completely different; it was clear and white, and the huge windows were shiny clean, letting the evening light pour in.

Two red sofas, deep and luxuriant, sat on either side of the white wooden fireplace. Red-and-white-striped chairs provided extra seating. On the other side of the room, near the spotless stainless-steel kitchen, was a large circular table with a large bowl of green apples sitting on it. Large abstract canvases hung on the wall. Lizzie realized immediately it was how she'd like her flat to be, if she ever had a choice in the matter.

"Uh, hello, yeah?" came a drawling voice.

61

Sitting on the sofas, as she took in more than just the furniture, were three skinny creatures. Two of them were blond, including, she noticed, Penny, who was not, in fact, being held hostage in an eighties fan's torture cellar after all. The other was dark and dusky, absolutely gorgeous in the manner of those who get off with married footballers.

"Uhh . . . I'm from upstairs," stuttered Lizzie, finding, annoyingly, that she was intimidated just because she was standing in front of such good-looking people.

"This is obviously our night for having the neighbors drop in," said the brunette with a sleepy look.

"I think having the neighbors drop in is a bit common," said the blonde, who had a pinched face and ridiculously long pin legs. "A bit *EastEnders*."

"Shut up, Minty," said the brunette. She made an inquiring face.

"Oh," said Penny from the sofa, looking up at Lizzie for the first time, as if surprised to see her there. "Yah."

"*Yah?*"

"This is my . . . my sister."

The brunette gave a slight smile. "Oh, you didn't mention her."

There was an uncomfortable silence.

"Penny was just telling us she works for an art gallery?" said the brunette, who was obviously the only one with manners more advanced than that of a stick insect.

"That's right," said Lizzie. "She sells crayons."

The girls didn't even smile.

"I'm Lizzie," said Lizzie, conscious that she hadn't changed out of her stained top. If she tried to sit down on their beautiful sofa they'd probably shoo her off.

There was a momentary pause before the girls raised themselves from their exquisite longeurs to respond.

"I'm Brooke," said the brunette. Araminta was the pinched-faced blonde who didn't seem the slightest bit interested in suggesting Lizzie call her "Minty." Penny looked a little bit uncomfortable and moved up from the sofa. Lizzie noticed they were all drinking white wine but hadn't offered her any.

"Well, I've got to go," said Penny. "Busy schedule." She cleared her throat when they looked at her expectantly, and Penny thought of the newspapers she pored over, where celebrities were always getting into trouble for throwing punches at the paparazzi. "Boujis?" she ventured.

"Who goes there these days?" said the one called Minty. "It's common."

Penny bristled. "Really? I saw Prince William there last week."

"We'll see you there," said Minty.

Penny nodded.

"You're going *where* tonight?" said Lizzie as she trailed her sister upstairs.

"I don't know, do I? I've read about it. The kind of place these nobs go and there's photographers outside. It'll be in gossip pages."

"So you're definitely going out?"

"Yes!" said Penny. "I've always wanted to go to these places. So I'm going to, and you're coming too."

"Are you sure they're real places and not something you just made up?"

"Yes."

"We don't have any money."

"We'll share a soda."

"How're we going to get in?"

"I'm going to hide you behind my breasts. Would you shut up with these really stupid questions?"

"But we've got work tomorrow."

"Yes, and forever, if I don't pull Prince William."

Lizzie sat down on one of the broken chairs back in their own apartment. It creaked ominously. "But I don't want to."

"Don't be daft, Lizzie."

Lizzie hung her head. "Why don't you go with your real friends, rather than drag me along everywhere?"

Penny snorted. "I don't think Kelly Anne and Dwaneesa would really fit in with Brooke and Minty, do you?"

"Oh, I don't know," said Lizzie. "They're all horrible. Just Kelly Anne and Dwaneesa are probably more inclined toward actual physical violence."

"It was just that one time," said Penny in a bored tone.

"That one time," said Lizzie. "That one and sole time I had my first period and they flushed my head down the bogs." Lizzie could never quite get over her resentment at having to hang out with Penny all the time, and the misery it had caused her.

"Well, that's all over and in the past and ages ago and they're not like that anymore." Penny had never understood why Lizzie bothered trailing after her at school; it wasn't like they let her join in. Penny'd never made the connection between Lizzie's calming influence and the fact that she was the only one of her group not to be expelled.

"Dwaneesa's got an ASBO!"

"That policeman was racist."

"She threw a fox at his head!"

"Just get dressed," said Penny.

"No!"

"Get dressed."

"No."

"OK, well, come in that dirty thing that makes you look re-tarded."

"I'm not going."

"Please."

"No."

"Please."

"No."

Penny pouted when it became obvious this wasn't going to work.

"But we're celebrating," she said. "We both found jobs on our first day out. And we live in Chelsea! And it's our duty to have fun and get to know the beautiful people and get our pictures in the back pages of *OK!*"

"You never recognize anyone in the back pages of *OK!*"

"That's not the point, is it? I want to be someone people go, 'Who's that cow and why on earth is she always in the back pages of *OK!*?'"

"And that's your life ambition, is it?"

"Well, yeah. Followed by 'Royal Wedding Special Edition.'"

"Well, a fondness for old bags does run in that family."

"Fuck off! And get changed."

"No!"

Penny came up to Lizzie. "You know," she said sincerely, "this is all I've ever wanted. Just a chance. Just a chance to change our lives and try and do a bit better for ourselves. It's all I've ever wanted. For both of us. To have more than Mum ever got. To have our chance . . ."

"By going out to some overpriced nightclub?"

"It's our new life," said Penny. "It will be so good for us. Us, together, striving to make a new way of . . ."

"OK, OK, make it stop!" said Lizzie. Why was she so weak? But someone had to look out for Penny, otherwise who knew what she'd do? "I'll come. For half an hour. Then I'm going to bed, I'm cream crackered."

"Don't say cream crackered," said Penny.

"I'll stop saying cream crackered, when you *start* saying thank you," muttered Lizzie, stomping off to her own room to find her trusty mascara.

Lizzie realized, staring disconsolately at her wardrobe for the second time that day, that she had no idea what Georges was going to pay her. She tried to think of some kind of innovative mathematical formula that would allow her to earn a magnificent salary selling sandwiches and spaghetti in a box, but she couldn't figure it out.

So it looked like she'd be sticking to TK Maxx and George at Asda for a while yet. There probably wasn't a TK Maxx in Chelsea, she reflected.

Oh, well, what was it Trinny and Susannah always said? V-shapes to show off those big bosoms and generous waist. And wide hips and big bottom. She wondered what it would be like to buy something that wasn't an act of disguise.

Next door she could hear doors and cupboards noisily being thrown open, with loud music being played. The wine seemed to have perked Penny up considerably, which was worrying and encouraging all at once.

"OK!" she shouted eventually, and Lizzie went out—in her black V-neck top—to see what was up. She gasped. "You're not."

"What?" said Penny. "Are you going to say, 'You're not going out dressed like that?'"

Lizzie knew Penny desperately wanted her to say it. Lizzie flashed back to all the occasions of this in their lives, from high heels worn to school when she was eight to the boob tube fiasco of the Year 7 Christmas party. Penny had a history of wearing things that made her look like she was walking out of the house with the distinct intention of getting pregnant. Why did Penny always make her feel so old?

"Are you sure the girls here dress the same as you do down at Coasters?"

"What?" said Penny innocently. "They're worse here. You should see the girls who go to these places. They wear artillery belts over their nips and nothing else at all."

"And that's the kind of girl you'd like to be?"

"It's just a bit of fun!"

"Slutty, slutty, slutty fun," said Lizzie.

Penny was wearing a transparent black shirt—that had been designed to be worn over a tank top—without the tank top—and a see-through bra. Her nipples were obvious from almost every angle. She'd teamed it with a denim mini and pink cowboy boots.

"Penny, it's illegal to walk about the streets showing your nipples."

Penny rolled her eyes. "Well, I've got something for that, haven't I? Look. I found it in one of the cupboards."

She threw a fur stole around her shoulders.

"Oh my God," said Lizzie, genuinely shocked. "You can't wear that!"

"Why not?"

"Well, one, it's not yours, and two, it's not anybody's, it belongs to an animal."

"An extremely old animal," said Penny. "Smell it, it smells like the Second World War."

# Chapter Four

There were more than a few raised eyebrows on the bus but while Lizzie felt mortified, Penny didn't seem in the slightest bit concerned; she was more worried that the girls downstairs would see them leaving to catch a bus. Not quite knowing the protocol with guest lists, etc., they'd decided to arrive at Boujis super early and sit and nurse a drink in the corner.

Even so, there was an early queue forming outside the club, the place Penny had chosen on the basis that according to the 3 a.m. girls it was a dead cert if you wanted to pull an ex-member of a boy band or a third-division footballer.

There were one or two boys, nervously tugging at their Ted Baker shirts, but overwhelmingly the queue was formed of girls; and girls whose clothes made Penny's outfit look like a shelf-stacking uniform in Tehran. Tall girls, model types shouting loudly and cavorting around up the front, nervous fat girls, freshly bronzed, wearing the latest glittery halterneck from

Morgan with their striped hair piled high on their heads; black girls and white girls in tiny little strips of dresses; girls from out of town who appeared to be wearing every piece of jewelry they owned simultaneously and more blue and green eye makeup than Lizzie had seen since secondary school.

Everything was tanned, squeezed, plumped, and primped to its very limits. Hair spray and heavy musky perfumes hung in the chilly night air like a dark velvet curtain. Across the road a small bank of photographers with huge lenses and heavy over-coats was limbering up for the evening in case they got lucky with a Page Three girl flashing her norks or a rap star out pub crawling. It wasn't that different from Brandford after all—just, Lizzie suspected, a lot more expensive.

Lizzie realized she felt terribly nervous for some reason, al-most as if she was about to be judged. Then she remembered that she *was* about to be judged, by some clipboard Nazi on the door who was going to bar her entry on the grounds that she'd kept her lip liner to the inside edge of her lips.

"Are you sure about this?" she moaned. She didn't usually go to nightclubs. She went to pubs with Grainne, where they sat and ate a lot of dry roasted peanuts and prawn cocktail crisps. When they'd finished eating from their crisp bags, they'd fold them up into perfectly neat triangles and place them tidily in the ashtray.

In fact, she only went to nightclubs proper for their bloody birthday because Penny would insist on a night out with the girls. They usually went to Coasters in Walthamstow because Penny knew the barman and they'd get free drinks. Lizzie sup-posed they weren't exactly free because Penny would repay the bar staff by flashing them and dancing wildly on the tables of the "VIP" section, which had never seen anyone more famous than the roofer out of East 17, and was bookable by anyone who didn't mind buying a bottle of horribly overpriced and revolting Jampagne ("It's just like champagne," the owner Billy was always saying, "except it comes from Japan"). Lizzie would sit in the dark and look after people's coats for ages, then suddenly get pissed very quickly and jump up and dance her head off and the next day everyone would say, "Oh, Lizzie, you were totally outrageous," and she'd want to disappear into a big hole and die.

She didn't want to be outrageous. She'd just like to move as easily through the world as other people seemed to, without blushing and feeling as if her hips were too wide for the available space.

Lizzie heaved a big sigh.

"Just stand behind me," ordered Penny, and she sashayed into the shorter queue. This was patently the queue to be in, with fewer bridge-and-tunnel-style ASOS knockoffs and a lower BMI.

At the front was a scary-looking but beautiful dark-haired woman with a severe expression and a large clipboard, which she was hugging to her chest. She looked extremely grumpy, except for when a young actress Lizzie recognized from *Coronation Street*, together with someone else from *Hollyoaks* (Lizzie made a mental note to watch less television now that she lived in Chelsea), flounced up to the front, wearing between them about three diamanté studs and some fringing.

"Hello, darlings!" said the scary woman, and the flashbulbs started going off. A little whisper of excitement went through the other queue, the one that didn't think it was on the guest list. After all, *Coronation Street* already, and it wasn't even half past ten!

"Have a few voddies on us!" shouted one of the photographers, "and we'll see you later. Falling over, hopefully." There was a nasty snigger, but the girls beamed big white smiles and waved chirpily.

The dark-haired woman was growing ever closer. Lizzie felt her heart in her mouth like she was being sent to see the head-teacher. This was ridiculous. Penny's earrings twitched as she approached the podium. The woman barely glanced up.

"Minty de Lougis," she announced, in her very best "I'm not from Essex" voice.

"Oh yes, of course, that's here," she said. "Minty! How's Brooke?"

Penny jumped back into the shadowy doorway and turned her head away in a bored fashion so that all that could be seen was her long blond hair.

"Yah, fine," she said.

"Wait a minute," said the woman, as the bouncer was pulling across the red velvet rope. "You're not—Krystanza!" she exclaimed suddenly, as, to their right, the most ridiculous thing Lizzie had ever seen got out of a stretch Hummer.

It had long skinny legs colored easyJet orange and balanced on a pair of six-inch heels made of Perspex and feathers, wore a tiny miniskirt made of denim and lace, and, juddering above this, floated the most absurd pair of balloon breasts imaginable. Two huge footballs were stapled to a chest above a tiny waist. They were so plump and bouncy on the top you could let kittens use them as trampolines. Barely held in with a tiny piece of stretchy pink tiger-skin fabric, they cast their own shadows over the waiting crowds, who drew back oohing. It was like the spaceships landing in *Independence Day*. Above the robo-bosoms, which were at neck height, was a vast mane of blond hair that looked to be made of several types of synthetic fiber, crowning a shiny mahogany face swimming in at least half a kilo of lip gloss. The apparition batted her eyelids.

"What is that?" said Lizzie, standing stock-still before Penny grabbed her by the elbow and pushed her through the double doors while everyone's attention was still diverted by the huge top-heavy apparition who was clunking past the bouncers; a horde of voices yelling, "Pull your top down, love," and flash-bulbs popping behind her. "And who are you? Did you just pass yourself off as our downstairs neighbor?"

"Well, I knew she'd be on the list."

"How?"

"She seems like the kind of person who'd be on the list. And I nicked her surname from the post. Right, let's go."

"OK, Sherlock Holmes," said Lizzie. Behind them came gasps as Krystanza tottered carefully down the lit-up stairs.

"Is that a man in drag or what?"

"No," said Penny, glancing behind her. "That's Krystanza. I think she's fantastic. For a dirty old slapper, of course. She's slept with four premiership footballers and most of her record company."

"Oh, yeah," said Lizzie. "I just didn't think she'd look so . . . weird up close."

Penny looked around. "Now, where were we?"

The club was already jam-packed, and people in the room—it was much smaller than Lizzie had been expecting—looked up hopefully as they descended the staircase, only to look down again dejectedly when they realized that the new arrivals did not play for a football team or star in Hollywood movies.

There were girls draped everywhere, up against pillars, over the bar, here and there huddled in small groups around men, who were laughing and smiling indulgently as the women fluttered and twittered over cocktails. On the dance floor were girls with fabulous figures grooving with one another and showing off their moves, which were, to Lizzie's unpracticed eye, bordering on the obscene.

"Are they lesbians?" she asked.

"No, they just pretend to be to get the blokes to notice them," said Penny.

"That's moral. What are we going to do for drinks?"

Penny tried to look like she knew what she was doing but she didn't really.

"Uh, well, I think we just hang around looking decorative."

Lizzie swallowed. "Look, I brought twenty quid. It's all I've got, but we should at least get a couple of drinks if we're going to be here."

"I thought there'd be more men around," said Penny. "This looks more like a—"

"Bordello?" said Lizzie.

"No. No." Penny looked around. "It's nice really."

A huge girl with a massive Afro elbowed them out of the way to get to Krystanza, whereupon she started showering her with kisses.

Finally they compromised; Lizzie bought one cocktail (she'd asked for beer, but they didn't serve it—it was champagne cocktails or nothing), which used up almost all of her twenty quid, which almost made her weep but didn't—and they found a tiny space by the toilets where they crouched, sipping it morosely. Every so often Penny would announce she was going to do something—get up, dance, introduce herself to some people—and

Lizzie would nod encouragingly, then Penny would hear the squeals and giggles of everyone greeting each other like old friends and yelling with glee and change her mind.

"Actually this place is really past it," she announced after an hour. "You can tell. It's shit really."

"Isn't that Will Smith?" said Lizzie, who as she hadn't been asked to do anything embarrassing yet was actually having not that bad a time. It didn't hurt that, for once, Penny was feeling just as uncomfortable and out of it as she was.

"No," said Penny without turning around.

By one in the morning Lizzie was wondering if they'd mind terribly letting her have a little lie-down in the cloakroom.

"Well, hello, you lovely ladies," said the DJ. Everyone yelled. Lizzie had been trying to work out if DJ "lovely ladies" was being ironic or not but she didn't think he was. It was obviously cool now to behave like you were about to put a Bros record on.

"I'm about to put a Bros record on," said the DJ. The crowd screamed. Obviously not as young as they were trying to look then.

"But first, there's a special prize . . . for tonight only . . . a bottle of champagne . . ."

Penny's ears pricked up.

". . . for the first girl to get them out and have a bit of a dance on the table."

A roar went up from the few men stationed around the room, most of whom looked disconcertingly seedy.

Lizzie closed her eyes. No. No, no, no, no, no. Please. Just call the night a bit rubbish, then they could go home. Just hop on the bus and chalk it up to experience, and they could relaunch the central London experience again tomorrow. Please. When she opened them, Penny had gone.

The first, familiar bars of "When Will I Be Famous" had started up. To Lizzie's utter amazement, several other girls were already tearing at their thin bikini straps.

"Help me with these goddamn buttons," hissed Penny from a few feet away, striding toward the center of the floor.

"No!"

Penny took a panicky look around. Already a petite Tara Reid lookalike had nearly finished wrangling two big plastic melons out of her cerise Barbie top.

"Bollocks to it," said Penny finally, pulling off the rest of the buttons which scattered on the floor. "Grab my bra, Liz!"

Lizzie tried to crouch down behind the nearest table as Penny tugged at the elastic. Mission accomplished, Penny hauled herself, in a most ungainly fashion, onto the nearest table, knocking over someone else's glass in the process.

"Oh, for fuck's sake," came a female voice that was purest Essex. The man also sitting at the table, however, whom Lizzie recognized from her peeping vantage point as having once, many years ago, appeared in a soap opera, was clearly delighted.

"Up you get, love," he shouted, proffering a hairy arm.

Red-faced and slightly out of breath, Penny finally succeeded in getting rid of the bra and threw it straight at Lizzie. It landed on her head.

"Hold on to it," she hollered and began swaying gymnastically, if not necessarily rhythmically. The people around started to clap halfheartedly. To Penny's horror, though, there were at least four other girls dotted around the club, also with their tits out. And they undoubtedly outshone Penny in the mammaries department, as they universally had the exact same breasts, jutting out of their emaciated rib cages at a ninety-degree angle, like they'd been swallowing apples whole.

"And it's a dead heat in the Zeppelin race!" chortled the DJ as if he was being incredibly witty. "So, girls, I guess it's up to you to dance your way to that bottle of champers!"

Immediately, Penny sprang into action. Lizzie wanted to cover her face with her hands. It was so . . . undignified. Was that the right word for writhing about half naked in front of washed-up TV stars for a bottle of bubbly? Actually, undignified didn't really cover it.

Penny had stepped up her game quite considerably and was shimmying up and down like she'd made an unexpected stop on her way to Stringfellows. The television actor was completely mesmerized. The girl whose glass Penny had knocked over was making loud sighing and tutting noises and mouthing "slut" to her friends, but Penny was oblivious. That champagne was going to be won. She stuck out her little bottom and swiveled her rump down to the tabletop.

"Ooh," said the DJ. "Looks like there's a girl there that really, really wants it. So I think we're going to have to declare a winner . . . And, I know you'll find this hard to believe, chaps, but I think those might even be real!"

There was another loud holler. Penny raised her arms in the air and shimmied in triumph.

"Come on down then, hot stuff."

The other girls slunk off their tables looking slightly shame-faced as Penny put out her hand for the actor to take it as if she were stepping down from a carriage. She demurely put her hands over her bosoms and picked her way toward the DJ station. The DJ was a ridiculous white man in his mid-thirties with long blond dreadlocks falling over his shoulders, wearing a pair of dungarees with nothing underneath them. He beckoned Penny over, gyrating in what he evidently thought was a pretty sexy manner.

Just as Penny—reveling in the attention—nearly made it, there was a distinct *whoo* from the crowd as Krystanza strode off the dance floor and stood directly between Penny and the DJ.

"Excuse *me*," said Penny, but the DJ had already turned the music up.

Slowly, desultorily, Krystanza lifted her arms above her head and brought them down behind her back. Winking one eye, that was drooping slightly from the weight of the eyeshadow on it, she ran her tongue over her lips. The men in the club were on their feet.

Carefully, she unhooked the eye of her bra top. Lizzie screwed her eyes up, in case one of Krystanza's mega bosoms sprang out and hit her in the face.

Indeed, they popped out with an almost audible plopping, bouncing noise, as if they were full of jelly. The entire club went silent in awe. Like two enormous flying plum puddings they seemed to defy the laws of physics. The nipples alone were larger than Penny's perfectly nice pert pair. It was impossible not to stare at them. Lizzie tried but absolutely could not discern the attraction for a man of getting stuck between two things bigger than his head.

Krystanza was now fondling her two footballs with the same lazy uninterested air.

"And it looks like we have a new winner, ladies and gentlemen," announced the DJ. Krystanza extended an arm and grabbed the champagne.

"Oh no you don't!" shouted Penny suddenly, seeing all her efforts (and buttons) going in vain. "Give me that! It's mine!"

She launched herself at Krystanza in a feral leap, fingernails pointing outward.

Krystanza merely turned around, ensuring Penny bounced off her huge mammaries without leaving a mark.

"Rrr!" yelled Penny, plowing in for another go.

"Fight! Fight! Fight!" shouted the crowd delightedly.

Penny managed to get hold of some of the girl's hair, but it came out without causing her any noticeable discomfort whatsoever.

"*Urgh!*" shouted Penny. "What is this? Did you shave it off a starving Russian prostitute, you skank?"

The DJ, while clearly enjoying the scene, realized something would have to be done as Krystanza turned around, slowly, like a ship.

"How dare you talk to me like that?" she said poisonously. "Do you want a scrap? You'll get one."

"Fantastic," said Penny. "Have you seen *Million Dollar Baby*?" And she started bouncing up and down like a boxer.

Lizzie hid further down behind the chair, until she was practically kneeling on the floor, burying her face into her knees. From behind her fingers she noticed Brooke and Minty enter, wearing white jeans and glittery little tops.

"*Nobody* touches my hair, you bitch," Krystanza was screaming.

"You want a piece of me?" Penny was screaming back. "Do you? Give me my champagne, bitch."

Lizzie saw Brooke and Minty break into broad smiles as they

saw Penny in the middle of the floor. Clearly their new friend was going to prove excellent entertainment.

"Go, Penny!" shouted Brooke. Penny pushed her arm out again, grabbing another handful of Krystanza's hair in the process. Krystanza went wild and ran for Penny, looking exactly like Miss Piggy, whomping her on the chin with her crystal-studded handbag.

Lizzie rushed forward to see if her sister was hurt, watching her, feeling helpless as she cascaded through the air, completely off balance.

As she fell, with Lizzie diving over to grab her, she managed to make a punching motion out toward Krystanza's left leg. Fatally unbalanced, the blonde started to totter forward, just as Penny hit the floor and Lizzie landed on top of her. Like a tree falling (someone even shouted *"Timber!"*), with crashing slowness, Krystanza's nipples, followed by the rest of her, collapsed on top of the girls.

Lizzie felt as if she was being squashed beneath two giant bouncy balls as the place erupted into applause.

When they finally disentangled themselves, Krystanza was led off by an overly handsome man looking concerned, and the DJ was calming the crowd.

"I think *both* these lovely ladies deserve a bottle, don't you?"

"Yah!" Minty was shouting.

The DJ looked at Lizzie, who had managed to rip her top in the melee and was conscious that her hair was doing that frizzy thing again.

"Uh . . . yeah," he said, glancing past her. *"Both* our lovely catfighting ladies!"

Penny retrieved her top, panting, red in the face and somehow looking devastatingly sexy. Already footballers and the sons of once famous footballers were beginning to circle around her.

"You are crazy," said Brooke, in a voice that sounded admiring.

"Yah, Penny, you're so wild," said Minty. "That girl, fighting in public. *So* common."

"I started it," said Penny happily.

Bottles of champagne seemed to keep appearing from somewhere, but nobody had asked Penny for any money, so it was quite all right. Lizzie, a bit wobbly from her trip and long day, sat quietly in the corner with no one talking to her except every so often, when they'd say something and she'd perk up and try and look happy and interested and raise her eyebrows expectantly, and they'd ask her if she'd mind moving so they could go to the toilet. So she drank too much and wondered unhappily why, if this place was so incredibly expensive, they couldn't spare some peanuts to put on the tables. She slurred this to Brooke before she left, who looked at her with an eyebrow raised and said, "Darling, you know, I have this little dietician fellow you really *must* meet," and Lizzie had lurched backward like she'd been slapped. She couldn't bear to have her weight mentioned.

Suddenly it was after three-thirty: it was *so* late, and everything was winding down. Lizzie only just realized she was horribly drunk. People had been turning up with drinks for them all night and, madly, she'd just kept going. Their new neighbors had disappeared ages before—whether on to another club or just sensibly home to keep their perfect skin and glossy hair, Lizzie didn't know. There was hardly anyone left when Lizzie finally managed to drag Penny off the dance floor, where she was half dancing, half swaying with an incredibly sleazy fellow with slicked-back hair and shiny shoes, who obviously thought his luck was in and looked annoyed at Lizzie dragging his pissed-up dancing partner away, until he saw the determined set of her jaw.

"Home," said Lizzie. If only they'd gone with Brooke and the others they could have cadged a lift in their cab, but Penny had been dancing and Lizzie had been standing up to let someone go to the toilet and they'd missed them.

"I've had a *fabulous* time," said Penny. "Everyone really liked me. And I've got . . . this!"

As they fell through the front glass doors, she held up her trophy, a long blond lock of synthetic hair.

"I'm definitely going to be a Chelsea girl," slurred Penny. "I think I'll just stick this in my hair right now."

Lizzie shook her head as she felt the cold morning air in her face, freshening her up considerably.

"Look at me," said Penny, lifting up the hair. "I'm Krystanza and I'm a great big fucking slut, slut, slut. Ooh! I'm a slut! I'm a slutty slutty slut . . . with my stupid big tits and my tiny wee butt I'm a skank, I'm a ho, I'm a slut slut . . ."

Her last word, which Lizzie suspected might have been "slut," never had a chance to escape her mouth as the woman in front of them, waiting for a taxi, turned around and pounced.

"Hello, Krystanza," attempted Penny, as the other girl tried to pick her up by the throat. In the next instant they were rolling around on the ground again, as the few remaining paparazzi started flashing away wildly with their cameras.

"Oh God," said Lizzie. "Will you two stop that?" And she waded in to try and separate them.

"*Get off!*" shouted one of the photographers.

"Yeah, get out of it, podge," shouted another one. "We've got shots to get here."

Lizzie's head shot up. They couldn't mean her, surely?

"Yeah, get out of it. Shit, that arse is obscuring my lens."

There was coarse laughter as Lizzie stumbled backward, face flaming, to try and get out of the way. She lost her footing a little on the step and fell horribly, inevitably, her ankle vanishing from underneath her as she catapulted downward and landed on her bottom on the pavement.

Stunned, feeling drunker than ever, she sat there trying to regain her equilibrium, the chortling of the photographers ringing in her ears. The heel of her shoe had broken off. She noticed it had fallen in a dirty McDonald's cup. This was possibly the most excruciating night out she'd had since her and Penny's joint twenty-first, when she'd pulled a virgin and they'd sat on her single bed for four hours drinking Nescafé with milk that tasted slightly off.

Maybe she should just stay here, in the gutter, and go to sleep. Maybe she could lie down and put her head in a puddle and find some more fast-food wrappers and stick them to herself to keep warm. She didn't think it could be any more humiliating than the way she felt already. After all, nothing could get any worse.

"Uh, hello?" came a voice from above her. It sounded kind and concerned. This wasn't what she wanted right now. Kind and concerned was bad, in fact, because it implied she'd done something ridiculous that required patience and pity. Grudgingly, she looked up . . . and her night deteriorated even more.

"I *thought* that was my new employee. I was right!" said Georges. He held out a helping hand. "Are you OK? Have you been mugged?"

Lizzie realized how she must look, with the evidence of two fights all over her. She shook her head. "No."

He shook his hand at her and she took it and scrambled up. "Having a good night?"

Lizzie swallowed, suddenly feeling very drunk and awful. She wobbled a bit in only one shoe and had to lean against him. He held her elbow.

"Are you OK?"

"I am absolutely fine," said Lizzie, concentrating on not slurring her words. "Are you?"

"Me? Yes, I am great. I go to the fish market, there may be some lovely red snapper. Early bird catches the fish, yes?"

"But it's the middle of the night."

"Or very early in the morning. It's good. You should come, er, sometime."

"What about now?" said Lizzie. Penny could still be heard yelping behind her, and she felt like getting away.

Georges looked pointedly down at her missing shoe.

"I think you should probably get some sleep . . . I hear you start very important job tomorrow, no?"

Lizzie hung her head and leaned into him a bit. After all, he'd seemed to like her today, hadn't he? For a bit at least.

"Please?" she said, trying to sound a bit flirtatious.

"No," he said, gently extricating himself from her boozy hold. She felt him pushing her away.

"Go home now," he said. "Get some sleep."

"I didn't want to get off with you anyway," she said, upset.

Georges coughed and looked startled. "Er, excuse me?" he said.

"You're not my type," said Lizzie, thinking in her befuddled state that this would make her seem cool and unbothered. "I just don't have enough money to get home."

Lizzie bent down to fish her shoe out of the McDonald's container. For a second it looked like she was about to topple over again, but Georges grabbed her by the waistband—sadly elasticated. She wavered for a second before righting herself.

Georges smiled at her, concern in his eyes. He stuck up his hand and hailed a taxi, handing the driver a tenner.

"Is this enough to get this lady back to Chelsea?" he asked the cabbie.

"I don't know, is she going to be sick?" asked the driver.

"Are you going to be sick?" asked Georges.

Lizzie shook her head miserably.

"Off you go then," said Georges.

"I have to get my sister," said Lizzie. "I have to get her."

"Where is she?"

But Georges didn't have to wait long to find out. Able to sniff out a free cab from five kilometers away, Penny was flying down the steps, with what looked like half a wig in her hands.

"Fly! Fly!" she yelled, as she hit the pavement. "Who's this?" She looked at Georges without the faintest flicker of recognition that she'd met him less than twenty-four hours previously.

"It's Georges. I don't fancy him," said Lizzie.

"Oh, that doesn't matter. Is he rich?"

"Goodnight, ladies," said Georges. And he shut the taxi door and marched off down the street.

"Well, what a fantastic night," said Penny. And, like a cat, she stretched herself out on the back seat of the cab and promptly fell asleep.

# Chapter Five

"Well, there's no point in crying," said Penny, already making herself up very efficiently in the tiny square of bathroom mirror that wasn't completely obscured by boxes of pinned butterflies.

"You don't know how bad it was," said Lizzie. "I'm not a hundred percent sure myself when it comes to it."

"How bad could it have been? Wasn't he just sleazing you up a bit?"

"No," said Lizzie, through painfully hiccuppy noises as she tried to prevent herself from bursting into sobs. This was why she didn't like getting drunk very often. "I was sleazing him up. Oh, Penny, I'm a disgrace."

"You threw yourself at your new fat boss?" Penny raised an overplucked eyebrow.

Lizzie sniffled to herself.

Penny looked at her pityingly. "So what are you going to do—move jobs?"

Lizzie shook her head. "I can't . . . it was hard enough to find this one." She groaned. "I'll just have to do the whole thing without looking at him. Unless he sacks me, of course."

"Is that a big zit on your nose or did you fall asleep on a Jammy Dodger?" said Penny.

How anyone could look quite so perky when they'd been ten seconds off getting a police caution only a few hours previously was a mystery to Lizzie. Penny strode briskly up to the newsagent's on the corner and picked up a copy of a tabloid.

Sure enough, there she was, on page eleven. "Big Bust's BIG Bust Up!" ran the headline. "Page Three stunner Krystanza's night came to a shocking close at Boujis when she was set upon by a jealous fan. 'This girl was making a real fool of herself all night,' said a friend. 'Then when Krystanza went to leave she couldn't stand it anymore and jumped her. It was pathetic really.'"

This was emblazoned over a large picture of Krystanza, breasts akimbo, twisting alarmingly on the steps. Penny's fingernails could just be seen outstretched toward her bosoms.

"It's me!" said Penny. "I'm famous!"

Lizzie studied it, momentarily distracted from her funk.

"It says you were making a real fool of yourself all night," she said. "I didn't think it was *all* night, just the bit when you were taking your clothes off and that."

"Thanks," said Penny. She studied the newspaper closely. "I don't see a bit where it says, 'The beautiful mysterious stranger is still being sought as she disappeared into the night.'"

"Maybe they had to trim that bit for space," said Lizzie.

"Maybe I should call the paper and put in my side of the story."

"What's your side of the story? She stood up and you tried to fight her."

"She tried to nick my champagne!"

"She had the biggest tits in a 'Who's Got the Biggest Tits' competition!"

"She cheated!"

Penny was still feeling mildly exuberant when she rocked up to the gallery. Sloan was outside, opening up.

"Shocking hangover," he said. "A few too many brandies at the Officers' Club with an old guardsman, ahem, chum."

"Me too," said Penny. "Well, similar."

She showed him the newspaper and he shouted with laughter.

"You are a hoot," he said. "What a girl."

Penny smiled happily. At least someone approved. Why couldn't Lizzie understand she was only trying to have a little bit of fun, for goodness' sake, and nobody had got hurt. Well, maybe Krystanza had got a *little* bit hurt, but she'd be grateful for the column inches—Penny had done her a favor, really.

"Right, a gentle morning then," said Sloan. "You fire up the coffee machine over there and I'll leaf through *Harden's* and consider my luncheon options."

Penny went over and looked at the strange hissing contraption. She didn't know where to start.

"Don't you have any Nescafé?" she shouted.

"Are you sure you've lived in Chelsea all your life?" said Sloan.

"Of course," she said. "We just always had maids to make the coffee. And stuff."

"Of course you did, dear," said Sloan, smiling. He couldn't

help it: wherever she was from, he admired her chutzpah. "Watch carefully."

As he started to talk about steam pressure and grinding beans, Penny looked around the gallery—she'd glanced at the paintings yesterday, but Sloan had seemed so interested in her false nails that she hadn't really had time to take them in properly. Now as she did so, she realized they were actually rather nice. Large landscapes. They looked like photographs from a distance; only up close could you see the beautiful detail in every painting.

"Not challenging," Sloan barked when he noticed her examining them, "but they sell well and look gorgeous. The painter isn't bad-looking either, which always helps. Much better than those chaps who bring in their stuff made from piss and monkey dung." He shivered, while he did something complicated with some filter paper and a tube that whistled. "Practically sell themselves. So all you have to do, sweetheart, is sit pretty and smile widely. And *I* get my bloody lunch hour back. You know, I worried that when Maud left I would only get an hour or two!" He shook his head. "What way is that to get business done? See," said Sloan, pointing at the newspaper. "I can tell you are definitely the right person. If someone tries anything, feel quite at liberty to challenge them to a fight. Nothing like a little bit of scandal. They'll be *flocking*."

Penny wasn't entirely sure that being allowed to fight sexism with violence was quite the way they ought to be going about things, but Sloan seemed thoroughly satisfied, and so far this job seemed to involve a lot more sitting on her arse than being pinched on it, so perhaps this wasn't quite the time to bring up any human rights legislation.

"Ah, lunch," said Sloan, looking misty-eyed. "Now. Look here. If a painting has a red dot on it that means it's sold and you can't sell it again, OK?"

Penny nodded.

"However, if they really like it, tell them you might be able to have a word with Will, the artist. He can basically photocopy it and we'll sell it twice. Bingo!"

This wasn't how Penny had thought the art world worked, if she'd ever thought about it at all. But she could probably get used to it, she figured, as Sloan wobbled out the door at quarter to eleven, and she sat back with the paper.

Forty minutes later the door clanged open. Penny shoved her *Daily Mirror* under the desk pronto and tried to look smart. Lizzie had tried to stop her from using the lip liner this morning but she'd ignored her. Now she wished she'd listened; she felt far too pouty. Surreptitiously she tried to wipe it away.

"Hello," came a posh voice. "Are you eating a jam sandwich?"

She looked up. A man had entered. He was wearing a beaten-up old leather jacket at least thirty years out of date that somehow conspired to look great on him. Fair, with floppy hair over long-lashed eyes and an equally long jaw, he needed a haircut and had a twinkle in his eye. Rogue, thought Penny immediately, cheering up.

"I was," she said. "But now I'm all yours."

The man looked around the gallery. "What are these pictures? They're all crap."

Penny glanced down at her desk. Sure enough, there was his picture on the glossy folder that accompanied the exhibition; this was Will Brown, the artist.

"I know," said Penny. "We're kind of selling them for charity. I think it's for the mentally handicapped or something."

The man stifled a rather shocked snort. "That is a very strange thing to say," he said, looking at her more closely. "Where's Maud?"

"I wanted her job so I had her killed," said Penny, wondering if this mode of flirting was going to work or not. She figured that this cute-looking artist probably had women coming on to him all the time so she should probably look to stand out.

"Well done," said the artist, looking around. "So are you selling much of this rubbish then?"

"We give them away, mostly," said Penny. "Sometimes we use them as wrapping paper for other paintings."

The artist looked confused but slightly pleased, which Penny reckoned was probably the right way to go.

"I'm Will Brown," he said finally, holding out his hand.

"Penny Berry," she said, smiling and taking it. "Would you like a painting?"

He looked even more confused.

"I . . . er, those are my paintings. Do you talk to everyone like that?"

Penny decided to let him off the hook sharpish before he had her fired. "I know." She gave him the benefit of her widest grin. "We've sold loads. I think they're lovely."

Will held her gaze a tiny second too long, then dropped his eyes. Bingo, thought Penny.

"You've got lipstick on your teeth," said Will. Bugger, thought Penny.

Lizzie could feel herself beginning to sweat as she put her hand on the door to the café. Oh bugger. How could she have disgraced herself like that? She would love, love, love to blame it on Penny, but for once she couldn't quite see how. She sniffed. Was that pure alcohol coming out of her pores? Oh bugger. So as well as being a shiftless party girl and part-time slut, she smelled of booze in the mornings. Her new life was going just great. It took quite a lot of Lizzie's meager supply of courage to push open the door at all.

"Uh, hello," she said, staring at the floor and blushing furiously as usual.

Georges peered out from behind the counter where he was deftly flaying fish.

"Hello. Is that Paris Hilton?"

"I'm very sorry about last night," said Lizzie in a rush.

"I am amazed you are here," said Georges. "How is your head?"

"Terrible. And I don't remember a thing," she said quickly.

"Oh, well," said Georges, still looking severe. "You have nothing to apologize for then."

Lizzie winced.

"Would you like a coffee?"

She nodded.

"That is too bad. You've got lots to do. Come on then, get started. There's the bread—I need you to make a start on the sandwiches, and slice up the new ham that is just delivered, and I'm making risotto so you need to grate the Parmesan."

Phew, thought Lizzie. She'd got away with it.

"Oh," said Georges, "and you must please scrub the bottom side of the cooker."

Lizzie nodded and resignedly pulled on an apron from behind the door.

In a way, the hard work was helpful; cathartic. She still felt sweaty, but she was getting so unbelievably dirty it didn't matter much anyway. She scrubbed the whole place down, washing up everything before she started on the food, trying to lay everything out in a good place to make it as easy as possible for Georges when the lunchtime rush came around.

At eleven Georges popped his head around into the little washing-up area. He looked carefully at everything, quite impressed, then nodded.

"Good job," he said. "You can have a coffee now."

"Thanks," said Lizzie huskily. "Do you mind if I have a Diet Coke?"

He laughed. "You are far gone. Do your joints hurt?"

She nodded.

"You have a proper English hangover."

She followed him through as he tossed her a can from the fridge.

"So every day you will be like this, Lizzie?"

Lizzie shook her head. "It was—"

"Your sister?"

Lizzie nodded, surprised.

"Very naughty sister. Do you blame everything on your sister?"

"It was her fault!" said Lizzie, conscious she sounded about eight years old.

"So do you have much experience in the art world?" asked Will, suspiciously looking into the terrible cup of coffee Penny had just made him.

"Yes," said Penny. "No," she added quickly in case he suddenly decided to give her a quick quiz.

Will smiled. "So Sloan didn't take you on for your amazing history of art degree?"

Penny shook her head.

"Your marketing and design experience?"

"Nope."

"Your brilliant financial acumen?"

"Yes. It was that."

"Not your lovely smile and friendly manner?"

"I was only pretending to be friendly at the interview," said Penny. "I'm slightly worried about that."

"Do you think maybe your friendly skills need working on?" said Will. "Your coffee definitely needs improving."

"I'm a highly sophisticated art dealer, not a tea dolly."

"I forgot," said Will. He scratched his ear. He hadn't met many girls like Penny before—her hair spray alone was nearly choking him—and he was quite scared. But, on the other hand, he thought she was pretty sexy too. Very sexy in fact. She looked like the kind of girl who might wear a thong.

Most of the girls Will met wore footless black leggings with gamine dresses over the top of them and headscarves and wanted to talk about Cartier-Bresson and Sartre. Which he would, drearily, until he managed to get them into bed, where they would usually want to talk about what a spiritual experience they were having. Sometimes they'd cry. The girls he usually liked wore Chanel earrings and expensive shoes, but they tended to be trickier.

"So," he said, mustering his best suave-artist manner. "Those friendly skills of yours . . . do you think they'd like a tutorial over lunch?"

"I got hired so someone else could go to lunch," said Penny, delighted. "So, no."

"See, you're failing the tutorial already. That's not a friendly response at all."

"What happens if I fail? Do I get punished?" She smiled a tad suggestively.

"See, there, that's too friendly, spilling over into frightening." Penny smiled to herself.

"It's my first day. I'm just trying to stay out of trouble."

Will looked at her.

"Honestly?" he said. "You look like the epicenter of trouble."

The lunch rush went past so quickly Lizzie nearly forgot to eat a meal herself. She'd already forgotten her morning KitKat and prawn cocktail crisps. Oh well, she thought sadly at three o'clock, there was probably a coleslaw roll left over somewhere. She hadn't seen a KFC in Chelsea.

"Ta-dah!" said Georges, plonking a plate of risotto in front of her. "I saved you some."

Lizzie looked up at him gratefully.

"I thought we would not see you today but you did a good day's work."

"This is delicious," said Lizzie. "I don't think I've ever had it before."

Georges looked utterly shocked. "You've never eaten risotto?" She shrugged sadly.

"But what do you eat?"

"You know," said Lizzie.

"I do not know," said Georges.

"Well. Quick things mostly. Stuff you can microwave. Pizzas and things."

"You can't microwave a pizza," said Georges.

"You can, kind of," said Lizzie, mumbling a bit.

"What else?" said Georges.

"Curry and things."

"You microwave this curry too?"

Lizzie nodded. "And lasagne."

"Ah. The easiest thing to make. You can't make that in a microwave, can you?"

She nodded again. Georges looked absolutely aghast. He sat down beside her.

"Ooh, Lizzie, Lizzie."

Lizzie was blushing furiously. She knew her eating habits were terrible. There never seemed any point in cooking as Penny didn't eat anything. So she'd grab something and heat it up. On the pictures on the packets they'd usually have a serving with something green or some lettuce next to it, but she never bothered with that. Her mum had always just brought home some bland leftovers from school and heated it up, and they'd never progressed really. She kept telling herself she'd lose the weight when she was ready, when something happened that would be worth losing it for. So far, nothing had happened like that.

Not unkindly, Georges reached out and pinched a little of the wobbly flesh on her upper arms. Then he took her hand and placed it on his big belly. Lizzie flinched. She knew Mediterraneans were more touchy-feely than Brits, and she knew she was more uptight than most. This was the first time a man had touched her, she thought suddenly, in over a year, and that was a regrettable accident, after she'd run into Felix in Coasters. She hadn't been entirely sure he knew they'd broken up. Georges felt warm, and more solid than she expected. She felt her face turn scarlet.

"Now this," said Georges. "This tummy. You feel it?"

She nodded.

"This tummy is made from good chèvre, good goat's cheese, and calamar, and baklava, and tagliatelle with a wild boar sauce, and best chorizo, and potato cakes fried in the new oil, and good wine, yes? Every kilo of me is made from quality food and happy days and nights. So I am fat but I have many friends and much good food inside me. But Lizzie, you eat slop, yes? You heat up slop and eat it and taste nothing and watch television and this is not good, is it?"

Lizzie suddenly felt as if she was about to cry. She put down her fork.

"Thanks, Gillian McKeith," she said.

"I do not know who this is," said Georges. "Come now, eat."

"I don't feel like it."

"Of course you do. This is good Parmesan and good rice and good squids and—"

"Squid?"

"Calamar. Squids. Yes, of course."

"I'm eating a squid." Lizzie peered at it. "Isn't there supposed to be ink everywhere?"

"You've never eaten squids?"

Lizzie shook her head. "It was on a menu when we were in Spain once and we thought they were joking. We thought it was a right laugh, like eating donkey or something."

Georges looked pained. "But you are eating it and finding it good, yes?"

Lizzie looked at her plate. "Well, I suppose."

Georges winked at her. "You have a long way to go."

\*

"Is it time for my lunch now?" said Penny a tad sulkily, when Sloan rolled up at ten to five. He was clearly pissed as a fart and in a terribly relaxed mood.

"Of course, my dear girl . . . did you sell anything?"

Actually, Penny had. It was rather embarrassing. A poised young woman had come in with two large men and pointed to a frame. The men had taken it down and the woman, with barely a word to Penny, had left a card on her desk. Penny was hoping fervently this was a regular customer Sloan could send a bill to rather than a thief with a gimmick.

"Well *done*!" said Sloan overenthusiastically, spotting the card. "You must have perfect sales lady skills. This is one of our very difficult-to-please people. Russian oligarchs, you know." He said the last bit in a murmur, as if someone could overhear.

Penny emphatically did not know, but it sounded interesting. "I had to talk her into it. Do I get a commission, by the way?"

Sloan snorted. "No! You get to sit in my nice warm gallery out of the cold and read *Hello!* magazine and drink free tea. The fact that I'm paying you at all is a bonus when you think about it. Now, darling, shall we go for a little cocktail hour drinkiepoo?"

But Penny was already outlining her lips in the mirror. Having taken it off earlier, she had a shrewd suspicion that Will might rather like a slightly tarty look. Not that he'd admit it, of course.

"I've got a date," she announced. "You don't mind if I pull one of your artists, do you?"

Sloan looked slightly pained. "I'd rather you pulled one of our big spenders. No chance of that, is there?"

Penny shrugged on her short jacket. "Introduce me to a few of those Russian Olive Marks."

Sloan raised a single eyebrow. "I shall." He steadied himself and focused on her for a minute. "And go easy on that William now, won't you? He's a gentle soul."

"We'll see about that," said Penny. And she winked at her boss and hopped out into the crowded evening.

Lizzie looked around her on the bus. They'd been in London three days: it was time to pay her respects to the architect of their good fortune.

Barnet was as end-of-the-line as it was possible to go, endlessly long street after street of suburban houses. Their mother had sent the address, written on headed notepaper in a very theatrical handwriting full of loops and squiggles Lizzie had never seen before. But somewhere here, there was a nursing home. The good weather had not stayed; it was back to early spring drizzle. Conscious of not missing her stop, she squinted repeatedly at road signs and tried to follow her progress on the *A–Z* street guide. She was on the very top page of the *A–Z*; she hoped they didn't make any sudden left turns or she was done for.

No, that must be it, the building at the top of the road. Lizzie rang the bell to get the bus to stop, hopping up nervously. She suffered from a conviction that if she got on a strange bus in a new place, the bus driver would attempt to trick her and drive her all the way to the depot.

"Uh, yes, stop here, please," she barked.

There was no one else on the street as she stepped down, just rows and rows of houses and parked cars, televisions casting blue shadows from behind the curtains. Lizzie pulled herself together and headed up the tilt of the road to the large building at the end.

The Larches was a huge Victorian house with netted windows.

On the brochure it was shot in bright sunlight with a lawnful of daffodils in front of it and it looked rather like a stately home where you might take tea in the garden. In the early evening gloom of a London March, however, it looked forbidding and chilly. The windows were lit, but with strip lighting, not lamps.

Approaching the front door she smelled the nasty institutional smell of boiled veg and too much bleach swilled into too many corners, a smell masking a far nastier, occasionally whiffed undercurrent.

"Hello," she said to the grumpy-looking fat nurse sitting behind a reception grille. The foyer was sparsely decorated, with large emergency exit signs, six different types of fire extinguishers, and one gray chair with a defeated-looking potted plant next to it.

"I'm here to see Mrs. Willis."

She nervously fingered the lilies she'd bought, half expecting the nurse to tut that she couldn't come in without an appointment. The other half of her thought that the nurse might give her a radiant warm smile for being such a nice caring girl as to come out all this way to visit her mad old granny.

The nurse did neither of these things, simply nodded and pressed a buzzer. The glass door separating the foyer from the rest of the house clicked open.

"Uh, which room?" said Lizzie. The nurse looked up, completely confused, then started tapping at the computer.

"Four, eleven," she said finally, annoyed to be caught out.

"Thanks," said Lizzie. "I'll try not to steal any old ladies while I'm up there."

But the nurse didn't respond, and Lizzie went through the door alone.

To her left was a room wreathed in smoke, from which a

television game show was blaring. Glancing in, Lizzie saw a roomful of old people, mostly in nightclothes, staring straight ahead, not necessarily at the TV. It was like *Day of the Dead*. A shiver went down her spine and she rushed to the lift, which was big enough to get a bed in and out of. For all the dead people, she supposed, getting more and more creeped out as it ascended.

The room was down a winding corridor distorted by oddly shaped protuberances, like any old property adapted for a lot of extra plumbing it wasn't designed for. The door was tightly shut.

"Uh, hello?" said Lizzie, rapping her knuckles lightly against the wood. There was no answer. She gently pushed the door.

The old lady was lying on the bed with her eyes closed. She was tiny, a little bird-doll. Lizzie remembered her, from her brief visits in childhood, as being big, big and smelly. But she couldn't be, this tiny frail thing. Her hair was so thin Lizzie could see her white scalp.

The old lady opened her eyes and fixed them straightaway on Lizzie, who jumped. "Who are you?" she said. Her voice was stronger than her appearance.

"Uh, I'm Lizzie," said Lizzie. "Your granddaughter."

The woman craned her neck, staring at her for a long time, and let out a sigh. "The little twin?" she demanded querulously before falling silent again. "You're a bit of a chunky one, aren't you?" she said finally.

Lizzie let the door bang shut behind her. "Actually," said Lizzie, "if I want to get insulted about my weight, I can easily do it at home."

The old lady grunted and slowly pushed herself farther up on the pillows. "I'm not being insulting," she said. "I'd love a bit of weight on myself."

"Exactly," said Lizzie. "Compared to you, Nicole Kidman looks like she should be cutting down on the pies."

The lady beckoned her over. "Who did you say you were again?"

"I'm Lizzie. Penny and me are staying in your house."

A look of worry passed over the old lady's face. "I want to go back to my house," she said. "Why are you in my house?"

"You told us to stay in your house. We're the twins, Gran. Gran." She realized she'd never said the word out loud. "You're our gran."

"The little twins?"

Lizzie nodded.

"Someone's let the little twins run my house?"

"I'm one of the twins, Gran," said Lizzie, starting to despair. "Here. I brought you some flowers."

The old lady looked less confused when she picked up the flowers. She buried her nose in them for a long time, breathing up their rich scent. Finally, when she looked up again, she seemed much clearer.

"They give me lots of drugs," she said. "I get mixed up."

"I know," said Lizzie. "That's why you're here."

"Why are you in my house?"

"You said we could stay in your house while you were in here."

"Why would I let the little twins stay in my house . . . Oh. Because you're not little twins anymore."

"Would you like a glass of water?"

"Are you looking after my house?"

Lizzie nodded vehemently.

"They're terrible here, you know. They take the newspaper away as soon as you've read it."

"That does sound terrible."

"And they keep cleaning up after you."

"Awful."

The old woman looked around. "I'm not happy without my things about me."

She beckoned to Lizzie, who approached the bed. Her grandmother grabbed her wrist, holding on to it with surprising strength. "Don't throw out any of my things," she hissed loudly.

"I won't," said Lizzie.

The old lady's eyes misted over. "Oh, I miss Chelsea. This place is a fetid shithouse. You should have been there during the war. All the bombs falling, but we still went out dancing all the time. Misbehaving, too. Not much time to be hanging about during a war. Not many men around either."

"I'm not sure life's changed that much," said Lizzie.

"Hmm."

"How did you meet Grandfather?" asked Lizzie eagerly. She knew so little about this side of the family.

"Who?" said her grandmother. "Sorry. Who are you again?"

"I'm one of the twins," said Lizzie sadly.

"The little twins? The little twins are in my house?"

"So, apart from being bats?" said Penny. She was lying on the sofa painting her nails with a dreamy expression on her face.

"Nope, that was it, mostly. Apart from fessing up to being a bit of a slut in the forties. Then I read her *OK!* magazine for half an hour."

Penny returned her attention to her nails.

"So, aren't you interested?" asked Lizzie.

"In what?"

"In whether Dad's been in."

"Has he?"

"No."

"Imagine not even going to see your old mum."

"Prick," said Lizzie absentmindedly, from years of habit. Her father not exactly cutting the mustard as a family man wasn't what you'd call news.

"So anyway, aren't you going to ask me how my day went?" said Penny, a smile creeping onto her lips.

"I ate a squid," said Lizzie, cheering up momentarily. "It was nice. Like a chewy fish finger."

"Ugh," said Penny. "That sounds rank."

"Well, it wasn't. It was nice."

"Well, I suppose I'm going to have to be prepared to eat lots of exotic foreign food from now on," said Penny, rolling over on the sofa and pushing out her nails to dry. "Now I'm going out with an international artist and jet-setter."

Lizzie sat down. She was starving, but this news was too good to wait.

"You're what?"

"Oh, you know. Dating the artistic aristocracy, that kind of thing."

"No, I don't know. What kind of thing? Your last boyfriend owned fifteen lock-up garages. Spill."

Penny had been feeling good walking into the bar, despite the night before. She was made up, and she'd backcombed her hair so it bouffanted up high on her head, and tugged down her shirt a little.

Once she entered the crowded noisy wine bar, however, she felt a bit different. The place was heaving with men in expensive-looking pin-striped suits and very polished shoes, and the women were tiny, frail almost, with flat, very straight, glossy blond hair—more honey color than the Barbie shade she favored. These women's nails were done, but with short French manicures, not long fakes. And they all had perfectly shaped, but quite full, eyebrows. Penny had been drawing on her eyebrows since she was fifteen.

She suddenly felt out of place, and wondered if it was safe to tug her skirt down. It had been all right last night when everyone was dressed to impress, but here the women were in cashmere overcoats and cream shift dresses. Always fascinated by money, Penny found this was a new breed altogether.

A few of the men started ogling her as she walked in on her three-inch heels. Normally confident, she almost stumbled as one of them leered at her. She remembered suddenly the extra layer of lip liner she'd put on to wind up Will. None of the women here were wearing lip liner like that. She looked toward the bar, where the barman lifted an eyebrow. Shit.

From the corner Will watched the whole scene, feeling for her. Here she was, the little rich girl up in the proper city for the first time. What presumably ruled the suburban footballers' nightclubs and tanning salons wasn't working here at all. He went from imagining her as hard as nails to seeing the vulnerability in her and, somehow, he found it an incredibly attractive mix.

"Over here." He waved confidently. He stood up. "You look wonderful," he said loudly. Some people next to him rolled their eyes and stared at him rudely.

"This is a nice place," said Penny, as Will brought back her vodka and tonic. Penny had wanted a Bacardi Breezer, but had forced down the impulse.

"Come here a lot?" said Will, amused.

"Oh, yes, all the time. I think their vodka and tonics are just to die for," said Penny, wondering how Brooke and Minty got that kind of flick in their voices when they said "to die for."

"So. Tell me about you," said Will.

Penny had been dreading this.

"Well, I live in Chelsea and I work in an art gallery. For fun, you know?" she added hastily.

"But of course," said Will. "Where were you born?"

"Chelsea," said Penny quickly. "Lived here all my life."

"Right."

Must be one of those self-made daughter types, thought Will. Cardboard-making dad gets lucky, that kind of thing. Probably a daughter of the much more attractive second wife. That accent was weird though. You'd think school would have rubbed it off a bit.

"Where did you go to school?"

"Are you investigating me on behalf of MI6?"

"No," said Will, smiling. "Sorry. Just making conversation."

Penny took a swig of her drink.

"I didn't go to school. I had, you know, a governess, nanny-type thing." Penny hoped they still existed. "She came from Chelmsford."

Will nodded. That explained the accent then. "You're lucky," he said. "I hated school."

"Were they always beating you up and calling you gay and that because you liked art?"

Will frowned. "Um, no. I was head of the art club actually. Used to organize gallery tours and stuff."

"Ooh, head of the art club. Oooh," said Penny sarcastically, unable to help herself, until she remembered she wasn't meant to have been to school at all and thus would have no view.

"That sounds really interesting," she added quickly. "Sometimes I feel I missed out, I really do."

Will smiled. "I'm not sure about that. Another drink?"

Penny realized hers was finished while Will was only half-way through his. Whoops. She must try to remember to be ladylike in a Chelsea manner, not swig like someone who might later on misbehave with a wine bottle on national television. She looked at his long lean back as he went to the bar. Nice. She just had to get him to stop talking about schools before she got herself found out completely. Anything about the local turf in fact was probably best avoided.

"So tell me about your paintings."

The amazing thing, as Penny explained to Lizzie later, was that it wasn't dead boring at all. "Most blokes, right," she explained to Lizzie as if Lizzie had never had a date before, "most blokes, you ask them about their job, and they can bore the crap out of you for ages. And they'll start talking about some bloke that you don't know who's their boss and who's a complete prick for some reason, and they'll go on and on about them, and who really knows best and how they showed them and how if they weren't in an office they'd give them an arse-kicking they'd never forget."

Lizzie nodded.

"And you just have to listen and nod and go, like, 'Wow, you're really brave' and "What a bastard.'"

"They must see right through that though," said Lizzie.

"You'd think," said Penny. "*Anyway*, the thing is, when Will was talking about his pictures, it wasn't boring at all. He was interesting. And he didn't hate his boss because he didn't even have a boss. He just did what he liked."

She lapsed into a reverie again. Lizzie looked at her sharply. This wasn't like her sister. Usually Penny wanted a credit check and a cost/benefit analysis.

"So has he got tons of money, then?" asked Lizzie.

"Well, he must have, mustn't he?" said Penny. "He's an artist and he went to nob school. But we didn't really talk about money."

This was a first.

"We just talked about the countryside and our lives and pictures and things. It was lovely."

Penny threw back her head and cackled heartily at a well-timed crack Will made about Sloan. At the table next to them, very well-dressed people who looked on their way out to a stultifyingly boring dinner, tutted to themselves and one of the women rolled her eyes. Will made up his mind.

"Come on," he said. "Let's get out of here."

"Uh, where?" said Penny. She'd been having a good time—a surprisingly good time—sitting here with Will. She hadn't had to feign interest or anything, and he seemed genuinely interested in talking to her rather than, for example, talking about how much money he was making and how powerful and respected he was at work while simultaneously trying to fondle her kneecaps.

"It's a surprise," said Will. Penny's super-thin eyebrows twitched. Surprise? What did he mean? She thought longingly of

*The Thomas Crown Affair*. Maybe he was going to whip her into his helicopter and they were going to go to the Bahamas for a drink. She smiled happily.

"OK!"

But when they were outside he didn't immediately summon a chauffeur or nod her over to the back of a big shiny motorbike. Instead, he led her down a maze of back lanes toward the Embankment.

"Is this where you live?" she asked curiously. Will sounded like he was suppressing a giggle. "Uh, no. I live in east London. Where the artists live," he said, seeing her inquiring look. "Round Hoxton."

"Oh," said Penny. "So where are we going then?"

"Are you always this impatient?"

"Yes," said Penny. "I've found it speeds things up."

"What things?" asked Will.

"Important things," said Penny. "Getting served in bars, getting the best of the sale bargains."

"Ah. Important things," said Will. "You're a very urban creature, aren't you?"

"A what?"

"A city girl."

"Yeah. Compared to what, cows?"

"A bit of natural beauty."

"I don't see what's so brilliant about natural beauty," said Penny, critically checking out her nails as she clopped along in her high shoes, trying to keep up with Will. "I think it's overrated."

"Can you climb in those shoes?"

Will had come to a full stop in front of a high, pink brick wall that stretched on for a long way.

"I can do anything in these shoes."

"Excellent. Hup! It's a soft landing."

And with that, Will, half pushed, half lifted her up onto the top of the wall.

"Wh-aa!" screeched Penny.

"Shh," said Will. "Just jump. Trust me."

"Trust you? I just met you . . . ahhh."

Penny found herself on the top of a large compost heap, the setting sun reflected in her eyes from the river. She looked around, completely confused and shocked, until, with a scrabbling noise, Will made it up and over the wall, and bounced down past her.

"Come on," he said, holding out a hand.

"What the hell are we doing?"

"Just . . . just get down, then you'll see."

Penny worried about her ruined shoes as she tentatively clambered down the hill of manure.

"What the hell . . ."

"Shh," said Will. "I bet you've never been here at this time of day, have you?"

"I've never been here at all. Where the hell are we?"

Will looked at her, confused. "This is the Chelsea Physic Garden."

"Oh, yeah," said Penny rapidly, trying to cover her mistake. "Course it is. I've never been here though."

"Why not?"

"Uh, my sister . . . gets hay fever and that."

"Oh. Well . . ."

Penny looked around, and gasped. She was in a huge, beautiful garden. The trees were in full blossom, and the evening sun caught their delicate petals as they shimmered to the soft green grass. There wasn't another soul there.

"Oh my God," she said. Will looked at her undeniable delight and grinned.

"I can't believe you've never been here. Come on, let me show you around. I've spent hours drawing the botanics."

Penny didn't know what he meant, but she followed him anyway as he motioned her down the wide gravel path.

"That's when I found out about the manure thing," he said. "Not very romantic, I know."

"It's not bad," said Penny, looking at the long rows of perfectly labeled plants and flowers. It was extraordinarily beautiful.

"They used to train doctors here," said Will. "That's why it's called the Physic Garden."

"So do you bring all your girls here?"

"No," said Will. "I come here a lot on my own. I prefer it when there's nobody else here at all, just me. But I thought . . . I thought you might like it."

She smiled at him, and he thought again how gorgeous she was.

"Come on," he said. "Let's go look at the cornflowers."

"Why?"

"I don't know. I just like them."

Will had liberated a bottle of wine from the wine bar and, with the aid of his palette knife, they eventually got it open and, as the sky darkened into a deep blue, they sat, then lay down, on the grass by the cornflowers, talking about—well, almost everything, thought Penny later. She told him about her sister and her mum. But perhaps she had implied that the family was wealthier than it was—he did ask lots of questions about them, and, emboldened by the attention, she had embroidered them so far that they had spent too many summers in France and winters in the Caribbean to have ever heard of the Physic Garden, and she was only working for the fun of it.

But he laughed when she told him about the restaurant (contracting eight years to a week), and she laughed when he told her about his terrible school, and by the time he reached over to kiss her gently in the deserted garden, she realized she'd forgotten even to find out how many paintings he sold and what kind of car he drove, and even more weirdly, she didn't even care. When he walked her to the door of the flat (at which point she panicked about asking him in and having her cover blown completely), he merely told her he loved her street, kissed her again—rather spectacularly this time—took her number, and walked off down the road.

"*And* he paid for all the drinks?" said Lizzie, lost in admiration.

"Well, duh," said Penny. She examined her newly perfect nails, no longer bright cerise, but a delicate shell pink. A smile kept tugging away at her mouth. "He's minted, isn't he? He's an artist, with stuff in a gallery and that."

"So there's just one question left," said Lizzie, looking at the microwave lasagne she'd taken out of the freezer and, for some reason, not feeling like it just at the moment. "Why are you here and not in his swish flat, knobbing his brains out?"

Penny blew on her nails and a most uncharacteristically shy smile crept across her face. "Oh, Lizzie," she said. "Us Chelsea girls, we just don't behave like that."

# Chapter Six

"Let me see you," Georges commanded Lizzie the second she walked in. She jumped a little, flustered, as he stared at her. Just like yesterday, his Mediterranean sense of personal space meant he crept in closer than she was used to.

"What?" she demanded.

"I want to look into your eyes."

Lizzie couldn't help it: her heart fluttered. Oh, for goodness' sake. What a daft pushover she was. She'd probably be like this if a traffic warden said something nice to her. Had anyone ever been more susceptible to a bit of male attention?

"Why?" she said, conscious of her pulse speeding up.

Georges crouched down gravely. His huge arms against his legs were like hocks of ham.

"They're clear," he said, with some surprise. "Yesterday they were red like tiny tomato pips."

Lizzie backed away. "Well, that's because I didn't go out

clubbing last night. In fact I never go out clubbing. That was a complete aberration."

Georges nodded.

"In fact, I was visiting my sick grandmother."

Georges let out a guffaw.

"Ah, Lizzie, so close was I to believing you!"

"It's true!" maintained Lizzie. "I promise!"

"Could you start on the peppers and mushroom? I'm planning something good with chickenses."

"Chickens," said Lizzie.

"And I don't want to tire you out too much for tonight, when you have to go and tend orphans."

"Shh."

"Or for tomorrow, when you have to go and put bandages on the feet of small, slightly wounded ducks."

Lizzie picked up her knife and set to work.

Three hours later the café was a smoothly running machine of organized chaos, full of contented-looking punters, and Georges was wiping sweat off his brow as Lizzie's phone rang. It was Penny.

"I just got into work," she squeaked.

"Glad to hear it," said Lizzie, wiping some sweat off her forehead too.

"Two wonderful things have happened!"

"Only two?" said Lizzie crossly. She could almost hear Penny smiling down the line.

"So, first thing this morning I run into Brooke in the hallway . . ."

"First thing, eh?"

"Well, ten-ish, you know."

"Mmm hmm."

"And she says"—at this point, Penny attempted to launch into an imitation of Brooke's amused drawl, not entirely successfully—" 'Darling, we're having a little party on Saturday night—do join us!' "

"Why are you putting on a Welsh accent?" said Lizzie.

"So, we're going to be really good friends now."

"Well, that's great," said Lizzie. "You can tell me all about it when you get back. Or maybe I'll just lie on the carpet with a glass to my ear."

"Oh, you're invited, you idiot."

"Really?" said Lizzie, annoyed to feel her heart leaping, despite herself.

"Well, I asked her how she defined 'little' and she said, 'Oh, darling, bring everyone you know.' "

"I suppose the fact that she didn't then say, 'Except for your chunky sister' means I should take that as her begging me to attend,' said Lizzie.

"Don't be so chippy," said Penny. "I think they're really nice and good fun."

"I think they're evil and quite frightening," said Lizzie. "But I'm willing to be a bit more open-minded about women with scary gaps between the tops of their legs, and white jeans."

"Fabulous," said Penny. "We'll find you a lovely Chelsea boy yet. Yes, Sloan, ten-thirty *is* time for a cocktail. Everyone knows that."

Lizzie rolled her eyes. "What was the other wonderful thing?"

"No, I don't want one, thanks. I don't know what preprandial means."

"Penny?"

"What does preprandial mean?"

"I have no clue. Pregnant?"

"OK, got to go."

"What was the other thing?"

Lizzie could hear Sloan squawk over the top of the telephone. "Could you move these bloody flowers, darling? They're giving me hay fever. It's like Kew fucking Gardens in here. Who sends cornflowers anyway?"

"I think I'm seeing Will again," said Penny, with a little glow to her voice. "I think I might ask him to the party."

Parties made Lizzie anxious, possibly even more anxious than nightclubs. At least in nightclubs there was usually a dark corner to hide in. And if you hid in the toilets in a nightclub nobody tried to bang the door down and accuse you of ruining everyone's evening.

And a posh party. What was that going to be like? Maybe they'd have little cucumber sandwiches with the crusts cut off. Lizzie groaned to herself. And now Penny was going to fall madly in love with some gorgeous rich artist and they'd spend all evening cooing and being all cuddly-wuddly in the corner. And they'd get married and buy their grandmother's flat and live in Chelsea and raise lovely posh Chelsea babies and she'd have to go back to Essex and look after their mother. She heaved a great sigh.

Georges popped his head around the door.

"What's the matter with you? Are you worrying about all those koala bears you are going to save in Bosnia?"

"No," said Lizzie.

"You look tragic."

"I have to go to a party."

"That is tragic. That is the saddest thing I have ever heard. Watch as I start crying immediately—boohoo, boohoo. When is this party? Is it tonight? Will you need someone to pick you up and carry you home?"

"No," said Lizzie. "It's Saturday. And it's just downstairs from my grandmother's . . . I mean, my flat."

"So why don't you want to go?"

"Because I won't know anyone and my sister will have her new boyfriend."

Georges squared himself around.

"It's OK," he announced gravely. "I shall escort you to this party. No funny stuff. Just for friendliness. I am a very friendly person. I shall make some friends for you, then I shall go."

Lizzie almost giggled. She could just see big fat foreign Georges walking into that immaculate snooty sitting room. Her and Georges, the gruesome twosome. They'd be the cabaret.

"No, it's OK," she said. "I'm sure I'll be fine."

"But I don't mind!" said Georges.

"Really, it's all right," said Lizzie.

Georges turned back to his chickenses and started chopping them up with unnecessary force.

"So, I feed you, employ you, save you from falling in the gutter, yes, but you are ashamed of me? I am, what, too fat to go to a party with you?"

"No!" said Lizzie plaintively.

"You are prejudiced, yes? Against foreign people?"

"I would love you to come," said Lizzie, as more hungry customers started to march through the door.

*

"Hey." Penny had been uncharacteristically nervous about calling Will to thank him for the flowers and ask him to the party. Normally she didn't give a damn. But normally they weren't quite as handsome as Will.

"Hey yourself," he said, smiling. "Would it sound cheesy if I told you I was drawing cornflowers?"

"It would sound a lot less cheesy if you were drawing me among them."

"Uh, would it?" said Will.

"Oh yeah. Umm, I called to ask you something."

"Good. I like things. Ask away."

"Would you like to come to a party with me?"

"I would like to do anything with you."

"Really? I have a dental appointment next week."

"I'll hold the spitbowl."

"I don't really." Penny hadn't been to the dentist since school. She'd been lucky. So far.

"So, do you have a real party or was it just an excuse to phone me?"

"Yes. There's a party."

"Double date!" Penny was smugly doing her makeup in the bathroom mirror.

"It's not a double date," said Lizzie. "It's more . . . he's kind of escorting me. In case you and what's his name want to sit in a corner all night playing suck face."

"I would never behave like that," said Penny.

"You strip in public for a bottle of champagne."

"Don't mention that." Penny flicked a perfect line of black eyeliner to the very corner of her eyes.

"Don't mention it? Isn't that why Brooke's invited you? Because you're the amazing naked party girl from upstairs? I think you're the professional entertainment."

Penny put down the liner pen. "Well, that doesn't matter, does it? They're not going to get it, and I am going to get a lovely boyfriend whom I actually like for a change, so butt out, would you? You bloody hate seeing me happy."

"That's not true," said Lizzie, wondering about it. She'd occasionally like her to be a little less troublesome, that was all, surely.

"Well don't ruin it for me," pouted Penny. "Oh, I forgot, you did already, you're bringing Ape Face."

"Don't call him Ape Face," said Lizzie. "It's just five o'clock shadow."

"Chins and chins of it."

"Anyway, maybe everyone will think he's a shipping magnate or something."

Penny raised her eyebrows. "A shipping magnate that smells of cooking oil? Let's have a drink."

Lizzie obediently fetched two Bacardi Breezers out of the fridge.

"Where are you meeting him?" Lizzie asked.

"Down there," said Penny, looking around. "I don't know, I'm just not sure he'd enjoy the taxidermy collection."

"I'm sure that's a rat," said Lizzie, looking unhappily at the small furry stuffed animal in the corner. "But why would anyone stuff a rat? It doesn't make sense."

"Plus, he thinks I'm rich," said Penny. "He might not get too involved if he knew the truth."

It was nine before the girls felt they'd heard enough door-bells and screamed greetings to feel they could risk heading downstairs. Penny looked slightly odd. She'd shrugged off her Jordan-style micro mini, and stuck to a fuchsia pink minidress she'd worn as the winner of Butlin's lovely legs competition five summers ago. But to make it look not too tarty she was wearing jeans under it, with stiletto shoes. Lizzie could see what she was aiming for, but she wasn't entirely sure she'd succeeded. This wasn't like Penny. Parties were her lifeblood. Which could only mean one thing—who *was* this chap? Despite herself, and the Bacardi Breezer for Dutch courage, she even felt a little nervous herself.

She was in her black crossover top that Trinny and Susannah decreed was the right way to go if you had "wonderful big hand-fuls of cleavage," which she knew actually meant "are a big fat pig." She was equally doubtful about the cheap bottle of rosé they'd bought, but who'd notice?

"Just chill, OK? It'll be fine."

"I know," said Penny irritably. Then she softened. "Do you really think so?"

Lizzie nodded. "You're irresistible."

Lizzie's buzz disintegrated the moment they pushed open the large heavy door into the noisy thronged apartment. Two gor-geous specimens were chatting each other up in the doorway, and looked absolutely insulted to be interrupted just because some people wanted to walk through the door. The huge sitting room was full of tall, attractive, confident people, sipping drinks and laughing loudly. Lizzie suddenly felt as dumpy as a wombat in a deep submarine.

Penny swallowed loudly and tilted her head up.

"Right," she said, and marched straight ahead. There was, amazingly, a small woman there holding a tray with glasses of champagne on it. Lizzie stared at her. She didn't know people actually did this outside of *Sex and the City*. Penny immediately swept up two as if this was the most natural thing in the world, and handed one to Lizzie, before she took off into the throng. Not having the faintest clue what to do, Lizzie rather apologetically followed her.

"Brooke!" said Penny, marching up to her. Brooke's hair shone in a long tawny mane. Her backless top showed off her flawlessly even tan. She had the cutest, most petite nose Lizzie had seen.

"Hello!" said Brooke, looking slightly surprised as Penny launched over to kiss her on both cheeks. She stood back from the two tall men she'd been whispering to.

"Sven . . . Rob . . . this is my upstairs neighbor I was telling you about . . ."

The boys' eyes widened.

"Well, hello there," said Rob, the darker of the two. "Hey, you've forgotten to take your jeans off."

"Maybe later, eh, Penny?" said Brooke. "She is *such* a party girl."

"Excellent," said Sven. "Another glass of champagne?"

"No thanks," said Penny. "Actually, my boyfriend's coming. He's an artist."

"Really?" said Brooke.

"I'm your boyfriend?" came a voice behind her.

Penny whipped around. Oh, bollocks, she'd messed that up fast. There stood Will, in that same beaten-up leather coat, looking absolutely gorgeous.

"Will!" screamed Brooke. "My darling! How *are* you?"

"Hey, Brooke," said Will, suddenly looking a tad uncomfortable.

"Oh. You all know each other," said Penny, feeling her face flush.

"Well, of course . . . Will here was up to all sorts of naughty business with Minty last year, weren't you?"

Will flushed too. And suddenly Minty was standing beside them, looking stiff and annoyed.

"Hello, Will," she said, in an elaborately casual tone. "Fancy seeing you here at *my* party."

"I didn't realize it was your party," said Will.

"You just hate missing a Chelsea party, right?" Minty's face was tight.

"Uh, yeah, right," said Will, staring furiously at the floor. Penny looked at him, momentarily discomfited.

"Have a cocktail!" squealed Brooke. "They're wicked!"

Everyone immediately grabbed a glass from the passing tray and slugged it as quickly as possible. Penny slunk her way out of the group, making it extremely obvious she thought Will should follow her.

"Do you know her?" she hissed, from the corner.

Will shrugged. "Hardly."

"Look," said Penny. "When I said boyfriend just then—"

"You didn't mean me? You meant your six-foot marine boy who's on his way over to smash my brains out?"

"No," said Penny. "I just didn't want those guys . . . you know."

"To hit on you? Quite right too. You look luscious." Will glanced at Brooke and Minty. "Look, do you want to get out of here?"

Penny looked around. The room was really full now, with girls laughing hysterically, men in Pink shirts, waiters balancing full trays of champagne; while the cigarette smoke and expensive perfume made the place seem hazy and slightly hyper-real. She wanted to stay, to become the life and soul, to be standing next to Brooke, throwing back her head and laughing at the nice, charming people who wanted to be her friend. In one room . . . here . . . this was the life she was after.

"Can't we stay for a little while?" she asked. "I've just got here."

"But they're all idiots," said Will.

"How do you know? Have you been out with all of them?" asked Penny. "Is there a terrifying revelation about your past at every step?"

"Maybe," said Will, softening a little and taking a sip of his extremely strong drink. "Why don't you ask your boyfriend, Andy McNab?"

"Who?"

On the other side of the room, Lizzie felt herself sinking in quicksand. She had, nominally, ended up as part of the group that included the two tall boys, Rob and Sven, but they were patently talking over her head as if she wasn't there. Worse, they were speculating on the qualities of the other females present, as if she was a dog or something.

"What about that one over there?" said Rob, pointing out a supermodelesque Russian-looking girl with legs as thin as pins.

"Fat arse, wouldn't you think?" said Sven.

Woof, thought Lizzie sadly.

"Do you know who I'd like a crack at? Saw her at Ascot."

"Who?"

"Elle Macpherson."

"Ooh yes. Ding dong."

Lizzie made a quiet cough.

"Are you wearing a smock?" said Sven suddenly, in a rude way Lizzie hadn't encountered since the school bus. "Are you a lesbian?"

"Yes," said Lizzie, tongue-tied and short of something to say. Immediately she realized her mistake.

"Are you?" said Rob, looking at her for the first time. "Cool. Do you, like, snog women and feel their knockers and stuff?"

"Yes," said Lizzie, feeling herself sinking into a deep hole with no clear way of escaping. "Obviously."

Sven looked fascinated too.

"Very naughty," he said in an approving tone of voice. "What else do you do?"

"Oh, mostly we go to whole-food shops, that kind of thing," said Lizzie, looking around desperately for an exit.

"No, in the bedroom."

Well, this had backfired badly; now two strange chaps wanted her to talk dirty to them. Why couldn't she just get over her shyness and be herself with people?

"Sorry," said Lizzie. "I have to go over there to chat up a girl."

"Can we watch?" said Rob.

Looking at Will, Penny realized how much she wanted to kiss him. Not marry him, or take him for a ride, or shag him—yet—or get him to take her out to dinner, or show off to Dwaneesa about who she'd managed to pull, or even tell Lizzie about it, which was usually half the fun. She wanted to kiss him, for hours and hours on a park bench, like they were teenagers.

"Why are you looking at me like that?" said Will. "You look like a wolf licking its chops."

"No I don't," said Penny, hastily finishing her cocktail.

"So your place is just like this then?" he said.

"Yeah, it's the one above. Exactly like this," said Penny, looking at the gleaming modernist chandeliers, huge paintings, expensive mirroring, and halogen lighting. "Just like this."

"Maybe you could show me around sometime," said Will, and Penny cursed herself for falling into the trap.

"Cheeky!" she yelled, in a tone that came out much louder and brasher than she'd intended.

"Uh, sorry, I didn't mean it like that," said Will, backtracking desperately, as Penny hurriedly pulled another couple of cocktails off the tray. Free drink; who knew when it was going to run out?

"That's OK," said Penny, her mind working furiously. Well, she'd just have to pretend to be very, very pure and make sure he never got back there. Plus, he must have some really funky pad in Hoxton, surely. Somewhere really cool, a big loft with all-white walls and huge blown-up photographs on his wall and polished floors and sunny spots for the cat to lie in.

"What's your place like?"

"It's all right, you know," said Will, and he gave that self-deprecating grin that made her insides go all wobbly.

Minty came up to them, her legs looking like a baby giraffe's on long spindly heels.

"Will," she said, in a voice that she obviously thought sounded calm. "Could I . . . could I have a word with you, please?"

"Uh, no, he can't," said Penny immediately. Her hackles rose. She wasn't going to have this anorectic cow smelling of Diorissimo and gin slobbering all over him.

"What's the matter, Minty?" said Will, looking concerned.

"It's private," said Minty, glaring at Penny with a barely hidden snarl in her voice.

"Well, I can't really . . ."

"It's very important. It will take only five minutes. I think you owe it to me, Will."

Minty was looking really tragic now.

"Well, if she's *begging* you," said Penny nastily. She was giving Minty major evils, but she was clearly not a girl new to this. Minty immediately began examining a nail and looking coyly up at Will as if Penny had vanished into thin air.

"OK," said Will. "Five minutes." He turned to Penny. "Then we really should go somewhere that isn't full of people taking coke, vomiting up canapés, and telling each other how expensive their hairdressers are."

"Fine," said Penny, only just resisting the urge to stick her tongue out at Minty. Not that it would have mattered, as Minty had immediately grabbed Will's arm and was leading him somewhere Penny suspected was the bedroom. Penny checked her watch. Well, they really *were* getting five minutes, then she was going in. There were some circumstances where subtlety would get you nowhere, and this was definitely one of them.

"Aha," said Rob, appearing to her right with a fresh cocktail. "There you are. We've just met the most *extraordinary* midget lesbian."

This was more like it, Penny couldn't help thinking. Now there were chaps around, who'd attracted more girls, and there was a big group around them and she was quaffing the absolutely delicious cocktails and having a hilarious time, telling stories about other nightclubs she'd been to and the third-division footballers she'd met—everyone seemed so impressed—and her fight with Krystanza and how you could see her fingernails in the paper. The boys in particular were laughing heartily and refilling her glass. Will was nowhere to be seen, but that didn't matter because as soon as he came out he'd see how popular and pretty she was and be incredibly impressed and realize that she was a Chelsea girl; it was completely obvious that she couldn't fit in any more.

She'd forgotten about Lizzie completely.

Lizzie was trapped in a corner. She'd gone to the toilet as usual, to give her something to do, and heard lots of whisperings following her, along the lines of "the new lesbian in the building." When she emerged, an enormous woman wearing a purple hat and huge, flowing robes was blocking the landing.

"DARLING," she said, swooping down and giving Lizzie an enormous kiss that reeked of Poison. "I hear we must welcome you to Chelsea!"

"Well, that's nice," said Lizzie, but her voice was muffled as she was still under the woman's armpit, jammed next to her vast bosom.

"Always lovely to get a bit more LOCAL COLOR," the woman boomed, then held Lizzie at arm's length—which meant Lizzie still had her head in her breast—and examined her. "Well, better than nothing, I suppose," she said. "Now, sister, tell me. Did you know? Sylvia Plath used to live just around THE CORNER?"

"I did not know that," said Lizzie, looking around desperately for her drink.

"Terrible story. Spent her life with a man, you see. Could have sorted it out MUCH BETTER, don't you THINK?"

There was no way past this lady. She was the only person at the party wider than Lizzie was.

"Here," said the woman. "Try this. I brew my OWN WINE."

Lizzie gave up and sank down slowly onto the chaise longue.

Penny couldn't quite focus on who she was in the bathroom with. That was confusing enough in itself. Also, the bathroom was massive, clean, white, and airy, with candles flickering along the window ledge and a claw-foot bath lined with Jo Malone smellies.

"This one bathroom," she pronounced with some difficulty, "ish nicer than my entire house. Was. I mean, a house. In a dream I had."

"Never mind that," said the man, a rather foxy-faced character who had slipped into the group as Penny had been loudly debating whether or not to take her jeans off underneath her minidress, and the boys were voting vehemently in favor. "Here, try this."

Penny lurched around. The man had wracked out two lines of white powder on the toilet cistern.

She'd seen it around, of course, but had never had the cash to indulge; nor the desire, come to that. Her vices usually ran to a few cheeky sodas, the odd spliff, and the occasional E at holiday times. But a different life . . . different tastes.

The man proffered a rolled-up twenty-pound note. In for a penny . . .

Lizzie realized she'd just agreed to apply for a shared allotment when she saw Penny reel out of the bathroom. Her eyes were wild, her pupils huge.

"Lizzie! Lizzie! My darling Lizzie," she squealed. "Oh, I must tell you, I think you look absolutely fabulous. And I think isn't this just the most amazing party? It's just amazing, I'm having such a fantastic time and . . . do you like this lipstick? What do you think, I wasn't sure, but . . ."

"Stop chewing your lips for a second and I'll try and tell you," said Lizzie, annoyed.

"Ooh," said the woman, whose name was Beulah. "Is this your other half?"

"My sister," said Lizzie.

"Whoo," said Sven, passing through on his way to the champagne bin. "Sisters!"

"Why don't we go now?" said Lizzie, ignoring them.

"Don't be ridiculous," said Penny. "I've just started to have a great, really brilliant time. I need a drink. And a cigarette."

"You don't smoke."

"And my bloody boyfriend. Where's my boyfriend?"

"Who?"

"You know. Will."

"Are you sure he's your boyfriend? You don't seem to be spending lots of cozy nights in together."

"Well, I'm just going to find him right now. He better not be cheating on me."

"Your serious long-term boyfriend, whom you've known for all of ten minutes? Penny, no. Don't. Let's go home, you're a mess."

Penny had discarded her jeans now, and her minidress was far too high in the leg and low in the breast for the tottering stilettos she was wearing, particularly coupled with her crazed stare and slowly meandering mascara.

"Please, Penny. Come home," said Lizzie, begging.

"Shut up," said Penny, tottering over. The foxy-faced man came up behind her. "Looking good," he said, cupping her bottom quite openly.

"Yeah, going to give us a strip?" shouted Sven.

"*Penny*," yelled Lizzie in exasperation. "No more stripping!"

But Penny stepped away, letting the horrible foxy man keep on groping her, and did "ta-dah" hands. Lizzie looked around desperately for Will. If he saw this, he'd be out the door faster than a greased otter, and her poor sister would be mortified.

"I'm having fun," said Penny. "Will's fucked off, hasn't he? He's back there copping off with his old girlfriend, isn't he? No nice blokes for me." She gyrated to the music playing. "But that's OK, because I feel just fine."

Lizzie watched her in horror as she stretched up to undo her dress top. Over on the sofa Brooke was sitting watching complacently, with a cream-licking smile on her face.

Suddenly the doorway was blocked by a large, bear-like figure. Lizzie glanced over in desperation.

"What is this?" came the accented voice. "This is a kind of seedy party, is it?"

Penny turned around and focused unsteadily.

"Ah," said Georges. "The famous Lizzie's sister. You are cold, yes?"

And just as she let her hands—and the top of her dress—fall to her waist, Georges whipped off his coat and pulled it around her shoulders.

"Much warmer now."

The boys started to boo, until Georges silenced them with a lift of one of his heavy brows.

"You live upstairs?" he said to Lizzie. "Shall we go there?"

"I'm not going home!" said Penny, struggling with the coat. "I have to show Will what a good time I'm having when he doesn't give a toss."

"No, we will go home," said Georges. Lizzie looked at him, and felt a little thrill in her stomach.

"Yes, Penny," said Lizzie. "Let's go home."

"While Will is fucking some fucking slut in the back bedroom?" said Penny. The room fell silent.

"While I'm doing what now?" said Will, leaning against the wall. Minty slipped out behind him, looking sulky and petulant.

Penny's face crashed. This wasn't how it was meant to be at all. This wasn't her lovely party. Now everyone was looking at her like she was making a fool of herself. She stared at Will's gentle face one more time.

"Come on," said Lizzie. "Let's just go."

And for once, Penny knew when she was beaten.

"Don't bring your girlfriend to our allotment," yelled Beulah. The three of them left the party in silence.

*

Upstairs, Georges looked aghast at the apartment, as Lizzie moved a collection of broken dog figurines off a broken chair and set about making tea.

"This is your home?" he asked incredulously. Looking around, Lizzie realized how quickly she'd gotten used to it.

"It's not really," she said. "It's our grandmother's. She would go crazy if we moved or touched anything."

She noticed Georges looking askance at an enormous open tea chest filled to the brim with macramé owls.

"Crazier."

She put the kettle on for tea. Penny was sitting glumly at the table, completely deflated and most of the way through a pint of water.

"My head hurts," she said.

"Don't take drugs," said Georges.

"It was an accident," said Penny. "My nose fell on them."

Georges shook his head. "You girls are a real teapot of fish."

Lizzie nodded, just as the doorbell went.

"Oh, God," said Penny. "It's downstairs, for sure. You know they want to be evil about me. In fact, I think I need a glass to hear what they're saying."

"I don't think you want to know what they're saying," said Lizzie.

"Don't answer the door. If it's Brooke asking about the carpet . . ."

"What did you do to the carpet?"

"Nothing. Red wine. Whatever. Oh God. I hate my life," said Penny.

"You are a very unusual person," said Georges.

"I'm sure loads of people hate their lives," groaned Penny.

"I think he meant 'evil' person," said Lizzie. The knocking at the door sounded again, more vehement now.

"Oh God, I'm not evil," said Penny. "Am I? Maybe that's why I don't get what I really want. Why a lovely bloke like Will won't talk to me. Maybe I should change my ways, be a bit less selfish. Do you think I'm selfish, Lizzie? Maybe it is all my fault."

Lizzie returned from the doorway.

"It's Will."

Penny leapt up, a huge shiny grin spreading over her face.

"Fantastic."

She hurried to the door, shrugging up her dress, leaving Georges's coat pooling in a pile on the floor.

Penny put on her best contrite face as she closed the door behind her and stepped into the well-kept hall. She was definitely going to play modest; no way was he going to get into her apartment tonight. It was simply too grim. She'd have to pretend it was lovely, then move into his groovy artist's pad as soon as was humanly possible.

"Hi," she said, hanging her head.

"Hi," said Will, looking equally contrite.

"I wanted to apologize," said Penny. "I was jealous and acted like an idiot."

He looked at her, amazed.

"But . . ." he said, "I came to apologize to you. We were meant to be on a date and I completely deserted you."

"Well, there is that," said Penny.

"Minty is . . . well, she wanted to tell me about how depressed she was and how she'd become dairy intolerant and stuff, and all about her parents' divorce, and every time I tried to get up she'd start crying, and . . . girls cry a lot, don't they?"

"I never cry in front of boys," said Penny.

"I bet," said Will. "Anyway, I am sorry. The whole Minty thing was . . . a terrible mistake. So don't be surprised if she disses me a bit."

"Apology accepted," said Penny cheerfully.

"Although, you know, if the reverse were true I probably wouldn't have started stripping, then screeching like a fish-wife."

"Oh, yeah, course you would have."

"And I think Minty wants to kill you," he continued.

"OK, well, if she comes at me, I'll blow at her and she'll fall over and get carried away by a high wind."

Will smiled and looked a bit embarrassed. "Can I come in?"

"No," said Penny.

"Good," said Will.

"Why's that good?"

"Cause if you didn't want to get off with me you wouldn't give a toss about whether I came in or not."

Penny paused for a minute and thought about it. "Bollocks."

Will looked around. "This hall's pretty nice though. Soft lighting, carpet, pictures on the wall . . ."

But Penny was already kissing him.

Georges and Lizzie sat in the kitchen, looking at each other.

"This is a very exciting fun party," he said. "I'm having a wow time."

Lizzie stared into her teacup, too embarrassed to answer. What on earth must he think of them?

Georges looked at the array of shocking junk piled up in the kitchen.

"You have lived here for a long time, yes?" he said. "Maybe one century. Are you a wampire?"

Lizzie giggled. "I'm not a wampire."

Georges smiled. "That's better, huh? You look so worried all the time. Which is how I would expect a wampire to look."

"It's *vampire*."

"Wampire. That's what I said."

"Yes," said Lizzie. "That's what you said. Well, I'm not one."

"So. This is your grandmother's house?"

Lizzie nodded. "We're staying here while she's sick."

"And then you're going again?"

Lizzie shrugged. "I suppose."

"Back to where?"

"Brandford, I suppose. If, I mean, when she gets better. She's very old."

"You like Brandford?"

"I hate it," said Lizzie savagely. "I mean, there's nothing wrong with it. I suppose. I just . . . I mean, it just doesn't suit me."

"But here in Chelsea you feel much better?"

"I don't know. Maybe I don't fit in anywhere."

Georges tutted. "Oh, Lizzie. Do not be so stupid."

"I know," said Lizzie. "I can't even do self-pity right."

Georges looked at her for a second and she felt most uncomfortable under his scrutiny. This was ridiculous. He was a chubby café manager who couldn't pronounce his V's. Why should she always feel she wasn't quite living up to him?

"I think it is time for me to go," he said. "I am up early, of course."

"Thanks for coming," said Lizzie, getting up.

"Not at all, it was . . ."

He let the end of the sentence trail off as he opened the door and saw Penny and Will literally all over each other in the hallway. Panicked, Penny immediately pushed the door back shut again before Will could turn around and see into the flat.

"OK," said Georges. "Well, maybe I didn't really want to leave yet anyway."

"Sorry about that," said Lizzie. Georges looked toward the windows.

"Second floor," said Lizzie. "I wouldn't jump. More tea?"

"No," said Georges. "I would like to go home. Could you tell your sister to take her boyfriend in or out or somewhere else, please?"

Lizzie twisted uncomfortably in her seat. "I'd rather not."

"She bites?" said Georges.

"No," said Lizzie.

"Then you can just tell her, no?"

"I don't want to get in the middle of something . . ."

"Have you got a water hose?"

Lizzie twisted in embarrassment. She'd never hear the end of it if she ruined Penny's night.

"OK, we sit here waiting for Penny to finish doing exactly what she pleases? Are you a welcome mat, Lizzie?"

"You mean doormat."

"Yes."

"No. I'm not."

"OK," said Georges. He looked at his watch complacently. Lizzie was suddenly furious with him and leapt up. She flung open the door. Penny and Will had vanished.

"Just go!" she yelled. "Happy now?"

"Lizzie, I just . . ."

"The doormat says goodnight!"

Georges left, giving her the same aghast look he had when he'd found her in the gutter. Bugger, bugger, bugger. Nobody could ever understand. She had to look out for her sister, that was all. Which meant that sometimes people . . . not anyone in particular, just sometimes . . . people should pay attention and notice that just because she was being sisterly didn't automatically mean she was being a doormat.

The doormat went to bed, thought about her terrible social skills, thought about being sad and lonely for the rest of her life, thought of the four thousand canapés she'd consumed at the party even though no one else had eaten any, and cried herself to sleep.

# Chapter Seven

Spring was definitely springing, and as far as Penny was concerned, the sap was rising. She bounced to work in the morning, then Will, with his delightfully relaxed artistic schedule, would come and hang around at closing time and they would go off and wander and have chats and talk about things. It was so unusual, and so delightful.

Not only that, but she was discovering a previously undiscovered knack for selling paintings. Years of hard pushing to the front of nightclub queues and shameless yelling had given her a certain tough edge when it came to alternately charming and bullying customers, men in particular. And the added incentive of Will's face every time she sold one of his pictures meant she was, for the first time in her life, in a job that didn't make her want to kill everyone in the place with a blunt instrument.

The only thing confusing her and slightly getting in the way was the fact that she and Will hadn't . . . done it yet. There'd been long sessions of snogging, cuddling, a bit of wandering hands here and there, but just as she'd expect him to invite her back to his place, nothing had happened.

It crossed her mind briefly that maybe there was someone else at home, but he didn't seem at all as if he had something to hide, or give any indication that he had something better to be doing. He didn't hide his mobile or glance at his watch or say, "I was out with . . . uh, nobody really."

"So what's your place like?" she asked him, as they wandered through Hyde Park one unseasonably warm evening in March. Everywhere couples were waltzing through the daffodils, and throwing bread to the ducks. Jumpers were being shrugged off; anoraks tentatively spread on the still wet winter grass.

"What's yours like?" he countered immediately.

"You've seen it," she said.

"I snogged you outside of it. That's not the same thing at all."

"I'd like to see your place."

"Why? Do you want an ice cream?" he asked as they passed a van.

"Of course."

"Excellent. They do Loseley."

"What? Can I just have a ninety-nine?"

"But that's their horrible aerated stuff. They've got tubs of proper ice cream."

"But I want a ninety-nine!"

"OK," said Will.

"I want a ninety-nine and I want to see your place."

Will smiled. "Oh, it's nothing really."

This wasn't going according to plan. Penny took her ice cream and stuck her tongue in it in a very suggestive fashion.

"A mystery, huh?" she said. "Are you on day release from prison?"

"No!"

"Are you gay?"

"Yes," said Will. "I'm gay. That's why I just bought you that ice cream. I was hoping you might set me up with Sloan."

"So . . ." said Penny. The sun was setting over the far side of the Serpentine Gallery. It was hard for her to believe she was within walking distance from home, just about. That London could be so beautiful, rather than filthy and dangerous and noisy . . . it was amazing, she thought. She'd already forgotten about her grandmother, really. She was such a distant figure. Lizzie was off visiting her again, thank goodness. They were spending their evenings playing Boggle. It was great Lizzie had something to do. And meanwhile, this . . . *here* . . . was home.

She flashed Will her widest smile.

"Well," she said, "pardon a girl for being forward. I just . . . I just wondered, you know, if you ever felt like being alone with a woman."

Will raised his eyebrows at her. The evening sun was making her gold hair gleam, and she looked absolutely gorgeous. Why on earth hadn't she invited him home? How hard to get was she trying to be? He hoped she wasn't after an engagement ring or something equally ridiculous. But, goodness, he was desperate to . . .

"I beg your pardon?" he said.

"Oh, nothing," said Penny, giving her ice cream a big lick. "I was just thinking about something grown men and women do . . . in private. In the privacy, in fact, of their *own homes*."

"What's that, then?" said Will, moving toward her.

140

"Uh, you wouldn't like it," said Penny.

"Perhaps you could show me now," said Will. He grabbed her hand and pulled her off the path and into the shadow of a huge oak tree. Then he took a huge lick of her cheap ice cream and started to kiss her long and hard, sharing it between them.

"Who are you?" The old lady was staring at her again. Lizzie wouldn't have thought it possible, but this place was worse on a glorious evening like tonight than when it was pouring with rain.

"I'm Lizzie, Gran. I'm Stephen's daughter."

"One of the little twins?"

"That's right. I'm one of the little twins."

The old woman glowered and peered at her closer. Lizzie geared herself up to explain the whole thing twice more. Maybe next time Penny could visit. Lizzie laughed hollowly to herself. She was exhausted. For the last few weeks, she had worked her head off in the café. To her utmost annoyance, Georges, while paying her hardly any attention at all, had started taking loads of time off. OK, it was his business and everything, but he'd come in in the morning, start things off, then disappear. As she'd vowed to behave frostily toward him it was frustrating to say the least.

Slowly, and grudgingly, she was bloody well having to learn to cook. And Georges said he was going off on business somewhere but she didn't believe him. He was just mooching about, enjoying her hard work, which was still netting her only the minimum wage, plus the odd pound some of her regulars slipped her here and there.

The fact that it was about a hundred times more interesting and stimulating than the stamp importers hadn't cheered her up that much.

"Are you a happy little twin?" asked her grandmother.

Funnily enough, she had caught herself feeling something close to happiness just that morning. Georges had shown her how to make a wonderfully fresh-tasting bruschetta—which she'd never tasted in her life; she'd thought it was just garlic bread showing off—and pretty much every customer who'd sampled it had mentioned how delicious it was. It had taken her a second or two to realize that she felt proud of herself.

"I'm all right," she said stiffly.

"Just all right? Not enjoying Chelsea, then? Your dad used to love it."

"Did he?" said Lizzie eagerly.

"Oh, yes. I used to take him down the Embankment, you know, and we'd watch the boats go by. They still had the barges then. After he lost his daddy . . ."

Lizzie knew about this; that her grandfather had died in an industrial fire. His settlement had bought the flat. Secretly she wondered if this meant it was cursed.

Gran was musing. "He was all I had, little twin. You'll understand one day when you have your own, how much you love them. And he was all I had left. I spoiled him. Yes, I spoiled him. Then I lost him."

"We lost him, too," said Lizzie.

"Aye, I know that," said her grandmother. There was a long pause.

"Well, to other matters," said Gran eventually. "Have you got a nice young chap?"

"No," said Lizzie.

"Have you got a horrid old chap?"

Lizzie looked at her grandmother for signs of smirking.

"No," she said.

"Quite right," said her grandmother. "Don't settle."

"Let's face it though," said Lizzie. "I'm going to have to settle, aren't I? Everyone says don't settle, like there's a million fabulous blokes out there looking for slightly below-average women. There's no doubt about it at all. I blame Colin Firth. He's an actor, Gran . . ."

"I know who he is," said her grandmother suddenly. "He's a hottie."

"Oh, OK," said Lizzie, "well, it's his fault. In *Bridget Jones's Diary* he says he loves Renée Zellweger just the way she is. But he doesn't really. In real life, his wife is really, really, skinny and looks like a model and speaks nine languages. And in real life Renée Zellweger is super thin and gorgeous. I don't think hotties really do have to settle or love someone just the way they are."

"Renée Zellweger settled down," observed her grandmother.

"Hey, I thought you were crazy and a bit out of it and stuff," said Lizzie, surprised by her gran's grasp of celebrity gossip.

"I am," said her grandmother. "Why do you think I have to sit about all day taking drugs and reading *People's Friend*?"

"Hmm," said Lizzie, shaking the Boggle box. "Well, anyway. Now I just have to decide how low to lower my standards. Every year they have to drop about five percent, I reckon. Every year and every pound over eleven stone."

Her grandmother looked at her. "Is Wayne Rooney free yet?"

"I could never pull Wayne Rooney," said Lizzie. "Why am I depressed about that? I don't know. I find something constantly depressing in being unable to pull people I don't even fancy."

"How's your sister?"

"She's madly in love with a gorgeous successful artist and

adores her new job," said Lizzie. "Apart from that, you know, just about all right."

The old woman sniffed. "Nice of her to come and see me. Or maybe she did come before—was that her?"

"No," said Lizzie. "That was me."

"You're not identical? Are you the little twins?"

Her grandmother's eyes were closing.

"Yes," said Lizzie. "Yes, we are."

Penny was in heaven. Minty and Brooke had asked her out on another drinks night too. This time Lizzie, strangely, had declined. Penny had felt quite at home relaxing on the large brown sofas of the Sloaney Pony, letting boys in stripy shirts buy them champagne and make remarks. The girls had been very interested to hear all about Will, and she'd been delighted to talk all about it until, on their way out, Minty had cornered her in the toilets.

"So, it's all going swimmingly," said Minty, touching up her flawless skin with a tiny amount of rose blusher. Penny was thwacking the bronzer on as usual, and wondered, for the first time, if she was going about her makeup quite right.

"Yes," said Penny, smiling.

"Well, be careful," said Minty, smacking her lips. "I'm only telling you this for your own good, Penny, but that Will's a user."

"What, like Pete Doherty?"

Minty swung her golden ponytail disdainfully. "I'm just warning you, that's all. He's trouble. Bad news. Stay away. That's all I'll say."

Poor Minty, thought Penny. So jealous. Will had dumped her and she'd never gotten over it. Well, the two of them were different.

*

Lizzie, meanwhile, was finding that between work and visiting Gran her world was, if anything, shrinking—she didn't even see her old friends now, it was all too much for them to make the trek. She had had one night out with Grainne, in a too-loud pub on the King's Road, music thumping around them, and gorgeous teenagers copping off with each other. It hadn't gone well.

"God, everything sucks," said Lizzie as a conversation starter, gingerly helping herself to another prawn cocktail crisp. She'd been off crisps for a bit—Georges wouldn't have them in the café—and she couldn't believe how strong and fake they tasted.

"Yes," Grainne had said. "It really sucks, living in a castle in Chelsea and running a restaurant. I'd hate to live in Chelsea and get off with celebrities and be a millionaire."

Penny grew rosy and happy with love—for the first time, as far as Lizzie could see. There were outdoor assignations, weekends away, parties that Lizzie, after the horrors of Brooke and Minty's, refused to go to.

Lizzie worked hard, ate fresh food, went to bed early. Penny danced all night. Georges left Lizzie to her own devices more and more, which she supposed was a compliment of sorts.

Penny and Will were lying entwined near the Serpentine. It was a perfect evening in a perfect park. People were feeding ducks and flying kites; taking strolls and generally, Penny suspected, feeling pleased with themselves and the world.

"I think," said Penny, lolling, "you should paint me in the nude. You know, like Kate Winslet in *Titanic*."

"Like who?"

"You know. In *Titanic*. Everyone's seen it."

"I haven't," said Will, eyeing the ducks.

"You must have," said Penny, shocked. Lizzie had cried so hard snot had come out of her nose. Dwaneesa had called her pathetic in front of everyone. Penny had laughed. She felt slightly ashamed of that now.

"Nope," said Will.

"OK," said Penny. "Well, what happens is a boy takes a girl to a nice room, and she gets naked and he paints a really beautiful picture of her in the candlelight."

"Really," said Will, leaning over to give her a quick tickle. "Why did I think it was about a big ship sinking and lots of people descending to their watery deaths?"

"Well, those are the kind of detaily things that happen later on."

Penny peered up at him and gave a hopeful look. Will sighed. He would like to take her home, he really would but . . . it just wasn't the right time. He had to be careful. It was such a big step. He changed the subject.

"So, what do you like?" Will was saying. He was playing with a stick, watching the clouds and trying to work out what colors he'd use to paint them.

"Raindrops on roses and whiskers . . . hang on, that's not right, is it?" said Penny.

"No," said Will, smiling. He couldn't get over how much fun Penny was, how much he enjoyed being with her. She wasn't like any of the other girls.

"I mean, what do you want? Out of life."

Penny smiled. "Like a Rolex watch? Or true love."

"Or both," said Will.

"Both then," said Penny. "A big house and a garden and a lovely home and a lovely family and, you know. Normal stuff. Not having to worry. That kind of thing."

"But you've got a big house," said Will.

"Oh, yeah," said Penny. She should come clean, she really should, but her feelings for him had grown so strong. She wanted desperately for things to work out, she wanted to meet his posh family, and spend time in his gorgeous apartment and meet more of his friends and . . . but to her amazement, it wasn't just about that, about what he drove and how wide his television set was. It was about how he made her feel—pretty, yes, but she was used to that. Smart, funny, and, more important, safe. Nothing bad had ever happened to Will, it was obvious. He was comfortable everywhere. He had money, and ease, and had always been sure of himself, and treated her as if she were just the same.

He'd never had to steal for a bus fare, or pretend to have been on an expensive holiday with his dad (Lizzie had loyally refused to deny it, even with Dwaneesa's taunting about her pasty skin still ringing in her ears). Will was secure. He made her feel secure. He was everything she'd never known she wanted. And it was scaring her to death.

She had to convince him she was the girl for him because . . . well. Because she thought she was. Because she wanted to fit in. Because she didn't want to be rejected.

She swallowed suddenly. The ground seemed to be shifting under her feet. Or was the sky tilting? Suddenly she felt incredibly light-headed.

"Oh, Will," she said.

"What?"

147

"I don't know, I just feel a bit . . ."

She stood up, but that was worse. She felt terribly sick and bleary.

"Oh, Will, I think it must have been that hot dog."

"I can't believe you ate a hot dog from a man in the park."

Penny had bought one, and wolfed it down—she'd been starving—without even noticing Will staring at her, aghast. Well, now she knew. Smart people didn't buy hot dogs from a stand in the park. She filed it away as a mental note, just as she suddenly, definitely, knew she was going to be sick. And soon.

"Will, I've got to go," she said.

"Well, let me come with you."

"NO! I mean, no, don't, I'll be fine."

"But I'll need to get you home to see you're all right."

"No, you don't . . ." She was practically running out of the park now. "See you later . . ."

Lizzie was attempting to dust around the fourteen ornamental toilet-roll holders on the floor of the bathroom when she heard Penny enter.

"Pen?" she yelled. "Are you still doing it outside all the time? It's disgusting, and it's getting grass all over the silver dog bowl collection."

"Out of my way," said Penny, only just managing to push past Lizzie and make it to the toilet in time, where she threw up copiously. Lizzie watched her in silence.

"Oh, OK," said Lizzie. "Forget what I said about the *grass* being disgusting."

Penny ignored her, continuing to hurl down the lav. Lizzie went over and patted her on the back.

"What's the matter with you, then?"

Penny shook her head. "*Bleeaarrggghhhh.*"

"Dodgy pie?" said Lizzie.

"No . . . *Bllleeeaaggh.*"

"Dodgy foie gras? Bad glass of champers?"

Penny didn't answer and Lizzie handed her a towel.

"Here you go, sport. Don't tell me, Will peeled back his perfect skin and revealed he's actually a lizard?"

Penny shook her head vigorously.

"Is he here?"

The shaking was even more vigorous.

"OK, OK. Are you finished? Would you like some water?"

But Penny waved her away.

Twenty minutes later she emerged, looking sheepish, into the sitting room.

"How are you feeling?" said Lizzie, looking up from *Hello!*, which she'd borrowed from her grandmother.

"Really terrible. I ate a hot dog in the park." Penny sounded shocked, like she couldn't believe something as strange as feeling bad could happen to her. She slumped down onto the couch.

"Ah, well," said Lizzie, who considered herself quite hot on health and safety these days. "If you will . . ."

"Yeah, yeah," said Penny, smoothing down her fitted tank top. "I wouldn't normally. It's just not like me, but I was so bloody starvin'."

Lizzie raised an eyebrow. "Did you miss lunch?"

Georges believed sitting down to lunch was a hallmark of a civilized society and that the plastic-wrapped all-day-breakfast sandwich was an abomination. Sloan believed in the lunch break too, though only for him, and for different reasons.

"Well, I have to, don't I? Will's hardly going to want to go out with some porker. No offense."

"There wasn't any," said Lizzie, "until that bit at the end, just there, where you said 'No offense.'"

Penny propped herself up on a weak arm. "Is it just me, anyway, or are you looking a bit thinner?"

"That's because I've been puking my guts up," said Lizzie, still stung. "Oh no, that was you."

"Stavros is obviously having a good effect on you."

"His name is *not* Stavros," said Lizzie. "And I've hardly seen him."

"Whatever," said Penny. "Oh God, I feel awful. I'm going to bed."

The following morning Penny crept out into the sitting room, looking, if anything, worse.

"Oh God, I still feel terrible."

Lizzie, making a lemon tea, looked up as Penny jumped up and ran through to the bathroom again.

"There's nothing coming up," she said when she came back in. She was pale and white-faced, with beads of sweat showing on her forehead.

"Oh dear," said Lizzie. "Sit down."

Waiting for the kettle to boil, Lizzie glanced through the huge windows over into the houses opposite. Those houses were beautifully furnished—polished tables and Persian rugs and untouched pianos in orderly rooms–and often empty as their owners flitted to the south of France, or skiing, or the Caribbean, or anywhere else Lizzie imagined they went. A minor chord was striking in her breast.

Penny was staring at the floor, a small island of pink pajamas amid the sea of junk. She couldn't look up and meet Lizzie's gaze; her heart was beating a million times a minute and her hands were feeling clammy.

"Well," said Lizzie.

Penny blinked rapidly. She couldn't, couldn't . . . I mean, it was so ridiculous.

"I wonder," said Lizzie, still looking out of the windows, "I wonder if there's some kind of test you could buy from a chemist if you were throwing up in the morning." She looked at Penny, who grimaced back at her. Lizzie noticed her eyes were red.

"Of course not," said Penny. "I mean, almost certainly not . . . I mean, it would be really unlikely . . ."

"Haven't you been doing tons and tons of alfresco knobbing?" said Lizzie.

Penny looked guilty.

"You know, scientists have discovered you can get pregnant doing it standing up."

"Is this the time for jokes?"

"You were careful, weren't you?"

"Yes. Yes. You know, mostly. Nearly all the time."

Lizzie looked at her.

Boots on a Saturday morning on the King's Road was heaving with beautiful young tourists. Lizzie couldn't quite believe she was doing this. The only time she'd even had a scare was one night with Felix when they'd had sex so stupefyingly dull that afterward neither of them could remember a thing about it, including the contraception.

151

The queue was incredibly long, as they stood trying to look innocuous while carrying a big blue box.

"You're going to be fine," said Lizzie. "We're probably infertile anyway."

"What makes you say that?"

"I don't know. The papers keep saying everyone's infertile, don't they?"

"Well . . ."

"And we're nearly thirty. And we drink cocktails and live in a built-up area with fumes and sleep with boys who've been drinking water that the pill gets flushed away in and stuff. I think we missed our chance to get pregnant when we were fifteen."

"D'you think?"

Lizzie nodded fiercely and, even though it was stupid, Penny felt comforted.

"It's true," said Lizzie. "The only way we're ever going to get pregnant is via IVF. Everyone knows that. It costs thousands of pounds and makes you really moody."

"You do that for nothing," said Penny, smiling weakly.

"Oh, yeah," said Lizzie, glad to see a ghost of a smile return.

"Yeah?" said the disinterested checkout girl, chewing her gum slowly in their faces. And I couldn't find a job, thought Lizzie to herself.

Penny held out the pack, hand shaking.

"Thirteen ni-ee nine," said the girl. The twins stood there.

"Go on then," whispered Lizzie.

Penny turned to her. "What?"

"Pay her."

"What with? I don't have any money, do I? Sloan hasn't paid me yet this month, and I owed Dwaneesa sixty quid."

"Well, I don't have it, do I?" said Lizzie, exasperated. It cost her more than that in bus fares up to Barnet, and she only had twenty pounds to get her through till Monday. Which she hadn't brought with her.

"You got it or wot?" said the checkout girl. Penny gave Lizzie an anguished look. "I don't, OK?" said Lizzie. "Can't you put it on your credit card?"

"They chopped it up in Argos."

Behind them the queue was getting distinctly restless. Lizzie hoped Penny wasn't going to do something embarrassing, like ask them all for a quid.

But then she saw Penny's face, and it didn't look tough at all. In fact she looked as if she was about to cry.

"Come on," said Lizzie. "Let's just go home."

"You put that back," said the checkout girl.

"Really," said Lizzie, dumping the test on the counter and manhandling Penny out of the store with uncustomary vigor. Maybe all these rude Londoners were having an effect on her after all.


Back home, Penny was quiet at first.

Lizzie sank down beside her on the sofa and put her arms around her.

"Sweetie."

From Penny came a great racking sob.

"How *could* I . . . how *could* it? I know I am. I just know it."

Lizzie patted her gently on the shoulder.

"I mean, this is just bollocks . . . this isn't how it's meant to happen at all." Penny, bleak with despair, shook her head, then covered her face with her hands.

They were startled by the phone as it rang. Lizzie couldn't help thinking, It's for Penny, it always is.

"Hey," said Will. "How are you? Are you feeling OK? It's going to be a gorgeous day. Absolutely wonderful. I propose a picnic, with smoked-salmon bagels, cream cheese, and some diet Fanta for you. You can read *Heat* magazine, then I'll snog you in the long grass. How does that sound?"

It sounded like heaven.

"Uh, I'm not sure," said Penny. "I'm not feeling too well."

"Really?" He sounded concerned. "Would you like me to come over and look after you?"

Penny glanced around.

"No!" she ordered, panicked. "I'll . . . I'll call you later, if I'm feeling better."

"OK, sweetie pie."

Penny put the phone down and turned to Lizzie.

"What . . . What am I going to do now?"

Lizzie looked at her, helplessly.

"I don't know, Penny. What, you think this is the kind of thing that happens to me every day?"

"Maybe I should ask Brooke."

"That's right," said Lizzie. "Posh people are much better at dealing with life's problems. That's why they're always going into rehab and insane asylums. Why don't you just ring Mum?"

Penny winced. "I don't . . . you know, I don't get on with Mum like you do. And it's the last thing I want . . . she'll just be so disappointed. Sometimes I feel like she's been waiting for me to do something like this my whole life."

Lizzie tried not to show how true this was. "She'll be OK."

"Look, she's happy for the first time in her life, doing this stupid drama school thing."

Unbelievably, RADA had deigned to allow Eilish in. She had taken to wearing colored headscarves and large earrings, and talked about becoming the next Brenda Blethyn. Penny had found it embarrassing, and had barred her from coming in the shop without several hours' warning so she could get Sloan out of the way before he was rude about her.

Lizzie looked at her. "You know," she said gently, "we're being very negative about this. How do you know he won't be . . . you know, pleased? I mean, you guys are in love and everything, aren't you?"

Penny swallowed. "Pleased?"

"Yes, you know, happy. Maybe he loves you, and you might be having his baby and that will be a good thing."

Penny looked away as her worst fears surfaced.

"Lizzie, he doesn't even know me. I'm supposed to be a rich bitch working for fun," said Penny, looking as disconsolate as Lizzie had ever seen her. "I mean, I'm just so different from him . . . he reads the *Telegraph*. He thinks . . . he thinks he's going out with someone else."

"No, he doesn't," said Lizzie. "You're his gorgeous Chelsea girlfriend, aren't you? And I'm sure he doesn't care a fig either way. You're his Chelsea girlfriend, who just happens to have his baby. Move into his flat, or just pretend you're . . . uh, an eccentric messpot. Who's to be any the wiser? You could sort the rest out later. As far as he knows you're just a nice girl. None of that shit matters anyway. You know, what spoons to use and stuff. Nobody gives a toss."

"You think?" said Penny, unwilling to admit to the world she'd described to Will. But she thought of the way those women looked at her when they went to bars and restaurants. Why had she never met his mother? What on earth would his mother think? Boys didn't care as much about these kinds of things but women . . . women knew straightaway.

Penny looked at her stomach sadly. How could she be so foolish, so ridiculously undone by a handsome face and a roll in the hay? This wasn't what she'd planned for herself at all.

But Lizzie's words had inspired a small hope. What if he did want to take on responsibility? They had had fun together, but it was so sudden, so soon.

She closed her eyes and imagined his face, spreading wide with delight.

"Oh my God! A little baby!" he'd say, then he'd pick her up and fling her around and spin her in the air, then put her down gently and carefully as if she were made of china. Then he'd take her to meet all his friends and his parents and they'd love her and . . .

A single tear ran down her face.

"Would you like to eat some French toast?" said Lizzie, who'd almost subconsciously started whisking eggs to calm her nerves. "Otherwise I'm going to eat it all, and I was rather near to getting into my old black trousers."

Penny paced up and down, still staring at the phone. There had been several cute and inquiring text messages from Will. Each one made her head for the door, determined to confront him head on, her heart full of hope. Every time she'd stop and wonder at the implausibility of meshing her life to his.

156

"I've got to know," she said. "I've got to know. There's no point putting it off."

"He loves you," said Lizzie loyally. "And what a beautiful baby it will be."

"Shh," said Penny. "That's not helping."

The phone rang again.

"Oh, come on, Penny," said Will. "It's gorgeous out there. I don't want to be stuck at home."

"I need to come and see you," said Penny. "At home."

There was silence on the other end of the phone. She had it on speaker so Lizzie could hear.

"Uh, are you sure you wouldn't rather go to the park? It's lovely."

"No," said Penny. "I want to come around."

There was another long pause.

Will hadn't been expecting this; usually girls were all too keen to get him to theirs; cook for him and show him how lovely they were around the house. He counted on it. But Penny was different: so mysterious.

Still. She was different. She was special. Maybe the time had come. Will blinked rapidly and took the plunge. She'd look after him . . . wouldn't she?

"All right," said Will finally. He sounded quiet, decided, rather muted. Penny looked at Lizzie expectantly.

Will gave an address in east London.

"I suppose you'll hop in a cab," he said.

"Uh, yeah . . ." said Penny, who was already fingering one of their grandmother's many, many bus timetables.

"What do you think?" she said to Lizzie the second she was off the phone.

"I think he knows already," said Lizzie. "He's a young bloke, his girlfriend is sick, and now she wants to come around to discuss something. What else is it going to be?"

"I think I'm going to be ill again," said Penny, sprinting for the toilet door.

The journey from Chelsea to Clapton was one of the longest of Penny's life. She watched as the beautiful mansion blocks and pastel houses gave way to the formidable square structures of Belgravia and Mayfair; along the tatty bustle of Oxford Street and beyond; past Centerpoint and on past the bookshops of Charing Cross Road, along the Strand, and Fleet Street, and on to Liverpool Street, to change and get on an older, tattier bus. Why buses serving cheaper postcodes should be nastier than those serving nicer ones she didn't understand at all, but just sat upstairs, her head leaning against the window, trying to keep the nausea down.

One second she would imagine a world where she inhabited Will's trendy loft, maybe sitting cross-legged on the floor, a neat baby bump in front of her while all their trendy friends (faces mostly blurred) came by and teased her, and Will announced she was getting more beautiful with every month that passed. And they would have a little girl and call her Chelsea. Or maybe that was common, she couldn't decide. Well, Bill Clinton's daughter was Chelsea, and so was that girl who used to date Prince Harry, so it couldn't possibly be.

And then she saw herself, pregnant, huge, lumbering through streets inexplicably covered in snow, crying to herself. Then she realized she was thinking of the film *Oliver!* Or a cold hospital room, filled with other silly girls, looking at a pair of howling twins . . .

*

125b Nitclose Road wasn't at all what she was anticipating. She was expecting a converted schoolhouse. Or maybe just a huge warehouse, like the home of the man from the old "Easy Like Sunday Morning" adverts, with an open wall and an industrial lift. Or a vast studio with great vaulting windows.

In fact, 125b Nitclose Road was a side entrance to a gloomy-looking Victorian terrace. It was filthy with soot, and the front garden was covered in black bin bags and an old sofa that sagged, looking soggy and disconsolate. Bits and pieces of various bicycles cluttered up the path.

There were five doorbells, all unreadable, by the small door. Penny picked up her phone to call, but just as she did, the door swung open, and Will stood there, at the bottom of a grimy flight of stairs littered with pizza delivery leaflets and brown envelopes.

He stood there, staring with a strange, apologetic look on his face.

"Well," he said. "Hmm. Have you heard of the new Bohemians?"

Penny felt as if she'd been knocked out by her second major shock of the day. Unsteadily, she followed him up the filthy stairs and into a tiny bedsit. There had obviously been a last-minute tidy-up—several pairs of trainers had been lined up underneath the cheap wardrobe—but there was no disguising the shabbiness of the brown carpet and green curtains.

Will winced. "So," he said, "welcome to my, uh, humble abode."

Penny looked at him, too shocked to speak. "But I thought . . . I thought . . . but you're a successful artist."

Will started boiling the small kettle in the corner. "Coffee? I've only got instant, I'm afraid. And powdered milk. I, uh, don't have a fridge."

"You don't have a fridge."

Will rubbed the back of his neck nervously. "Look, Penny, I know I've put off having you over."

"I can see why," said Penny, feeling chilled inside.

"But I thought . . . you should know the truth. I really like you and—"

"You're actually a tramp."

Will looked ashamed. "Well . . . I sell one picture every month or so . . . then there's materials and I have to pay off my student loan, and, you know, I like to use my money to socialize . . ."

Penny thought of all those expensive dinners she hadn't eaten, those nights out where he'd taken care of everything, in his suave manner. She looked at his battered brown leather jacket again, hanging on the back of the door, and had a sudden flash of realization. It wasn't battered because it looked better that way. It was battered because it was all he had to wear.

"Oh my God," she said.

"I really like you," said Will. "So I thought . . . you should know . . . I'm not quite in the same league as you, financially speaking . . ."

She looked at him. Now she knew why Minty had been trying to warn her off. She'd thought it was jealousy, but it wasn't. It was something else altogether.

"You were sharking me," she said quietly.

"What?"

"You're a shark. You go to nice bars to pick up rich people hoping they'll fund your art. Aren't you?"

160

And boy, did she know how that was done.

"No!" said Will, his face reddening. He wasn't a shark . . . he didn't mean to, but he'd found his looks and his accent made things easy and . . . well, otherwise, how was he going to live? He didn't want to live in Nitclose Road all his life, and was it so wrong?

"I mean, I go where, you know, patrons of the arts hang out, I suppose . . ."

Penny backed away cautiously. "Were you looking for a meal ticket?"

"No," said Will. Oh God. Agreeing to her coming here was the worst decision of his life. He gestured around slightly despairingly. "Well. I don't want to lie to you, Penny. I mean, it would be nice to be able to work somewhere . . . you know, get my own real studio, something like that."

He looked slightly ashamed for a moment.

"And, Pen, I really, really like you. I mean, I think I lo—"

Penny realized she was shaking. This could almost be funny. Two grifters, grifted. Well, it could have been funny. If it wasn't for . . .

"Uh, Will," she said. He stopped what he was saying and looked up. "You know, I don't have any money either."

He looked confused. "What do you mean?"

"I mean, I'm looking after my grandmother's flat while she's ill. That's why we've never had you over. She's my dad's mother and my dad was never really part of our lives and we don't even know him. It just came out of the blue. I'm from Brandford. Mum's a dinner lady."

Will stared at her, as if she was the one who'd just dropped the bombshell. "But . . . but . . ." he said. "You knew all those places to go."

"I read magazines all day."

"And you work in an art gallery."

"Sloan thought it would be good for business," said Penny. "You know. Little market-stall worker stuff. He thinks it's hilarious."

Will's mouth was actually hanging open.

"I don't believe this," he said, although of course, it explained everything. He'd just thought her money was a bit crass. Plus, she'd been willing to do things in parks that posh girls didn't mind doing either; it was only ever his middle-class girlfriends that were a bit uptight. It hadn't occurred to him for a second that it wasn't brash money; that it was no money at all.

I know something else you wouldn't believe, thought Penny, but all her protective instincts kicked in and she didn't say anything, just looked at him closely.

Will was fumbling with the neck of his T-shirt as if it was constricting him. He'd given up any pretense of making coffee, and had gone bright red. Penny swallowed hard. When she spoke, her voice was quiet, without its hard edge.

"But you still really, really like me, right? We're still, you know. In lo—"

Within a tiny millisecond, the space of a blink, there it was. It took him just a tiny sliver of a moment too long to look at her.

"Of course," he said. But everything had changed.

Lizzie made salami with fennel on pasta and took it in to Penny, who ignored it. Lizzie eyed it hungrily.

"Are you going to stay in bed forever?"

"Yes," said Penny, sobs still racking her frame.

"You know, it might be fun," said Lizzie. "Having a little baby."

"Being a single mum back in Brandford and raising a baby," said Penny. "Maybe I could get a job in a school. You know. Cooking. Hey, maybe I'm going to have twins."

Lizzie patted her on the shoulder. She'd never asked this question before.

"Did you . . . were you in love?"

Penny looked up. There were four hundred sodden tissues littering the duvet.

"Uh-huh!"

Through the day, Penny didn't get out of bed, and Lizzie was beginning to feel like a full-time carer. On Saturday night the doorbell rang just as she was taking Penny another mint tea. Lizzie's eyebrows shot up.

"Don't get excited," said Penny. "It's Brooke and Minty. I invited them up. Told them what's happened. People love to hear about misery and maybe they'll give some advice. Or cheer me up or something."

"Or something," said Lizzie definitely, as she jumped off the bed and went to answer the door. Brooke and Minty were standing there, both in jeans so tight they could have fainted and not fallen over. Minty looked almost triumphant.

"POOR Penny," she said loudly. "I'm SO sorry for her. I did try and warn her you know. Gold-digging rat."

"He's a cad," said Brooke. "We knew it, I'm afraid. Is this your place?" She peered into the room with a look of unfeigned horror on her face.

163

"It's industrial chic," said Lizzie.

"This smells like that old lady who lived here," sniffed Minty.

"Would you like to come in?"

"I can't stay long," said Brooke. "Charles is taking me to dinner at the Wolseley."

"Oh, how boring," said Minty. "We're going to Crazy Bear. It's so loud there, I haven't the faintest clue what Oscar is banging on about. It's great."

"Follow me," said Lizzie. "Uh, would you like a snack?"

She thought sadly of her lovely fennel and salami, which she'd hoped to tempt Penny with, then polish off.

The girls sniffed loudly.

"I'd like a *cocktail*," said Minty, striding into the room with her shiny boots.

"Ooh, yah," said Brooke, marching in too and yelling to Penny. They bustled through leaving Lizzie feeling like the waitress. The doorbell rang again.

For crying out loud, thought Lizzie. This better be good news.

Amazingly, her Brandford friend Grainne was standing in the doorway.

"Hi," said Grainne dully, staring at the floor.

"Hey, there," said Lizzie. "Come in. What brings you to this neck of the woods?"

"I thought you'd be in," said Grainne.

"On Saturday night. Well, that's good," said Lizzie. "I'm glad that's the kind of thing you'd be quite happy to rely on and come all the way from Brandford without a phone call or anything. You know, just to make sure."

"I'm very lonely," said Grainne. "Have you got anything to eat?"

"Salami and fennel?" said Lizzie weakly.

"I don't really like salami," said Grainne. "And I don't know what fennel is. Is it some pretentious new thing you have now you live in Chelsea?"

Lizzie shrugged.

"But it'll do, I suppose."

In the sitting room the girls from downstairs were sprawled about, long legs up on the sofa and coffee table, cigarettes dangling, as if they'd never had to worry about spilling or breaking anything in their lives. Which they hadn't, of course.

"Hiya, guys!" said Penny. Somehow Penny had managed to leap out of bed, squeeze into her super-tight jeans and a halterneck top—and a pair of heels for Christ's sake—and clear enough space on the sofa to lounge on it, looking nonchalant.

Brooke tilted up her indoor sunglasses and inspected her closely.

"God, Penny," she breathed. "You look like you've had a tit job."

Penny had noticed that her breasts felt a little bigger. She supposed this was part of it too.

"Lucky cow," said Minty. "I had ten days in hospital after mine."

"And you told us all you'd been having a torrid affair with an Argentinian gaucho," said Brooke accusingly.

"Oh, I was fifteen," said Minty. "What was I supposed to tell you?" She patted her neck-height crystal-ball tits affectionately.

"Yes, well," said Penny, giving a slightly fragile giggle. "There have to be some side benefits."

"God, yes," said Minty. "Count up the side benefits. There's

165

the big tits and . . ." She fell quiet. "Um, not having periods," she added. "That'll be handy."

"You still have those?" said Brooke scornfully. "God, how much do you weigh?"

"Of course I don't," said Minty quickly. "No one who's anyone has periods."

"So anyway, darling," Brooke said to Penny, "join the club."

"You're pregnant too?"

For an instant, Penny had an image of them bowling around with matching three-wheeler buggies, having a great time.

"Good God, no. Whatever gave you that idea? No, darling, three abortions at the last count."

Penny was amazed. "*Really?*"

"Oh, yes. Know this excellent chappie. It's like having a haircut."

Penny didn't think it was anything like getting a haircut.

"I can't believe you got knocked up. Will is *such* a bugger." She stifled a chuckle.

"Although of course if he'd been a bit more of a bugger you wouldn't be in this situation! Haaw!" said Minty.

"Minty, that's not very helpful."

"Of course not, darling. OK, hang on, I've got the doc's card in my purse . . ."

Penny squeezed her eyes shut, horrified that they both carried an abortionist's card in their wallets.

"Ah, here we go, darling."

Penny wrote the number down on a piece of paper and stared at it.

Lizzie came in from the kitchen area with a freshly mixed

jug of cosmopolitans. Grainne stood by her side like a suspicious toddler waiting for a vaccination.

"This is Grainne, everyone."

The girls couldn't have looked her up and down faster if she'd been a piece of dust.

"Hmmm," said Minty, possibly the lowest form of actual conversation ever invented. The other girls saw this as good enough to cover them too and didn't say anything at all.

"Can I sit here?" said Grainne, making Lizzie wince.

"Course you can," Lizzie said quickly. "Make yourself at home."

"This sofa is bigger than my entire flat," said Grainne.

"Really?" said Minty. "That's a shame for you. Are you terribly poor?"

"Well, you know, London's so expensive," said Grainne, purple with embarrassment at being singled out.

"So it's actually smaller than the sofa," said Minty wonderingly. "Do you have to curl up really small to sleep? How do you wash?"

"Well, it's nice really," said Grainne.

"It's very nice," said Lizzie.

"Oh, sorry," said Minty. "I thought you just said it was really squat and tiny. My bad." She helped herself to more cosmopolitan.

"So, D&G have started doing a baby line!" said Brooke tactfully. "That's exciting!"

"It is," said Penny. "Oh, I hope I get a little girl. So cute to dress. If I have it . . ." she tailed off.

"Little boys are cooler, though," said Minty. "Look at Liz Hurley."

"Little boys are definitely the way to go," said Brooke. "You can take him everywhere and dress him up and let him help with your makeup and he'll grow up gay and love you forever and never leave you. While girls, I mean"—she lifted her hands—"I can't stand my mother, to tell you the truth. And she's always bursting into tears when she can't fit into my clothes."

"It's true," said Minty. "My mother's on her fifth facelift but her neck is a complete mess. She's holding on to Belgravia by the skin of her teeth and I just don't think husband number four is going to turn up anytime soon. But she cries every time I mention this stuff. You'd think she'd be happy to know the truth."

"Little boy it is, then," said Penny. She reached out and popped a bit of Lizzie's precious salami in her mouth. Grainne had also been absentmindedly stuffing it away in a completely oblivious way, which went a long way to explaining her figure and her constant state of amazement at her size. ("But I hardly eat a thing.")

"You'll have to watch, though," said Brooke, looking pointedly at the salami. "Victoria Beckham managed to get back into her size six jeans this time in thirty-eight minutes."

"Gwyneth's still fuming," said Minty. "Took her nearly an hour and a half."

"I'll worry about that later," said Penny, licking her fingers.

Brooke glanced at her Cartier Tank watch. "Oh! Charles has been waiting . . . twenty minutes. Do I have time for another cocktail or not?"

"I'd better go too," said Minty. "Although if he hasn't got me an expensive present, he can whistle for that blow job."

"You give blow jobs?" said Brooke. "Ew, I can't believe you still do that. That is a very, very needy thing to do. It's so vulgar."

"Of course I don't give blow jobs," said Minty, standing up and tossing her long blond hair over her shoulders. "I suggest that I might and use it as a lure for gifts."

"God, your friends are *so* lovely," said Lizzie as she finally shut the door.

"They're all right," said Penny, letting her stomach out and kicking off her shoes.

"They're not all right! Grainne's a shaking puddle on the sofa!"

"I'm still here," said Grainne. "And my flat is bigger than the sofa, actually, it's just that it's a studio, that's all, and there's nothing wrong with that. It's sixteen by twelve, I remember from the plans. I'd be very amazed if you had a sofa that was sixteen by twelve, ha, ha, ha!"

"It's OK, Grainne, we didn't think that," said Lizzie gently.

"I mean, OK, so my sofa is like my sofa and a bed as well, and I don't always remember to fold the bed back into the sofa," said Grainne, "and OK, so you have to climb over the sofa to reach the sink. But it's not the same size as the room, no way."

She shoved the last piece of salami into her mouth.

"Shh," said Lizzie, patting her on the shoulder.

"And it's cozy, you know," said Grainne. "In the winter I don't really have to turn on the heating, cause I can feel my neighbor's radiator through the wall."

"Grainne," said Lizzie. "You bought your own place. With your own hard-earned money. They'll never do that. You should be really proud of it and really proud of yourself."

"Neh," said Grainne. "I hate it. Can I come and live here with you?"

*

"I don't want to go," Penny was saying.

"Well, you have to."

Monday morning and Penny was, if anything, worse. The visit from the girls had perked her up briefly, but when they'd dashed out on their glamorous assignations, leaving her in with Lizzie and the television, her misery had grown and grown. Also, the salami had made a speedy reappearance. She hadn't been able to keep anything down all weekend and looked terribly thin and weak and now Lizzie was sending her to the doctor's.

"You are taking the day off and you are going to the doctor's," said Lizzie. "Shut up."

"But I have to go to work," said Penny. "Sloan's got some big lunch on."

"He always has a big lunch on!" said Lizzie. "As far as I can tell, that's all he does."

"This one's really important, though," said Penny. "He's got to renew the freehold on the building or something, blah, blah, blah. I didn't really listen when he was telling me, but apparently it's absolutely crucial he takes them to Sketch and gets them mortal, otherwise he's going to lose the shop."

"Oh, Penny," said Lizzie. "Why didn't you mention this before? You must have known you'd have to go to the doctor's."

"Well, madly, I've had one or two other things on my mind," said Penny. "I forgot. Also, I thought . . . I thought I'd be better by now." She winced to herself. "I keep thinking I'll wake up and it'll all be better, you know?"

Lizzie nodded. "So, what are you going to do?"

Penny looked up at her. There were huge dark circles under her eyes.

"Well," she said.

"Oh, no," said Lizzie. "Oh, no. No."

"Lizzie, please."

"I've got a job, too, you know."

"Yeah, but you can twist that bloke around your little finger, can't you?"

"No!"

"And you haven't had a day off in ages. Jeez, when I worked in catering you were considered pathetic if you didn't dog it at least twice a week."

"I can't leave him in the lurch."

"You found him in the lurch. And Lizzie, if you don't . . . if you don't help me out the shop will go under and I'll lose my job anyway, and . . ."

"Could you be any more pathetic?" said Lizzie.

"Nope," said Penny. "God, I hate this."

# Chapter Eight

The sun came up huge and warm as Lizzie paced her bedroom. She couldn't believe she'd agreed to this. And she realized, picking up the phone at seven-thirty, that she hadn't spoken to Georges for weeks. Not properly, nothing beyond "we need extra peppers" or him passing over a recipe before he sped out the door. Not since the stupid night of the party when he'd made her feel like the world's biggest, most introverted idiot. Which, she noticed, she'd managed to change about herself, by doing nothing but staying in and sulking for the last two months.

Well, she had to do it. Her sister needed help.

"Yes?" He sounded gruff on the phone, harassed. She wondered what on earth he did when he wasn't in the café. Maybe some weird European thing she didn't understand, like marching in a saint's parade.

"Georges, it's Lizzie."

His voice softened straightaway.

"Hello, Lizzie. How are you? I feel I hardly see you, no? But you are doing a very good job of looking after my restaurant."

Well, restaurant was pushing it. Sandwich bar just about passed muster.

"I'm fine."

"You know, takings are up. I think the customers like you."

Lizzie couldn't help but feel pleased. She thought of her old job where, as far as she could tell, nobody at all had liked her.

"You gave me some good recipes."

"Good food is not hard, Lizzie. Just some good ingredients, you know, a little bit of love . . ."

"I don't know about love," said Lizzie, feeling herself go slightly pink.

"No," said Georges. Then his voice grew hearty again.

"Are you still using your microwave? And going to parties all night?"

"I'm not actually."

Seeing as she was welcome to take home the leftovers, Lizzie had been eating from the café every day.

"No? You are eating better? Ah, you will look beautiful. The tomatoes will make your skin bloom, and the spinach will clear your eyes and enrich your blood."

"You talk a lot of rubbish," said Lizzie. But it was true. She was looking better. The mirror kept hinting at it, and her waistbands were loosening. The other day she'd bought a smaller size in tights. From extra large to large, but it had given her a huge frisson nonetheless. And she wasn't sure, but she thought she was losing her microwave pallor a little too.

"Normally I am very serious," said Georges, but he didn't sound serious when he said it.

Lizzie steeled herself and dived in.

"Georges, I need to take a few days off."

Immediately Georges's light tone ceased. "I see."

"I need to . . . it's a family matter."

"Your sister is in a scrape?"

"No! Well, ish. Well, it doesn't matter, I just wondered if you would mind. Like, having a holiday."

"I understand 'a few days off.'"

"Uh-huh."

"Well, I think. Do you mean a few days off, or do you mean bye, bye, Georges, I am gone never to see you again?"

"The first one," said Lizzie. "I just need to help Penny for a few days."

Georges made a *pff* sound with his mouth. "This is not very convenient to me right now."

"Me neither," said Lizzie, quelling a very passing desire to say if it was convenient he could take his job and shove it up his portly bottom.

"OK. You will be back on Wednesday? When? I must come in and cover for you."

"Are you always so cross when anyone wants to take a holiday?"

"I am not cross, Lizzie. That is you, huh? Now, I have to go."

"Oh, Penny," said Lizzie. "What am I supposed to wear? What am I meant to do? What are my duties? Does *Sloan* know I'm coming?"

"Yeah, yeah, yeah," said Penny from the bathroom. "You'll be fine."

"*Penny!* You need to help me!"

There wasn't another sound from the bathroom.

"*Pen!*"

Silence.

"OK, I'm coming in."

"No! No, no, no, no, no!"

Lizzie cursed manfully under her breath and headed back into her room.

OK. Deep breath. Not to worry about it. It was just Penny's stupid job, that appeared to require the brain power of a four-year-old. No panic. What the hell was she going to wear? It didn't matter to Penny, she spunked all her money on designer shoes and bags in the sale, then wore pure black and white the rest of the time. Anything looks OK in a size eight.

Usually at work she wore . . . well, an apron.

But this place—God, they practically sold paintings on the smartness of some ditzy girl's buttocks. The keyword she was really looking for here was pert. Pert was not something ever applied to Lizzie. Pear, maybe.

OK, breathe. Black. That was it. Arty people loved black. Well, she had plenty of that. After a bit of rummaging she found a long black skirt she'd last worn to a Mission reunion concert with Felix. OK, fine. And maybe a white T-shirt . . . nope. It wasn't that white, and she looked like a waitress. Black again. Not the ironic Iron Maiden, that was never going to work. And didn't look ironic on her anyway, it made her look like one of those girls who follow heavy metal bands around the country in the hopes of finding a boyfriend through the law of averages. Which, it occurred to her, she should look into trying one of these days.

She finally found a basic V-neck top and slipped that on and stared at herself in the mirror. She didn't look like an arty boho chick. She looked like a plump girl trying to blend into the background.

She stomped through to Penny's room and used some of her expensive and patently shoplifted face cream.

"I'm just *accessorizing*," she called out. There came a muffled grumble that may well have been discontented annoyance mixed with an inability to prevent anything happening.

Inside Penny's jewelry box was some cheap silver and gold and a couple of tiny diamond baubles given to her by the slightly less cheap, but still not exactly fabulous, dodgy men of her past. Lizzie picked out a large brooch and pinned it to her bosom. There we go; arty eccentricity, and it drew attention to her best feature, which would surely be a good thing to do in the world of paintings. Emboldened, she glanced around. What next?

Penny's bedroom, over the rubbish, was a mishmash of clothes and sparkly things that attracted her like a magpie. Lizzie caught sight of a black fur beret hanging on top of the cupboard door. Aha! She grabbed it and clamped it down on her unruly hair, then squinted at herself in the large mirror.

There she was. If you squinted (quite hard) she looked boho, arty, and a tad frisky with the hat at a jaunty angle. This was perfect.

"OK," she yelled. "I'm ready."

"What are you wearing?" groaned Penny.

"Never you mind," said Lizzie. "It's perfect."

"Oh, God."

"What do I have to do in this stupid job again?"

"Just sit at the desk and look pretty."

They both paused.

Lizzie checked herself out again in the mirror. Perhaps some bright red lipstick, she thought. She picked up Penny's highly sought-after Chanel Red Bus, which Penny had always claimed to have found in the toilets at the All-American New York Diner, and started applying. Putting on lipstick wasn't as easy as she thought; she'd always made do with gloss. Oh well, no matter. She made a kissing face at herself in the mirror.

"OK. OK. I'm going to do this," she said. "Are you going to be all right?"

"Hhnnn," groaned Penny.

"OK. Keep your phone on so I can contact you with any artistic emergencies. And, you know. Call me the second . . ."

"Uh-huh."

Lizzie took a deep breath. She felt strangely excited. Maybe being an arty boho chick was the kind of person she really was after all. Maybe she could bring lots of art into Georges's café and turn it into a hip happening joint where people paid in paintings and got terribly famous.

"You know, I think I might even be glad you talked me into this," she said. "And, Pen . . . I don't know quite what this means, but—good luck."

There was still no sound from the bathroom.

Lizzie had been to Penny's gallery once before, for an exhibition where they had free wine. She'd stood beside Brooke and Minty, who'd practically ignored her, until Will had come up to say hi, whereupon Brooke and Minty had come over all friendly with her to freeze Will out.

Chelsea was coming to life all around her. Deliveries were being made to smart restaurants; beautifully dressed shopgirls hurried past; tall, smart-suited bankers stamped along briskly. Every single one of them glanced at Lizzie's hat. Admiration, undoubtedly.

Finally she turned up the little cobbled street and found herself outside Penny's workplace, the name of the gallery beautifully scripted in an elegant white font against a racing-green frontage. It was an ocean of tranquillity and breathed money and peace. Lizzie wondered why on earth she hadn't considered working here earlier.

In the window was one of Will's huge landscapes that Sloan had put on display. Oh God, what if he came in? What if she tried to say hello and accidentally shouted, "Penny's pregnant! Penny's pregnant! Penny's pregnant!" straight in his face?

"Uh, excuuuuuse me," came a ludicrously over-the-top voice interrupting her unhappy reverie. "Can I *helllp* you?"

Lizzie slowly turned around and found herself face-to-face with Sloan. He was wearing a large cream fedora hat and pastel bow tie that somehow contrived to look incredibly smart.

"Where did you get that *terrible* hat?" he said, then stopped himself. "Sorry, I really shouldn't be rude. But in your case . . ."

"Terrible hat yourself," said Lizzie, without thinking. "Uh, I'm sorry too."

"No, no, no, no, no," he said. "You're missing the point."

He took out a huge old-fashioned key and unlocked the heavy outer door to the shop.

"You see, my hat is beautiful, exquisitely tasteful and suits me. Whereas you have a dead otter on your head. Do you see the difference? Beautiful garment"—he indicated himself, then pointed to her head—"rotting maggot-infested carcass. Do you see?"

Lizzie followed him into the shop. What was with this posh/ rude thing? Would she ever learn?

"Are you following me?"

His self-confidence was galling, and Lizzie was remembering the circumstances she'd lost her last job in, still unconfident.

"Uh," she said unconvincingly.

"You know, there's a hostel around the corner."

"I'm not a bag lady!" said Lizzie in annoyance.

"That's not what your hat's telling me."

"You're the rudest man I've ever met."

"In that hat? I'm amazed."

"Shut up about my hat!"

She calmed down as he stepped into the shop.

"I'm Lizzie. Penny's sister."

Sloan eyed her carefully. "Are you *really*?"

"You've met me. Tons of times."

"*Have* I?" He sounded doubtful. He stared at her, hard. "I meet a lot of people. So, what are you doing here?"

Lizzie wasn't quite sure how to approach this. Maybe mention that Penny was taking one day sick, then take it from there.

"Penny can't come in today."

Sloan rolled his eyes. "Oh, my goodness, that's ridiculous. I've had some ditzy dollies work here before but your sister takes the biscuit. She knows this is a big day for me."

"No, don't say that!" said Lizzie. "You see, you can take me instead! I'll do it!"

Sloan's face cracked into a smile, showing brown and orange teeth. "You'll do what?"

"I'll fill in," said Lizzie, looking around. "How hard can it be? I've worked in shops before."

Sloan's smile looked, on closer inspection, more of a snarl. "Are you those psychic twins one hears about?"

"Nope."

"You sound nothing like her."

"She puts it on."

"And you look nothing like her."

"I do if I go like this."

Lizzie sucked her cheeks in as far as they would go and rolled her eyes. Sloan's mouth twitched.

"And you think you're just going to stand in for her?"

His phone rang. The ringtone was a little classical diddly number.

"Yes? Sketch? For nine people? Of course I made the booking. Uhhh . . . hang on a minute." He looked at Lizzie. "Is this a prank?"

"Is what a prank?"

He gestured impatiently. "Are you really here to work?"

Lizzie nodded fervently.

Sloan shut the phone with a slam. "I think I may just have made a very big mistake."

"Nonsense," said Lizzie. "I'll be good."

They were both facing each other as someone entered the shop. It was a tall blond woman with a Nicole Kidman nose and superior air, as if just having a Nicole Kidman nose was enough to make you feel superior. Maybe it was, thought Lizzie.

"Hello!" she said cheerfully. "Can I help you with anything?"

The woman stared right through her as if she was made of

invisible dust. Lizzie glanced at Sloan, but he was looking at her in exactly the same way.

"Well, I'll just be over here," said Lizzie, "if I can get you anything."

The woman made a tiny moue with her highly glossed mouth. She glanced airily around the gallery.

"Are these all you have?" she asked eventually, with a slightly European accent Lizzie couldn't identify.

"Uh, no, not at all, madam," said Lizzie, bouncing forward. "I'll just check in the back. What kind of color are you looking for?"

The woman stared at her. "What *color*?"

"You know. To go with your walls . . . on your yacht or whatever . . ." Lizzie's voice trailed away. The woman was staring at her in disbelief.

The woman's eyes flicked to Sloan, who jumped forward. "What this person was *trying* to say was that Brown's extraordinary use of color is truly what sets him apart from other artists in this area."

"But half of these are black and white."

"Are they though?" said Sloan. "Are they *really*?"

The woman peered more closely at the pictures in front of her.

"You. Champagne. Now," hissed Sloan at Lizzie out of the corner of his mouth.

"Thanks," said Lizzie. "But it's only ten-thirty in the morning."

"For *her*."

Lizzie stumbled into a large messy back room that was quite a contrast with the immaculate gallery next door. Frames were stacked in corners and a desk was completely submerged with paperwork. In the corner was an ancient fridge, held together with string, and inside were about twenty mini bottles of Moët. She grabbed one and looked around for something other than a chipped mug standing by the sink to put it in. There wasn't anything. She checked everywhere. Oh God. Maybe this was some kind of fashionable east London thing where it was cool to drink out of big builder's mugs. She poured it quickly.

Back in the gallery the woman and Sloan were deep in an animated discussion of just how many colors they could both see in the gray tones of Will's work.

"There's definitely some pink," said the woman.

"That's amazing," said Sloan. "You know, there is, but only a very highly developed eye could have picked it out. I couldn't—the artist had to show me."

"You know him well?"

"He's a very good friend of mine," said Sloan.

"Champagne?" Lizzie said, holding out the chipped cup which, she now noticed, had a cover of the *Sunday Sport* printed on it.

The woman recoiled. "Excuse me?"

Sloan immediately grabbed it.

"I washed it," said Lizzie as he pulled her to one side.

"I could smack you," hissed Sloan, and he looked like he meant it. "Go get another one of those little bottles, open it, put a straw in it, give it to the nice lady, then get the fuck out of my sight forevermore."

"What about Sketch?" said Lizzie bravely.

"I would rather have a robber's dog look after this store while I'm out than you. I think I'll just go down to the cellar and bring up some of the many rats who live there and invite them to take over. There's a chap in Shepherd's Market who looks after the prozzies with a razor and sells crack. I might ask him to step in for a couple of hours. After which I'll call up Ronnie Biggs, the great train robber, to do the stock check . . ."

"OK, I get your point."

"Following which I'll see if Pol Pot is available to do the totaling up and get the resulting accounts audited by Enron. Am I making myself clear?"

Lizzie nodded.

"Where . . ." came the woman's voice from over their heads, "*did* you get that hat?"

"There's nothing wrong with my hat!" shouted Lizzie, finally pushed beyond endurance. "If you bloody upper classes weren't so obsessed with things like bloody hats you wouldn't all be going inbred and mental."

The woman had moved forward, not listening to a word.

"It's really terribly chic."

They all paused.

"Uh, this hat?" said Lizzie finally.

"Yes. It's got an ugly chic to it. I like it."

Lizzie squinted at her.

"Please, madam, do take it if you like," said Sloan obsequiously.

"No, you can't!" said Lizzie. "It's Penny's."

"'Penny's,' eh?" said the lady. "I've never heard of them. Is there a waiting list?"

"Yes," said Lizzie.

"Fabulous. Well done you, I'll get my PA to look it up right away."

She swept toward the door.

"Oh, and Sloan, get those two big landscapes sent around, will you? The ones with the pink in them."

And the discreet bell of the shop politely twanged and she was gone.

"Stop it," said Sloan, after a time.

"Stop what?" said Lizzie, who was trying to compose her face while staring out of the window.

"Stop trying to keep that stupid smug grin off your face."

"Why should I have a stupid smug grin?" said Lizzie. "I've just made you tons and tons of money after being here for five minutes but you're still going to throw me out on the street."

Sloan's mobile went off again. He listened to it intently, then hung up.

"Did you know," he said, "that if you don't take up your lunch reservation at Sketch they charge your credit card anyway on what they think you might have eaten?"

"Is that the kind of thing a West End art dealer's assistant ought to know?" said Lizzie.

"Mmm," said Sloan. He wandered into the back room. Lizzie heard him throw the china mug against the wall. It shattered with a crash. Eventually, he came back in, with a new, freshly straightened cravat.

"I'm temperamental," he said. "Do you think you can handle that?"

"I'm temperamental, too," said Lizzie.

"Tough shit. Are you going to sell a few of these bloody paintings?"

"Yes!"

"OK then."

Sloan whooshed out of the shop and slammed the door, shaking his head to himself as he did so.

Penny sat in the waiting room of the local doctor's surgery looking around with some interest, even as her left foot twitched uncontrollably. It was much smarter than Brandford community health clinic. There were pictures on the wall that nobody had nicked, and a couple of smartly dressed businessmen, fiddling with their BlackBerries while waiting to go in. This might not be a bad place to look for men. Then she remembered why she was here and groaned to herself. Oh, for goodness' sake. It may look a bit smarter, but she was still having to wait. Although they did have the latest issue of *Vogue* rather than a five-year-old *Reader's Digest*. That was something. Her fingers were a little shaky on the keys of her mobile when she called her sister.

"So how's it going?"

"I realize why you spend so much time on the phone," said Lizzie. "There's really fuck all else to do."

"Yes, but when I spend time on the phone it's networking. You're just arsing about."

"Any news?"

"Nope, still waiting. Although, Lizzie, you should tart yourself up sometime and get down here . . ."

Sloan would be back soon from his liquid lunch, and she hadn't sold anything else. Was this normal? She knew when she walked past these places (which wasn't very often, and even then only on the way to John Lewis to buy thread with her mother), there never seemed to be anyone in them, browsing or purchasing.

She'd kind of assumed people bought over the phone or some-thing, but the phone hadn't rung all day. Penny's job was just literally sitting. When she thought of how busy she was in the café, running about, chopping, cleaning, serving, and chatting to the people coming in, she decided she had the better deal. OK, she had to start early in the morning, and she certainly got her hands dirty, and she didn't have a second even to glance at *Metro*, but her day flew by, and she got the pleasure of feeding people, of giving people things they liked. It had seemed that woman earlier hadn't even liked spending thousands of pounds on a huge treat like a painting, that it had been a chore rather than a pleasure.

But even just by being here, Lizzie could feel some of her suppositions falling away about these people. They weren't, as it turned out, any less mean or ignorant than the people she hadn't liked on her estate. They had the same expensive footwear (al-though shoes rather than trainers), flash motors, and an unearned sense of entitlement. But this, oddly, made her feel less intimi-dated. She really didn't care.

Lizzie let herself slump over on the desk, not even worried now about the state of her hair. Oh God, and she really, really had to go and visit Gran too. Excellent, a two-hour bus journey on top of this day of hell. She let out a huge sigh, just as the door to the shop pinged.

"Aha!" came the loud voice dramatically. "I guessed it! You are betraying me! But Lizzie, working for me is much, much better, no?"

Lizzie looked up and could not stifle a smile, even though she'd intended to treat Georges coldly the next time she saw him, after he'd been so short with her about taking time off. He was, for the first time, wearing a suit rather than a stained T-shirt with a striped apron tied around his middle or, at the party, a black shirt that simply screamed, "I am a black shirt donned solely for my apparently slimming qualities."

Now, however, he was wearing a very well-fitting gray pin-stripe, with a cream shirt and a darker gray and yellow tie.

"I'm just covering for Penny," said Lizzie. "Just for a couple of days. She's sick."

"You have not left forever?"

"No. Not at all. You look very smart."

"I am a very snappy dresser," said Georges. "Don't you think?"

Lizzie looked at the heavy gold ring and the little tufts of dark hair escaping from the cuffs of his immaculate shirt. Oddly, she found it rather sexy; the contrast between the pristine cloth and the animalistic man underneath made her shiver.

"Yes, you are. How did you guess I was here?"

Georges waved his hands. "Well, I recognized that drunk man. Sometimes he comes in and asks me if I have any wines and I say no, we don't have any wines, we are a lunchtime shop with no wines, and he says, OK, and then he forgets and comes back the next week and asks for wines."

Lizzie nodded sagely.

"And I am on my way to see my bank."

"Oh." Lizzie felt concern. There was nothing wrong with the business, was there? She hated to think of other places, who didn't care so much about their ingredients or how they threw their food together, getting the better of Georges by being cheaper.

"Is everything OK?" she asked worriedly, thinking of Sloan's meeting.

Georges smiled broadly. "Lizzie, it is OK. You do not need to worry yourself about us."

Lizzie rather liked him using the term "us."

"Oh good," she said. "It's a very good café."

Georges looked around. "What are these? They look like holiday pictures."

"They're paintings," said Lizzie. "Those ones there are by my sister's evil ex-boyfriend."

Georges raised his shaggy eyebrows encouragingly. There was no sign of Sloan in the street; perhaps he'd taken his meeting on to the Arts Club, where, according to Penny, he could sit in the corner smoking with a cigarette holder and discourse on contemporary art for hours despite being absolutely whizzbanged. "It's so boring it makes you want to kill yourself," she'd said. "I think that's why he gets drunk all the time. Otherwise he'd have to bash his own head in."

Lizzie told Georges the whole sad story ". . . and that is why she's at the doctor's."

"I know this word," he said, holding up a finger. "It is bounder. That is the word, yes?"

"Yes," said Lizzie. "That's it. And what he didn't think was, we don't have any money. He didn't realize."

"He didn't see your kitchen," said Georges.

Lizzie shook her head.

"I've seen your kitchen," said Georges. He looked grave. "And you work for me. Very few rich people work for me."

"Well, quite," said Lizzie. "Can I have a raise?"

"A raise? While I am in here talking to you while you are working for somebody else?"

"Oh, yeah," said Lizzie.

Georges walked around looking at the pictures closely. Lizzie wondered where he'd got a suit to fit him so well. Their mother's old lodger had had a suit, but he'd bought it at Burton's and it looked as if he was going to court, and not as a lawyer either.

"You know," Georges said finally, "I am a little sorry for Will."

"Sorry for *Will*? How can you be sorry for him? He got my sister pregnant, then dumped her because we're poor! Be sorry for *us*!"

"He doesn't know she is pregnant, no?"

"She didn't want to blackmail him into anything," said Lizzie.

"That's good."

"Plus she thought he still might not care. And that would make her feel worse."

"That's bad." He looked meditative. "You know, Penny will be all right. She's a survivor."

Lizzie let out a sigh.

"But to be a leech, to try to live off women's money, to pretend to make love . . ."

"He didn't pretend to make love," said Lizzie. "That's what got us into this mess."

"Well, I think that is a very sad thing for a man to do. Or do you think I'm old-fashioned?"

"Georges, you make your own bread and you don't use a microwave. I *know* you're old-fashioned."

Georges smiled. "I think I want to buy one of his paintings."

The doctor was a woman clearly younger than Penny, which made her sullen.

"You can just buy a test in Boots, you know," said the doctor crossly. "They're just the same and much quicker."

189

Penny looked at the floor. "I couldn't afford to," she mumbled.

"What was that?" said the doctor, as if the concept of not being able to afford something was entirely new. Which it probably was.

"Nothing," said Penny.

"Well, now I have to send it away to the lab. It'll take five days. Should I write down that this is a wanted birth, or do we have to discuss our options?"

Penny wondered if being told off by a sixteen-year-old virgin was some kind of cosmic punishment. As was, it seemed at the moment, the whole of the rest of her life.

Lizzie was so shocked she burst out laughing.

"You want to *what*?"

"Buy a painting. Then Will can give some money to Penny if she has the baby. From himself, not from playing kissy with a woman. And look, he is very talented."

"You're serious."

Georges nodded.

"Which painting?"

"You choose."

Lizzie almost giggled.

"Georges, they're thousands of pounds."

Georges shrugged.

"But . . ."

"Lizzie! You are working in a shop selling paintings! Sell me a painting! You are worse at this than you are at cleaning the big brass pot!"

"I hate cleaning anything bigger than me," said Lizzie. "Uh. OK. Now, I have to write it down, then we send it to you . . . I think . . ." She disappeared under the desk and started ferreting about.

"This isn't the kind of service I expect in an expensive Chelsea art gallery," said Georges. "Is that your hat? I like it."

Under the desk Lizzie smiled to herself. And found the invoice book.

"OK. What about this one?" She headed straight toward the smallest and cheapest, a tiny delicate seascape.

"That is the smallest! You think Georges Dos Santos takes the worst? Huh? No."

Lizzie looked around desperately. Georges pointed at the far wall, to a painting of a canopy of trees over an avenue stretching along a desolate landscape, with only the hint of a steeple in the distance.

"I will take this one. I like it. It says the road is long, but shady. And at the end of it there is home. Very nice."

"You're quite the romantic when you get going, aren't you?" said Lizzie.

"You'd better believe it," said Georges.

"But I don't understand," said Penny. She was sitting on the sofa, hunched up, working her way through a box of tissues on her left and chocolates on her right.

"I think he was just doing a really nice thing for you," said Lizzie. "I mean, the café can't make that much."

Penny looked confused. "Maybe it does."

"I cash up the till. I'm telling you it doesn't. Georges buys really good ingredients and has no portion control."

"Well, that much is painfully obvious."

"Be nice. He was trying to help you out."

"Did you say he goes out all the time?"

"Yeah."

"There you go, then. Maybe he does something else. Bets on the horses or something."

"How would that make you rich?"

But Penny didn't say anything. Her face crumpled up and she felt for the tissues again.

"Will'll be so happy," she moaned, "when he finds out he's sold some paintings."

"A big one too," said Lizzie.

Penny sobbed. "And he'll use the money to take out some bint, with diamond earrings and a tiny nose. I know he will."

Lizzie patted her gently on the shoulder. "Are you any closer to deciding what you want to do?"

"Yes," said Penny. "It's the obvious thing. And everyone keeps telling me there's nothing to it." She sobbed harder. "I've got to wait five days to get the results."

"Ah, well, no, you don't," said Lizzie, drawing the Boots package from her bag. "What does petty cash mean anyway?"

As Penny sat there, stunned, Lizzie stepped behind the coffee machine Georges had said he was finished with and let her take home. It was taking her quite a significant amount of time to learn how to use it and it was still liable to blast her with super-heated steam when she wasn't paying attention.

"Oh God," said Penny. "Either my life is a hundred percent ruined or . . . no, I think it's a hundred percent ruined. I didn't even know that it was possible to cry this much. How come I'm crying this much? I don't think there's any fluid left in my body. I've been squeezed dry, like an old lemon in last night's Bacardi."

Penny snatched the test from Lizzie's hand and dashed out. A second later she reappeared.

"It's the bloody crying! There's no moisture left in my body, I can't pee! There's no water in me at all." She grabbed a cup of Lizzie's coffee and sipped it furiously. "Bloody hell. Right, back in a minute."

Lizzie looked at the machine. As its pressure built up, the boiling water made a *wheee!* sound, as—from the bathroom—did Penny.

# Chapter Nine

"I'm not pregnant!" Despite what she'd said about being drier than the Sahara, some new tears were dripping down Penny's face.

"Great! I'm giving Georges his money back for that stupid painting he bought."

"No, don't do that," said Penny, "Sloan'd kill me. Just tell Georges he has to burn it."

Lizzie rolled her eyes. "Well," she said. "No harm done."

"No harm done?" Penny threw back the duvet she'd been sheltering under for days.

"NO HARM DONE? My relationship is completely screwed up . . . which was obviously going nowhere now I come to think of it, you've made me realize my new friends don't necessarily want the best for me, and it's made me give up drinking. How can you call that no harm done?"

"Well, at least I won't have to deal with your rude creepy boss anymore," said Lizzie, sitting next to Penny and patting her gently on the arm.

"Sloan isn't creepy," said Penny. "Not as long as you give him plenty of Midori to drink." She heaved a great sigh. Hot dogs, hot dogs, hot dogs. *Pff.* "What do you think it was with the tits?"

"The power of positive thinking," said Lizzie.

They sat in silence for a while.

"I just . . . you know, I thought for one tiny minute . . . just when I was on that bus to Will's house. I wondered what it would be like, you know. Me and him in—" she cast around—"in a nice apartment. With a little baby." She snuffled again.

Lizzie comforted her. "You hate babies."

"I don't hate babies. I just didn't want to be another one of the Evergreen Estate girls, you know? I just didn't want three babies, by nineteen, with different dads, and nowhere to put them and no money and not able to do anything with them and dressing them in England shirts and things. Those are the babies I didn't want."

She looked at Lizzie, blinking rapidly.

"And when I saw Will's place . . . it was such a dump, Lizzie, honestly. It made this place look like the Ritz. And I thought, even if he wasn't a gold-digging bastard, Liz . . . even if he'd been nice and good and kind and everything—I still wasn't sure I could do it. I still wasn't sure I could have the baby and live in that shithole and have absolutely fucking nothing all over again when I've had absolutely fucking nothing up until now."

Lizzie patted her gently on the arm again.

"Does that make me a bad person? I'm sick of it, Lizzie. I'm sick of scrimping on every fucking thing, then I look at what Brooke has got and what Minty's got and what bloody Sloan has got and just feel like shit all the time." Penny shook her head. "I'm sick of being poor. And that makes me just as bad as him, Liz."

A quiet week limped into a quiet weekend—Lizzie stayed on at the gallery (in case Will came in, but he didn't), until Saturday, when Penny forced herself out of the house ("I can't help it, Lizzie, I'm starting to smell of old lady") to the amateur pole-dancing night Brooke and Minty were going to in Shepherd's Market.

"Come with us, Lizzie," Penny had said. "I've got to get back on the horse and you . . . you've got to get *on* the horse. Come on. I'll pay. To say thanks."

"You want to take me pole dancing to say thank you?"

"It's something to do. And apparently lots of men go."

"I'll bet they do. No thanks."

Penny had sighed. "Up to you then."

The club had been great fun, full of daft girls up for a laugh. Penny had watched Brooke and Minty carefully though, especially Brooke. She watched how she refused every other drink, and encouraged other people on to mischief while never getting out of control herself. They'd been pleased to find out she wasn't pregnant, although Penny suspected Minty wouldn't have been that fussed. And now Brooke was pointing out the chaps to her.

"Look," she said. "Always check the watch. If it's too big it's almost certainly fake."

"And the shoes," said Minty. "They must be wearing shoes, not trainers. If there are tassels on them that means middle management and golf. Run, run, run."

"OK," said Penny. She'd had a couple of vodkas on her shrunken tummy and was feeling defiant.

"And the car," said Brooke. "That's important. You want flashy but not too flashy. If it's too flashy he's probably been saving up for it since he was six and still lives with his mum."

"After all," said Minty after a pause. "You did try falling in love, didn't you?"

"Yes," said Penny.

"And, did it work?"

"It bloody didn't."

"Exactly. Darling, you've got to go for what lasts."

"Money," said Brooke. She raised her glass. "To fun and money. And, darling, can we have a teeny tiny word about your miniskirt?"

Penny didn't look like their other friends, and Brooke had privately wondered about her, but Minty had never met anyone who hadn't been to boarding school before and was prepared to take Penny on trust. "She's probably from one of the minor counties," she'd said to Brooke sympathetically. "Somerset or somewhere equally preposterous. We should feel sorry for her really."

Lizzie was so bored by Sunday lunchtime—Penny wasn't up yet—that she'd started moving piles of things around slightly. She realized this was strictly *verboten*, but her grandmother certainly didn't seem to be getting any better or look like she was coming back, and she could always move them again later, and if she could just get to the window to clean it, the whole place would look better immediately.

She surprised herself by getting into the work, and having vigorously had a go at the window, she decided to attack the sink unit too. There was something satisfying about lifting up endless layers of gooey gunk, which somehow suited her mood, and as she swilled yet another bucket of soapy water down the drain she felt a little better, so she wasn't really paying attention when the doorbell rang.

Assuming it was the girls downstairs looking for sparkling water ("You still drink milk? I think milk is common," "Yuh, all dairy is definitely common"), or the young gentleman callers on the girls downstairs who often got confused (Minty thought locking men out was a hilarious prank), she went to answer it without taking off her rubber gloves or removing the old pair of tights she'd wrapped around her head to keep her curls out of her face, singing a Sugababes song to herself rather tunelessly.

"Hello," said Georges.

Lizzie nearly dropped the mop.

"What are you doing here?" she demanded. Georges stared at her.

"Hello. Welcome, traveler, to my home, where I shall show you kind hospitality and shower you with warmth, as I am a human being with normal human instincts, even when, as now, I resemble a frog wearing a pair of tights on top of my head."

Lizzie flushed.

"Well," she said. "It's a reasonable question."

Georges was wearing a suit again, but a different one this time, a lighter-weight khaki that made him look darker than ever. His bushy eyebrows came together.

"And I was taking my little sister to Mass, then she wants to go to Topping Shop. Is that enough or do you need a paper signed by many expert witnesses and the mayor? And I need to know if you are coming back to work tomorrow or will I have to get Marina to work instead, which I think will cost me much money in Topping Shop."

"Come in," said Lizzie. She was extremely pleased to see him, although mortified by the way she was dressed. "Would you like some coffee?"

"I'm very hungry," said Georges.

"Cheek!" said Lizzie. "I cook for you all week and now you want me to cook for you for free!"

"You look to me," said Georges, "well, you dress like that . . ."

"You are the most sexist dinosaur in the world."

"I am not," said Georges. "If I was sexist I would say, 'You do not look like you are dressed for cleaning and cooking, you look like you always dress like that and are a sad girl.'"

"Is that what you would say?" said Lizzie. "In that case you certainly get no breakfast."

"Ah, but when you smile . . . everything lights up and is happy again."

Lizzie couldn't help it. She smiled.

"See! Now any man would forget tights on head. What do you have? Eggs? Peppers?"

"Yup," said Lizzie proudly.

"We will have Portuguese omelette," said Georges. "It is like Spanish omelette, only good and not filthy and covered in rat hair and evil Spanish blood. Sit down. Where is your unfortunate sister?"

"I'm here," said the voice, not nearly as weak and tear-stained as it had sounded before. Penny rounded the doorframe of her bedroom and Lizzie nearly gasped. She hadn't been privy to Brooke and Minty's little directional fashion chitchat that Penny had taken to heart, so the effect was completely out of the blue.

199

Penny looked different. She looked dewy, and clear-eyed, with shiny pink lips and rosy cheeks. She was wearing a billowy, expensive-looking white shirt and a pair of soft faded jeans. Her bare feet were still quite brown, and the toes were perfectly manicured. She looked fantastic, like a black-and-white photograph of an American film star romping on the beach. Where was the fake tan? The five layers of mascara? Even the nails were shorter.

Lizzie's gaze darted to Georges. Sure enough, his eyebrows, which always betrayed exactly what he was thinking, had shot up.

"Penny," he said, and there was a new softness in his voice, "I should not know but I do know and I hear that congratulations is in order. You look like motherhood is going to suit you. Having a baby is always a wonderful thing, even if it is not always in the best of circumstances, no?"

Rather than contradict him raucously, Penny gave a shy smile.

"It was a mistake," she said, sitting down demurely on a chair and looking at Georges, eyes wide. "A silly mistake, I suppose."

Lizzie was incredulous. What was this with the "I suppose?" She'd just had the most narrow escape of her life!

"I am sorry," said Georges. "Maybe you are a little sorry too, no?"

Penny tilted her head in a Princess of Wales fashion, craning to see if she could get a glimpse of Georges's watch.

"Maybe," she said. Maybe nothing, thought Lizzie. What had happened to Penny? What was she up to?

"I am going to cook you a good meal," said Georges, leaping up.

"Wow," said Penny, looking straight at him. "I love a man who can cook."

Georges disappeared into the depths of the kitchen annex,

occasionally making disappointed noises as he pulled out antiquated and shockingly dusty kitchen appliances.

"What are you up to?" hissed Lizzie to Penny. "I thought you were getting over your heartbreak by being all sluttish and stuff."

"I was," said Penny, making her downcast face again. "But you know, Lizzie, I think I've changed. I think this happening has made me see things differently."

"Differently how?"

But Penny just smiled infuriatingly and padded over to the kitchen.

Georges was cooking with his usual élan, tossing the pan, letting the bread hop out of the toaster, and doing five things at once.

"That's amazing," said Penny, watching him as if he was the most wonderful thing she'd ever seen.

"It's not that amazing," said Lizzie. "I can do it."

"Not like that though."

"Yes, I can. It's just every time I offer to make you something you say, oh, boohoohoo, or you go and be sick or something."

"Don't be silly!" said Penny. She laughed a tinkling little laugh that sounded a lot like Brooke. "You're such a joker."

"Is Lizzie a joker?" said Georges, his bottom lip overlapping his top lip. "This is interesting. I did not know this."

Lizzie went to the bathroom to take the tights out of her hair. Then she decided that taking the tights out of her hair would be a really obvious thing to do and they would probably both pass comment on it so she'd better not take them out in case . . . well, in case Georges . . . anyone . . . thought something of it. She rubbed under her eyes in the mirror to get rid of any old mascara tracings, which seemed to congregate there, and took a scout around for Penny's makeup, but couldn't see any trace of it, the hoarding witch.

Penny's peals of laughter echoed from the sitting room just as Lizzie knew that if she hid in the bathroom any longer everyone would assume the absolute worst.

"This is *delicious*," Penny was enthusing, scooping up the omelette and—this was a first in a while—actually putting it in her mouth. "You're so clever."

"I listened to my mother," said Georges, grinding some black pepper.

"So did we," said Lizzie. "That's why I was such a bad cook."

"But you get better," said Georges. "That is the important thing. And you work hard. That is good too."

"So," said Penny, looking mildly discomfited to find the attention moving off her, "you bought Will's painting."

Georges shrugged. "I like paintings."

"You didn't have to do it."

"I know."

"It's quite expensive."

Georges shrugged.

"I wanted to say thank you. I know it was kind of for me."

"Not at all. I like paintings."

"Do you buy many paintings?"

"Sometimes."

Georges glanced at her, his face unreadable. Penny changed tack.

"So, how long have you been running your lovely café?"

"Well, my father started running it when I was a boy ... I came here when I was twelve, and I helped him with the shop.

Then he retired and went back to Portugal." He pronounced it "Por-too-gal."

"Uh-huh," said Penny, forking her food into her mouth.

"So I opened a few more shops, you know. It was good, my dad was happy when the business grew. And he could build a house in Portugal for my brothers and buy land for my mother to have her horses, and he was very happy about that." Georges smiled even when he thought about it. "So, you know, poor old Georges, I have to stay here and work and always open the cafés and work hard just so my mother can have horses, and my sisters can have these designer clothes, huh? It is a dog's life."

"I didn't know you had lots of shops," said Lizzie.

"You didn't ask," said Georges, buttering himself another slice of toast. "You say, Ah, Georges, I have dropped the mustard on the floor again. Ah, Georges, where is the taramasalata? Ah, Georges, once more I have cut open my finger and we must throw away the good meat."

Penny laughed again. Lizzie wanted to throw butter at her.

"That's amazing," Penny said, "to come to this country with nothing and build up a whole chain. You're quite the tycoon!"

Georges noticeably puffed up. "Well, I don't know," he said. "You know, I work hard."

"Well, I think it's amazing," said Penny. "I think you're so clever."

Lizzie was staring at her in disbelief. She couldn't mean it. Penny couldn't be serious, trying to pretend she liked someone like Georges. And Lizzie couldn't believe Georges had money. She'd thought he was just the fat sandwich-maker guy, who made her laugh and made her embarrassed and cheered her up and told her off. She realized as she thought this that she had begun to think of him in a proprietorial manner that wasn't exactly appropriate. It's just, Georges was *her* . . . friend.

"You must take me around some of your places some time," said Penny. "Mind you, if I can eat that well everywhere, you may have to roll me around!"

"I'm sure you would never get fat," said Georges. "Fat is only for old idiots like me."

As Penny laughed her high tinkling laugh, Lizzie realized her teeth were gritted.

Two days later Penny "popped in" to the café. Lizzie was furious. After everything she'd done for Penny . . . the help, the care. And now Penny was muscling in on the only part of her life she really enjoyed, that was hers. She spent her life looking out for her mum, her gran, her bloody headstrong bloody sister. Georges and the café were *hers*. Well, not hers, not like that but . . . how dare she? What a pig-selfish way to get over a broken heart.

"*Hello*," Penny said to Georges. "I thought you were never here!"

Georges shrugged. "I like to visit all my shops."

"Quite right. Very shrewd. I said to Sloan, we must see if you're interested in catering for any of our launches . . . we've got a very big exhibition coming up—"

"Oh yes?" said Georges. "We might be interested. Canapés, goat's cheese, that kind of thing is good, yes?"

Lizzie watched how enthusiastic he was getting over the new idea.

"We could take some small sunblush tomatoes and stuff them with rice and . . ."

"And pesto," said Lizzie. "That would be good."

"That would be very good," said Georges. "And take some pecorino cheese and—"

"Hang on," said Penny. "I did say it. But Sloan said, no, if you handed out food nobody ever ate it, and it interfered with good drinking time and the drunker people got, the more paintings they bought."

"Oh," said Georges.

"It would have been good," said Lizzie loyally.

"I know," said Georges.

"Anyway," said Penny briskly. "What's good on the menu today? It all looks so delicious."

"El Bullitt," said Georges proudly. "Portuguese stew. To our secret recipe."

"As long as it's dairy free," said Penny. She'd been saying this for years, ever since she'd read in a magazine it was a good way to avoid eating fatty foods. Georges looked genuinely upset.

"But no cheese? No fresh milk? No hot lattes or Greek yogurt?"

"Uh, I seem to be OK with yogurt," said Penny.

"Oh, well, if you can eat yogurt you can eat Parmesan."

"Just a juice, please," said Penny. "So. Georges. What do you do to relax?"

Georges stopped chopping up aubergines for a moment.

"What do you mean, relax? I do not understand this English word. Aha, that is me making a very funny joke."

"Well, you came out partying," said Penny. "So you can't be all square."

"I am all round," said Georges. His English, Lizzie had noticed, seemed to deteriorate a little when he got nervous. "I must stop with the very funny jokes, I will cut myself like with a knife."

"Me and the girls," said Penny—nothing ventured, nothing gained, she was thinking, "were going to try out a new restaurant tonight. Would you like to join us?"

That was fast, thought Lizzie.

Georges looked at Lizzie.

"You are going to try out new restaurant?"

"I'm not invited," said Lizzie, trying to busy herself with something.

"Of course you're invited," said Penny, sounding irritated. "Do I have to send you a golden ticket to get you to do anything? No wonder you never go out. It's a celebration to, you know, start off the rest of my life and all that. Plus, Brooke's got us into an opening, so the food will be free."

"Well, I promised to go see Gran."

"Join us later then. Sheesh." Penny looked conspiratorially at Georges. "And next time I'll remember to send the footman with the engraved scroll."

"No, almost any invitation would do for me," said Lizzie.

"It's tough, living with a martyr," sighed Penny.


"I'm not a martyr!" said Lizzie, brushing out her grandmother's hair. The journey up had been worse than ever and she'd had to sit next to a group of giggling scrawny teenage girls. Lizzie remembered when the only thing you had to worry about with teenage girls was that they would take the piss out of your clothes. Now, according to the papers, they were also into happy slapping and general physical violence, so she had trained her eyes out of the window and kept them there.

"You are a little bit of a martyr, little twin," said her grandmother. She'd seemed a lot more lucid today. Lizzie wondered, deep down, if she mightn't be getting better. Could that happen? She'd have asked one of the staff, but there was rarely anyone to be seen, and anyway, she was slightly frightened of them.

"You do complain a lot. Especially now you're not looking so, well . . . bountiful. And you should go out more. You don't need to come and see me every night . . . I know I'm just a boring old lady. You're young and should be going out and having fun."

So even her old gran, half crazy and confined to a bed in Barnet, thought she was a loser, pondered Lizzie gloomily, in what she realized was a martyr-ish manner.

"Do you know, I'd like to see my son," said her gran, out of nowhere. "I think he'll come to see me. Don't you?"

Well, seeing as he had disappeared without a trace almost twenty-five years ago, no, thought Lizzie. Maybe she was overestimating Gran's improvement.

"Yes, I would like to see him," her gran continued dreamily. "Anyway, why aren't you getting ready for dinner? They're going out to dinner? You must go. You like the man, you have to chase him."

Lizzie stared at her hands.

"There is a man I like," she admitted quietly.

"Oh yes?" said her gran.

"But I think Penny maybe likes him too . . ."

Her gran leaned over and patted Lizzie's hand. "I liked a man once. But I didn't chase him. Then he died in the war. So, the moral is obvious."

"Chase a man or he'll die in a war?"

"Exactly."

"Like, the sex war?" said Lizzie.

"Oh, any war," said her gran. "And you can tell me all about it the next time you come. But not too soon, all right?"

# Chapter Ten

The new restaurant was everything Lizzie had expected it to be, and worse. She had always dreamed, when she was working in the stamp firm, of what it would be like to come to a place with real napkins and mood lighting. She remembered for their seventh birthday their mother had brought them up to Leicester Square and taken them to Garfunkel's and they'd been allowed to eat as much ice cream as they wanted; Lizzie had eaten so much she'd been sick in a Technicolor fashion all the way down the toilets (something which hadn't seemed to surprise the staff).

At the time she'd thought this was the pinnacle of fine dining and had continued to do so for a long time. But no, she saw every day now, pin-thin women on the streets of Chelsea slipping into restaurants where a bowl of spaghetti cost twenty pounds. Genuine ladies-who-lunched then slipped back into cars after two glasses of mineral water and a leaf. What would it be like, she wondered, to go out for lunch, right in the middle of the week, to just wander in and sit and chat to your friends for two hours? What would they even talk about? Handbags probably. She couldn't really talk to Grainne about much these days.

Still, she was looking not bad in a simple black wrap dress she'd bought from Hennes, now she'd finally been paid. It was cheap, but it didn't look it. Well, it didn't look *that* cheap. And it suited her, which was a first, and, she thought, twisting around and examining herself from a few different angles, she looked definitely "curvy" rather than "plump."

The restaurant, just off the Fulham Road, was called Daffodil, for no earthly reason Lizzie could work out, but its food was, according to the invite Penny had left for her on the kitchen work surface, a new fusion between raw foods and Mongolian cuisine. There was a sample menu, but from the looks of it, it mainly involved uncooked carrots and porridge. The aim of the restaurant was stated to be "leaving mind and spirit in a harmonious spirit of freshness" rather than, she noticed, feeding you and making you satisfied and happy.

Across the front was a strip of smoked glass, and the lighting inside beautifully gleaming, making it extraordinarily soft and flattering. Only the heads and feet of punters were visible through normal glass, so it looked like lots of disembodied golden mannequins laughing and screeching. At the doorway, several wafer-thin girls were hanging about smoking furiously and giving each other dirty looks through smoky dark eyes. Into the monkey pen, thought Lizzie, handing over her card to a ridiculously well-dressed bouncer person and squeezing her way inside.

"Lallie," said Brooke, waving happily. Lizzie went over crossly. She didn't want a nutty posh-o nickname like everybody else, thank you. After her little stint in the gallery, she'd resolved to stop letting people treat her like a pushover. Well, like so much of one.

"It's Lizzie, actually," she said, as stiffly as she dared. "I live upstairs. We've met. My hands smell of garlic, I never get any post and my sister's a tart."

Brooke paused for a minute, then broke into a smile.

"Here, try this, *Lizzie*," she said, handing her a glass. "It's a thistle cocktail. Disgusting, but effective."

Lizzie accepted the proffered drink and took a hearty gulp. She couldn't believe that had worked.

"Jesus. That's repulsive."

"I know," said Brooke. "But apparently it gets you drunk while performing a full body detox!"

"Great," said Lizzie. Rob and Sven passed by, looking sharky as usual. They appeared to be wearing zoot suits.

"*Sven*," said Brooke fulsomely. "You remember *Lizzie*, don't you?"

Sven tried to look as if he did. Obviously, thought Lizzie, this dress wasn't quite doing the job. Or, if you looked at it another way, it was.

"Have you tried the canapés?" he said, making a face. "It's, like, black pudding served with a radish, and spinach and cream and shit."

"Excellent," said Brooke, patting her tiny hips. "Inedible canapés. This place is going to do fantastically."

Penny swung around. Keeping to her new simple regime, she was wearing a white top with subtle diamanté sewn into it, so it glinted in the light.

"Hey, Lalls! How's Gran?"

"She's fine, *Pens*," said Lizzie. "You'd know if you went to see her."

"Yes," said Penny. "Imagine, me going to see someone who wanted nothing to do with us, whose son abandoned us, and who has never given us an iota of support or encouragement throughout our entire lives. My bad!" She scooped up another cocktail from a passing waiter and took a large swig. "Oh God, I thought these things might get better, not worse."

"So, Penny," said Minty, flouncing up and kissing Sven on the lips, "where's the new man then?"

Penny shot a quick glance at Lizzie. She wished she hadn't mentioned Georges to the girls. But it was like they said—she had to get back on the horse, decide what she wanted, and go for it. Just because Lizzie was making this big deal of not approving of her behavior so soon after Will. Well, Will was different. Penny had thought he was special, then he'd turned out to be a gold-digging fink, and she wasn't going to let herself go through that again. She was *not* going to be one of those women, like her mother or her classmates, who just assumed all men would let you down, who sang "I Will Survive" on the karaoke down the social after too many rum and Cokes.

Penny was going for security—real security—and Lizzie could stop getting her knickers in a twist; you'd think *she* fancied the hairy short-arse.

"Don't be stupid," she muttered. "There's no new man."

Lizzie stared at her. She couldn't mean . . . she couldn't be serious. I mean, a mild flirtation maybe, but surely not enough to tell her friends about him. But Penny was definitely looking pink, as Georges, dressed in a smart black polo neck that did nothing to hide his girth but went extremely well with his black hair and blue eyes, pushed his way through the revolving doors.

Fuck, thought Lizzie. Fuck, fuck, fuck. And she even chucked back another cocktail.

"Hello, Lizzie," said Georges, looking, as always, delighted to see her.

"Yeah, hello, whatever," said Lizzie, feeling sulky and awkward.

Georges looked confused. "You look nice tonight. Though I miss the frog tights."

"Ooh, what are the frog tights, Lizzie?" said Brooke, bursting into the conversation.

"Nothing," said Lizzie, feeling even more sulky and annoyed at herself. She bucked herself up. This wasn't what her grandmother had meant. It wasn't Georges's fault. "You look nice, too." She smiled at Georges.

"You think?" he grimaced. "You know, I must go on diet. I went to Borough market today and ate so much cheese I think I am blowing up like giant balloon. Ooh."

He grabbed two canapés off a passing plate and stuck them in his mouth, then his eyebrows made a comic twitch of disappointment.

"Now, this is not food. You must come with me to Borough market, Lizzie. You would love it there. Everything is so fresh, and good. And they let you taste it. Too much, maybe. They know me there, so they say, 'Georges, cheese!' They know I am a soft touch."

"If you had me there I wouldn't let you."

"You wouldn't? You would be worse, I think. You would say, 'More cheese!'"

"I would not! I would be discerning!"

"You would say, 'Ah, orange cheese. Yellow cheese. Green cheese. Yes please!'"

"OK, that's enough, Dr. Seuss," said Lizzie.

"Perhaps I need to appoint a cheese consultant for my business. I wonder, would anyone here be interested?" He squinted around the room, as if confused, while Lizzie giggled.

"GEORGES!" yelled Penny, although she was only about a meter away.

"Penny," said Georges. "Hello."

Penny pushed her chest out a little and smiled a dazzling smile.

"You know, Rob and I here were just talking about cars."

Rob nodded. Lizzie didn't think they had been talking about cars at all, but a man couldn't deny talking about cars. Brooke nodded at Penny approvingly.

"Lizzie and I were talking about cheese," said Georges gravely.

"Yeah, whatever," said Penny. "So, anyway, Georges, what are you driving these days?"

Georges looked perturbed. "Uh. I don't drive."

Lizzie felt a small stab of triumph. For sure, they were barking up the wrong tree with this one. She could see what Penny was trying to do, but Georges wasn't rich. He didn't behave like someone rich.

"Oh," said Penny, trying to keep the disappointed tone out of her voice. She could already tell Brooke and Minty weren't exactly impressed with his looks.

Georges looked at the floor. "I have a service. I am too lazy to drive, yes?"

A service? That meant, what, a chauffeur? Lizzie's face fell. The other girls perked up.

"Oh, yah," said Minty immediately. "Much easier."

"Definitely," said Penny. She moved closer to him and, as if on cue, the other girls took a step back.

"So, tell me more," she said, leaning into him a little. She looked beautiful, Lizzie thought wistfully, as her perfume reached her. Georges couldn't help it. He looked dazzled, as Penny gazed at him—they were about the same height—with wonder in her eyes.

"Well," said Georges. "I thought about buying a car, then I thought, Why not let someone else do the hard work, eh? And I don't care much about cars. I think they are silly boys' toys. Not important."

Penny nodded. "I think that's really true," she said, a tad breathlessly. "There's a lot more important things to think about."

"Yes!" said Georges.

"Like cheese," said Lizzie. But nobody heard.

Of course, it was her fault, thought Lizzie, licking her wounds in the corner. Even the cocktails had started to taste better. If she'd told Penny or asked her to back down she would have. They did *not* have a history of having the same taste in men. But protecting her sister by letting her take anything she wanted—that wasn't right, was it?

Penny was steeling herself. She'd done this before. It was the only way for her. She wasn't calm and grounded like Lizzie, or full of confidence like Brooke. She had looks, cheek, and about three more birthdays to do what she could with them, or she'd be spending the rest of her life in the All-American New York Diner, and no mistake.

And she was getting somewhere. Georges certainly seemed surprised, and a bit fascinated. I mean, surely she could get used to his . . . build. She looked around the room. It was full of gorgeous skinny tall women with little fat men. That was the way it worked. Nobody got everything. If she did manage to pull one of the four good-looking rich straight men in London they'd be too busy forming an orderly queue of other women to spend any time with her. Plus, she knew her limits. She couldn't ski, couldn't ride a horse, her accent probably wasn't fooling anyone. So. Time to get on. Be pragmatic.

"So I like to take the car to the strawberry-picking fields."

Oh God, did this man never talk about anything other than food? No wonder he was so gross.

"Wow," said Penny. "That sounds fabulous."

Suddenly her eye was caught by a movement near the door. Someone was skirmishing with the black-clad bouncer. Inclining a little toward the noise, she could hear a familiar voice.

"I'm on the list! I'm sure I'm on the list."

She moved nearer the door.

There, struggling his way through the revolving doors, looking very gaunt, still wearing the beaten-up leather jacket, his handsome face looking strained, was Will.

The gold-digging fink had been pacing the pavement for a long time. He'd heard of the party on the grapevine, and knew he had to see her, had to see Penny. He couldn't sleep, couldn't eat, and, most important, he couldn't paint, which meant his loss of appetite was about to become less of a problem when he couldn't afford to buy any food.

Finally he scrambled through and, conscious of the entire room staring at him, instantly tried to dust himself off and look inconspicuous.

"Well, look what the cat dragged in," said Minty loudly.

Will stared at the crowd until he found Penny.

"Penny," he said.

Penny leaned back into Georges.

"Penny." He strode toward her. A waiter offered him a cocktail, but he waved it away angrily.

"Penny."

She stared at him. He looked gorgeous, and so tired. Her heart felt as if it was cracking in two.

"I've been thinking," he started, "I know . . . I know we're two of a kind, you and I."

"I don't know what you're talking about," said Penny, considering whether to take Georges's arm.

"You know . . . looking for an easier life. But Penny. I've never . . . I've never felt about anyone the way I feel about you. It's different."

Lizzie heard Minty give a large tut.

"Please. Come back to me. We'll . . . I don't know. Live off canapés or something. In fact"—he turned around to the still-hovering waiter and grabbed two of his prawn concoctions off the tray, proffering one to her—"come to dinner with me?"

Penny stared at him, taking in the glowing ambience of the restaurant; the chink of expensive glassware; the scent of expensive perfumes. Then she looked into Will's kind, desperately worried-looking face and thought about love.

"You're hesitating a long time," said Will nervously.

She knew she was. But . . . could she change everything and

settle—settle for less, even, than she'd left behind before? Could she trust *him* to? She thought of everything she'd longed for and everything she'd dreamed of. Then she looked into his face and . . .

Minty couldn't take another second. "*I'll* tell him," she screamed. She threw her cocktail into his face. "How dare you dump our friend just because she was pregnant!"

Will looked comically outraged, covered in sticky stuff.

"*What?*" he bellowed.

"You chuck her because she's pregnant and she might cost you money you don't have. Well, she doesn't need you, so you can just piss off."

"How was that?" she said to a shell-shocked Penny, patting her on the arm.

"Uh . . . unexpected," said Penny, staring at Will, who was staring back at her. His forehead was creased, trying to understand it all.

"But. But . . ."

Then his face hardened. He'd misunderstood. This had all been a complete waste of time. How could she do something like that? Just because of *money?*

"Not good enough for your baby, was I?" said Will coldly. "Knocked it on the head as soon as you saw I wasn't quite the meal ticket *you'd* been hoping for?"

"Of course not," said Penny. "Of *course* not."

He looked at her with narrowed eyes.

"I'd thought maybe we were just two of a kind," he said. "And that, you know, I loved you, so it wouldn't matter as much as all that. But now I see . . . I don't . . ."

His face seemed to crumple. Will trying to be an ice-cool

man of punishment wasn't something he could sustain for very long.

"A baby . . ." he said. Then he turned around and pushed his way out through the crowd into the bustling street beyond.

Penny immediately turned to follow him, but Minty held her back.

"He's not worth it," she said. "Let him go."

"No!" said Penny. "You don't know what you're saying."

And she dashed after him, elbowing past women who tottered on their needle-thin heels and turned their sharp eyes to watch as Penny pushed at the heavy gold crossbar of the door.

"Will! Will!" she shouted on Fulham Road, which was full of dressed-up women, drunk men, confused-looking foreigners, smoking waiters, youths trying to look hard, couples worrying about starting times, European students knocking one another with backpacks: everyone in the world, it seemed, except the one person she was looking for.

# Chapter Eleven

Summer flattened into its dog days. Chelsea, Lizzie discovered, went quiet in August as everyone took off to their yachts, or their other houses, she supposed, or went on their international grand tours, or to the moon perhaps.

Georges was gone; back to Portugal to see his family. On the one hand, Lizzie was pleased. It stopped Penny hanging around and asking after him all the time. On the other, she missed him horribly. He'd left her in charge of buying, and she couldn't even feel an aubergine without remembering him yelling, "Baby's bottom, Lizzie! What must it feel like? Hairy camel bottom? No! Big monkey bottom? No! You must listen to me. I am good teacher. And also, you must teach me something. For good balance."

"I don't know anything," Lizzie had protested.

"Lizzie!" He was shocked. "You must do. I wish to know how much is one stamp to Por-too-gal, please?"

"I don't know," Lizzie had giggled, blushing as usual.

"Uh-huh. My stamps experts. Now, you must tell me then, what is happening in *EastEnders*. I must know."

And she'd giggled again, but oddly, had rather enjoyed telling him, and they'd both got quite engrossed in her retellings as they chopped the veg in the mornings (he'd started coming into the café again, more and more), and now Lizzie couldn't put on the television without thinking of him, and instead tended to take long walks on the nights she wasn't visiting Gran.

She'd never looked so healthy. So why did she feel so dull?

Penny was refusing to discuss Will in the slightest, but seemed to be dressing much more in her old style when she went to work. The skirts were getting shorter, the lips larger. It was with a certain sigh of relief that Lizzie felt the light winds of September come and the freshness in the mornings.

Gran, while always pleased to see Lizzie, seemed no better and no worse, and had stopped mentioning Redmond Street at all. As a result, Penny and Lizzie had gradually begun to feel that it was their own. They still didn't dare throw anything out, but had started adding their own touches.

As the weather turned colder, Lizzie noticed that none of last year's huge winter woollies seemed to fit her; they were massive, baggy black things. In fact, she thought, looking at them, they were horrible. She suddenly felt the urge to get moving, do something new with the way she looked. Georges had given her a pay rise too, and no longer having to pay even the tiny amount of rent to their mother definitely helped. Maybe she could get Brooke and Minty to help out . . . show her how to be a little bit more stylish. Obviously she hated stupid fashion and everything stupid that went with it but, she thought, looking at herself in the mirror . . . it couldn't hurt.

She mentioned it one Saturday to Penny, whose face lit up. Lizzie'd been waiting for this for a long time. It was the most animated Lizzie'd seen her in weeks.

But Lizzie changed her mind just as Penny started hustling her out of the house.

"No, no, no, no," said Lizzie, clinging to the banister.

"Come on. It's a makeover! It'll be fun."

"How will it be fun, again? Standing naked and being judged in front of a bunch of emaciated strangers. How will that be fun?"

"Because they're going to help you look better. And feel better. It'll be great."

"Great as in undeniably humiliating?"

"Come on!" said Penny. "You need to be getting a life, stop staying in and watching *Celebrity Partner Swap on a Crocodile-Infested Island*."

Lizzie stuck out her bottom lip.

"Oh, yes, what I'd much rather do is watch you parade around in a size six *Footballers' Wives* outfit for three hours while nobody gives me any food."

"Trying on designer outfits and eating lots of food just don't mix, how many times do I have to tell you? If you're that desperate, make like your friend Grainne and bring some crisps. But don't get any greasy fingerprints on stuff."

"I won't do that," said Lizzie, "because I don't eat crisps anymore and because I've just decided *I'm* not coming."

"Do you really not want to look glamorous just once in your entire life?" Penny said.

Of course she did. If she hadn't looked like a pig in a wig every time she'd run into or worked for Georges, might things have turned out differently? She couldn't stop remembering the

way he'd looked at Penny that night at the restaurant. He was . . .
bewitched. He couldn't help it, even if he thought Penny was
nuts in real life.

But getting there felt like it would be terribly hard work.

"Well," she said, twisting her fingers around the banister.

"Course you do," said Penny. "And you've got to start somewhere."

"OK, OK," said Lizzie. "I just meant, forgive me if I'm not
totally in the mood for lots of harsh personal criticism."

"Then why are you wearing your shirt buttoned up wrongly?"

"Oh, shut up."


Where did Penny meet all these people?

"Beautiful," Rodrigo, the worrying personal shopper said. "So
curvaceous."

Lizzie rolled her eyes. She'd been waiting for this. Next they'd
say they didn't have anything in her size, and would she mind
heffalumping the hell out of their shop?

"What?" said Penny, who had perched on a high stool sipping
champagne while Lizzie stood in front of the three-sided mirror
in the beautifully swagged personal shopping suite, slumping her
shoulders and trying not to catch glimpses of her graying bra and
slightly scuzzy pants. She'd looked for nicer ones in her drawer
and it had hit her with a shock that she didn't have any.

Buzzing around them was a beautiful junior giraffe. Lizzie
couldn't imagine what being a trainee personal shopper could
possibly involve—maybe you started off on socks and worked
your way up, but she seemed to have the sneer down to a tee.
Who knew personal shoppers even existed in high street shops?

Rodrigo eyed Lizzie sternly through his ridiculous 1950s

women's spectacles and leaned over and whispered something to Penny, who nodded her head seriously as if they were having a debate at the UN.

"What?" said Lizzie miserably. "Stop whispering about me."

"It is nothing," said Rodrigo. "Nothing which someone of your Rubenesque beauty should ever worry your lovely head about." He stared at her. "You must embrace the sensual," he said. "Feel the fabric. The rich, dark purples and deep jewel-green velvet."

Lizzie recoiled in horror as the giraffe wheeled in a long rail of non-black items.

"I'll look like a sofa," she said, gazing at a leather burgundy skirt.

"You won't," said Penny. "You'll be making a statement."

"Yeah—'I shop at DFS,'" said Lizzie, looking furiously around for her perfectly serviceable black skirt. She couldn't help it. Tears sprang to her eyes.

"Ah, you cry with the drama of fashion discovery. Happy tears, happy tears."

The giraffe handed her a purple velvet skirt and a soft, small-looking gray top.

"Why don't you try it on?" said Penny.

Lizzie did as she was told.

"*Bravissimo!*" said Rodrigo.

She risked a glance in the mirror.

It was beautiful. The skirt had chic little French buttons that fastened down the side; it was less purple on, she noticed, more of a dusky lavender which, with the soft woolen top, enhanced the grays in her eyes. It was . . . she looked . . . for the first time in her adult life, Lizzie thought, she looked nice. Better than nice. Pretty.

And she could see behind her in the mirror Penny, both thumbs up, grinning like a Cheshire cat.

For some reason, she wanted to cry.

They bought the lot. Lizzie felt sick; but Rodrigo kept murmuring "investment . . . investment . . ."

The hairdresser's was even better. Or maybe, Lizzie thought, she was just more used to being insulted by hairdressers.

"Who cut your hair before?" asked the snotty uninterested stylist, although, as it was a smart salon Penny had modeled for years, the stylist was rude but also gave Lizzie a glass of champagne.

"A badger," said Lizzie. Her inhibitions about responding to London rudeness had vanished forever. "I think he was drunk."

"He shouldn't be cutting hair," said the stylist, who hadn't listened.

"He shouldn't," said Lizzie. "Animals without opposable thumbs should very rarely be cutting hair. Can I have another glass of champagne?"

"I'll have to charge you for that," said the stylist. Lizzie felt her traditional panic, like when she was on that cheap flight they'd taken to Ibiza and she hadn't known whether she had to pay for the drinks or not so she had to get up and get her wallet out of her bag and pay for it in euros and everyone on the plane had been looking at her. But it was OK. She had a bit of money. She deserved to be here. She was fine.

Then she glanced at Penny, who was having new ultra-blond super-Gwyneth highlights put in. Penny waved over the bottle and put her thumbs up. Of course. It was OK to have champagne.

"Now are you sure you don't want to go blond?" said the stylist. "Only, that's kind of what we do here. For most people. Most people want to go blond."

"I'm not most people," said Lizzie proudly.

"Only, cause your hair's a bit pubic, you know, and if we dyed it it wouldn't look quite so frizzy, you know."

"Well de-frizz it then," said Lizzie, less proudly. But the stylist still stood there, hovering unhappily.

Penny came over to help. "They don't know what to do without coloring," she whispered to Lizzie. "Everyone's got colored hair."

"Everyone?"

"Everyone in the country. Every single person."

Staring into the mirror, Lizzie realized uncomfortably that her hair was very mousy, really. She didn't, she supposed, look in the mirror that often. Not that carefully anyway, otherwise she got depressed. She stared harder. For all this time she'd just thought her hair was a particularly flat color and everyone else's was shinier, just as Penny had got the lovely straight hair and she'd got the frizz, even though their hair had been similar when they were children. Now she had an uncomfortable sensation.

"*Everyone?*"

"No," said Penny sarcastically. "Everyone in the country has sun-lightened highlights and we're a nation of natural blondes and shiny redheads. Oh, and burgundy hair is real."

"It's a lot to take in."

Lizzie stared at herself.

"Oh, and everyone has really straight hair naturally," said Penny.

"Well, you do," said Lizzie.

Penny gave a do-you-believe-this? look at the stylist, who shook her own poker-straight scarlet locks.

"Eh, Lizzie."

"Yes?"

"We're twins, remember? We have the same hair."

"We're not identical."

"No. But, trust me, we have the same hair."

Lizzie stared at her sister.

"Oh, God."

"Do it," said Penny to the stylist. "Just some light streaks, don't scare the horses."

Lizzie shook her shining, straight, gently streaked hair in the mirror. For the nineteenth time.

"Yes," said Penny. "It's lovely."

"But how am I going to keep it this way?"

"With a bit of care and attention," said Penny.

"I was afraid you were going to say that."

"And some nice expensive hair products."

Lizzie screwed up one eye and looked at Penny.

"Which you buy," said Penny hurriedly.

"Hmm." Lizzie went back to flicking her thick hair in the mirror. "So. That 'invisible makeup thing' . . ." she started.

"Yup. Tons of it," said Penny.

"I thought as much."

Lizzie couldn't stop looking at herself all the way to work. She was wearing a neat little gray woolen jacket over a slightly gathered jewel-green skirt, with soft makeup and her new hair. Penny had grinned widely at her.

"Go now, Grasshopper," she'd said. "My work with you is done."

It was a perfect autumn day, and the red and brown leaves were lying on the ground for the four seconds they were allowed to in Chelsea before being swept up by smartly dressed road-sweepers. The sky was a bright chilly blue and Lizzie had an absolute bounce in her step as she marched toward the door of the café.

"*Lizzie!*" came a huge roar from the other side of the road. And standing there, looking as merry and bear-like as ever, was Georges, getting out of the back of a smart black car.

"*Lizzie!* I am back! I am back! And you have not burned down the café! Truly, my happiness could not be more complete."

His smile was so broad and his cheeks so rosy, Lizzie couldn't help but crack open a huge smile in return, and she dashed across the road to see him. As she stood in front of him, he regarded her gravely.

"Oh, madam, I am terribly sorry. I thought I was addressing Elizabeth Berry. But now I see that I was quite mistaken and you are a very beautiful model on her way to a high-fashion modeling shoot."

"No, it's me, Georges," said Lizzie, giggling and feeling ridiculously happy that he'd noticed. He peered into her eyes and she caught the sharp black spirit of him as he did so.

"So it is!" he said, standing back. "You are a miracle."

Lizzie kept looking at him and, slightly, his face seemed to change.

"A miracle," he murmured, almost to himself. "Well, well."

Lizzie smiled at him again, more hopefully, wondering why

his face suddenly looked a little sad. Then there came a noise from inside the car.

"Georges!" came a heavily accented voice. "Georges! *Comece sobre aqui!*"

Lizzie didn't understand a word of the string of speedy high-pitched sentences that came out in a stream from the back of the car, but she saw Georges's face as he hesitated, then put on a wide smile and extended a welcoming hand toward the back seat.

From the car arose a shortish, sturdy figure, dark hair, dark eyes, and heavy-looking brows, which were presently pulled together in something approaching a scowl.

"Maria-Elena, I would like you to meet my friend and co-worker, Lizzie," said Georges.

Maria-Elena glanced at Lizzie, then let fly with another long flurry of Portuguese.

"And now we are in England," said Georges gently, "we should speak English, don't you think? Especially in front of our friends."

"Hello," said Lizzie timidly, wondering what was going on. Was this his sister? It could be.

"Hello," said Maria-Elena, not sounding too thrilled about it. "It is wonderful to be here in your very cold country."

She looked toward the café. "Is that your shop?" she said to Georges.

Georges nodded proudly.

"This is one of the cafés, but I must say," and he smiled at Lizzie, "it is my favorite."

This provoked a new torrent. Lizzie had never had a talent for languages, but at a guess it wasn't an entirely positive critique. She looked at Georges, raising her eyebrows. Georges, uncharacteristically, looked wrong-footed. He coughed and cleared his throat, fiddling a little with his tight collar.

"Uh, Maria-Elena . . . she is my third cousin," he said to Lizzie almost apologetically. Lizzie thought she knew what was coming. Maria-Elena was going to be her new boss. She was going to move into the café, start running it, she would never see Georges again, and Maria-Elena would be difficult and shout at her a lot. Her good mood started to evaporate.

"So, uh, when I was in Portugal . . ." started Georges, but stopped again, as if this wasn't quite right. Maria-Elena gave him an impatient look and fired a volley of Portuguese at him again.

"Yes, yes," said Georges. "Well, I spent a lot of time with my family and it is decided. Maria-Elena and I are getting married."

Lizzie stopped dead and looked from one to the other. Sure enough, Maria-Elena was wearing a huge, almost grotesque ring on the fourth finger of her left hand. She smiled complacently. Neither of them, though, was exuding the obvious joy that normally accompanies such announcements.

"Well," Lizzie said. Inside she shook herself for being an idiot. Of course Georges wasn't just swanning around waiting for someone like her to pull herself together and then, one day, magically notice her . . . of course he was going to get married and have lots of beautiful Portuguese babies. And, of course, it would never have been her anyway, it would have been Penny. In fact, Penny was going to take it even worse than she was. Imagine, the two of them being sad over some short fat sandwich maker. It was ridiculous. Except that he'd become so much more to her.

Lizzie swallowed loudly. Of course it was ridiculous. And it would always have been impossible, and by the looks of things he would never even have considered it: he would always have gone back to his town and married a nice local girl, of course. She was probably a virgin. She got a glimpse of Maria-Elena's slightly feral teeth. Definitely a virgin.

"Congratulations," she forced herself to say. "It's . . . it's wonderful news."

"The family thought . . ." said Georges. "It is a very good thing."

"Can you marry your third cousin?" asked Lizzie, in what she'd intended to be a playful tone but came out as slightly aggressive.

"But of course," said Georges. "Nearly everyone is third cousin in the world. You are probably my third cousin also."

She looked at him for a moment then, but Maria-Elena was tugging his wrist.

"Also I am very good businesswoman," she said in English. "Will help with smartening up all the business. I want to look at . . . hmm, in English, how do you say? Profit margins. Yes. My English is very good also."

Georges nodded. "Exactly," he said. "It is very much a good thing."

"So when . . . when are you getting married?" asked Lizzie.

"In six week," said Maria-Elena. "I will organize it magnificently."

"Are you getting married in London?"

Maria-Elena snorted rather wonderfully.

"Yes," she said. "We are getting married in London. With the rain. And we would like to eat bacon and fried eggs for our wedding feast and we would like to drink beer and have a cup

231

of tea, yes, please excuse me, I am so terribly sorry, thank you very much."

"We will get married in Portugal," said Georges. "All our families will come."

"Just the one then," said Lizzie, but quite quietly.

"There will be four hundred people there," said Maria-Elena. "To watch Georges do his duty."

"Your duty?" Lizzie couldn't help asking with a smile.

Georges looked slightly haunted for a moment.

"Yes. I have been away for too long. It is time for me to settle down and get married and have children and make a good family in Portugal."

"And that's what you want?" said Lizzie gently.

"Of course it is," said Maria-Elena. "Now, let me see how you work at this restaurant, please. Then, Georges, we are going to Harrods."

"Bollocks!" said Penny. "That is *so* unfair! I don't understand it. Every time I get hold of a millionaire, they slip through my fingers. Or turn out to have been ratbags."

"The world is standing in the way of your true destiny," said Lizzie, who to her annoyed surprise had stopped off at the corner shop on the way home (of course it was a Chelsea corner shop, which meant it was hard to buy things that weren't Bendicks bittermints and vintage Pol Roger) and bought a whole loaf of cheap and nasty white bread and some Nutella. She was methodically working her way through the whole loaf, next to the toaster, and loathing herself.

"You say she's ugly?" said Penny. "Maybe there's still time."

"She's not ugly," said Lizzie. "She just looks a lot like Georges."

"That's quite ugly," said Penny. "Especially on a girl."

"No, it's not!" said Lizzie hotly, before quickly turning back to the toaster. Penny stared at her.

"Oh, no," she said, realization finally dawning. "Of course, of course. Oh, Lizzie! I didn't realize! You've got a massive thing for him."

"I do not!"

"You do! Oh my God, all this time I was pulling him . . ."

"You were not pulling him!"

"I would have pulled him. Oh my God, Lizzie, I had no idea."

"I didn't . . ." Her voice petered out. Was there even any point in denying it? "Well, I thought . . ."

"What, you'd have pulled the millionaire?"

"I didn't know he was a millionaire. Not until he came into the art gallery."

"Which is when you started fancying him."

"No, it's not," said Lizzie, hoping she wasn't about to cry. "I fancied him a long time before that."

"You can't have done," said Penny. "He's short and covered in hair, like an ewok."

"You wanted to go out with him," said Lizzie defensively.

"I didn't fancy him. I . . . uh, respected him."

"And his big fat wallet."

Penny rounded on her.

"And you think I'm about to start apologizing to *you*."

Lizzie moved backward, slightly startled by the strength of the onslaught.

Jenny Colgan

"What do you mean?"

"You of all people. You know what I've been through."

"Exactly what I've been through," said Lizzie.

"Which is why you should *understand*."

"Understand what?" said Lizzie. Suddenly, she was furious. "That you should get everything you want just because you're blond? That you could treat Georges like a toy and play around with him just because you don't like working for a living? That you can't see what is patently obvious in front of your eyes—like your sister liking someone, which would have been *completely* bloody obvious if you'd ever paid attention—you know some twins have that secret communication thing? Maybe we should work on our *basic* communication thing—and even our grandmother who is one hundred and thirty years old and lives in a bed in an eight-by-eight room, which by the way you'd also know if you ever went to visit her, if you could take time out of your own selfish bloody lifestyle, even *she* spotted that I really liked this bloke, at which point you went all out to ruin it for me, and for him and, well, it doesn't matter anymore, OK? I'm used to coping with disappointment in my life. But don't you fucking *dare* to ask me to sympathize with you."

When she finished talking, Lizzie realized she was completely out of breath and quite shocked by how much she'd said. Penny too was completely taken aback, mouth open.

"I didn't mean—" Penny started to say.

"Save it," said Lizzie. "Really. Save it for people who don't see completely through you."

And she unplugged the toaster, picked it up, placed it under her arm and retired to her room.

*

Although they bickered a little—well, nonstop, Penny realized—they didn't actually have stand-up fights that often. And, well, she just wasn't used to seeing Lizzie so shouty. Testy, yes, but usually in a slightly low-key way, under her breath, which Penny could usually quite happily ignore. This whole Lizzie doing home truths thing was new. A lot of things about Lizzie were new. How could she not have noticed? But she hadn't realized Lizzie'd really had a crush on fat Georges. She supposed it made sense when she thought about it—the new interest in food, the losing weight, the fact that she hadn't complained *that* much when they'd given her her makeover—yup. It was all there.

But the fact that Lizzie fancied Georges suddenly made him much more attractive in her eyes. She could see why you might *like* Georges, as well as how you could *admire* him, and want the security and life he could provide. *Fancying*, she hadn't really figured on. But if Lizzie could see it . . . and had seen it even before she knew about the money. An uncharacteristic thought came to Penny—could she help?

Lizzie stomped to work the next day feeling sick and grumpy. Suddenly, without the chance of bantering with Georges and hearing him pronounce on things and teach her what to do with chili peppers ("No! No, Lizzie, you want to kill all my customers stone dead?"), it was just another job. In a café, basically. She was coming up to thirty and buttering sandwiches for a living, while staying in someone else's borrowed apartment without even her stupid idiotic sister to talk to. Things didn't look good. Maybe she should call Grainne; hearing about her life always put things into perspective.

When she got to the café, she was surprised to see some-one already waiting outside it. There were a few regulars who popped in for their excellent coffee, but they were well aware what time the café opened. She'd seen Sloan there a few times, apparently on his way home from the night before, but he was usually wobbling on the pavement inquiring loudly about the availability of wine, so it wasn't him.

"Hello?"

The figure, skinny and wan, slowly lifted up his head and she recognized him immediately.

"Will?" she asked incredulously. "What are you doing here?"

Will didn't look terribly good. Well, thought Lizzie, if you weren't being too harsh, the stubble slightly suited him, and being so thin gave him the look of the starving artist, and his gaunt face made those puppy-dog eyes look even bigger. But on the whole he looked unkempt, uncared for, a million miles away from the confident charmer she'd met earlier that year.

He looked at her rather piteously as she opened up.

"Will . . . are you *hungry*?" she asked as he followed her in.

He shrugged. "Well . . ." He looked around the little restau-rant, his eyes coming to rest on the panini toaster.

"Would you like some breakfast?"

"Why, are you having some?"

In fact, Lizzie was so ashamed of her previous evening's stress-related carb blowout that she had vowed to stick to fruit until lunchtime.

"Of course," she said encouragingly. "Full English OK?"

"Well, if that's what you're having," he said, looking incredibly grateful.

Lizzie quickly stuck the frying pan on the burner and started chopping mushrooms.

"Where have you been? You look like you've been dragged through a hedge backward."

Will shrugged. "Oh, I've been . . . about . . . not in this end of the woods, really."

The first two pieces of toast popped up and Lizzie buttered them speedily and sent them over to him, just as the Gaggia squealed and the first espresso of the day squeezed out. Will immediately guzzled both down so quickly that at first Lizzie couldn't quite work out where they'd gone.

"You really are hungry," said Lizzie worriedly.

Will shrugged. "Well, my canapé diet has . . . uh, suffered a bit. I miss those mini fish and chips they used to do."

"But Penny sold loads of your paintings," said Lizzie. "Even I sold a few."

"I know," said Will. "Just covered my materials, really. And the two years it took to do them. Anyway, the exhibition is over now. And I don't think I can expect another one in a hurry; apparently Sloan's put the word out. I'm untouchable."

Lizzie brought over some more toast and checked the frying sausages.

"That can't be true. Sloan can never remember to tell anyone anything."

"Hmm," said Will.

"What about your parents?"

Will straightened his back and spoke in gruff tones. "You want to leave a perfectly good university and try and make it as an artist, boy, you'll be standing on your own two feet with no help from us, do you hear?"

Lizzie finished his fried eggs and flipped them up into the air artistically so they landed perfectly on the plate, feeling slightly pleased with herself.

"Thanks," said Will. "Where's yours?"

"Oh, I don't need it," said Lizzie. "Could do with losing a few pounds."

"Really?" said Will. "I think you look smashing." And he bent his head to his food.

After ten minutes, he finished a second cup of espresso and mopped up the last of the egg yolk with the fried bread, letting out a big sigh of satisfaction as he did so. Noticing Lizzie watching him, he immediately pulled out a very bashed-looking wallet and started counting out twenty-pence pieces.

"Don't be daft," said Lizzie. "You just ate the staff breakfast. Don't give it another thought."

"OK," said Will, shaking his head in relief. "God, you think good days are going to last forever, don't you? I spunked it all away."

He swallowed and went quiet.

"Literally, I suppose. Sorry, that's horrid."

Lizzie took her own cup of tea, and a banana, and rounded the counter to sit at the table.

"Will," she started. As soon as she did so, he looked up at her, his eyes shining.

"Lizzie," he said, "I didn't know there was a baby. I promise I didn't. I wouldn't make someone get rid of my baby in a million years. I'd love to have a baby, really I would. Someday. But it would have been all right. We'd have got over it. It's just as soon as she came to see me we both realized . . . we both realized that it's not . . . it's . . ." He couldn't finish and stared at the table, clutching his cup. "I can't believe she killed my baby without even telling me."

Lizzie stared at her fingers until he'd composed himself.

"Listen," she said. "You have to listen to me."

"What?"

"There wasn't a baby. It was a mistake. A real mistake, not something to wind you up or anything. She just got a bit sick and we jumped to conclusions and, well, it doesn't matter now."

"She didn't have an abortion?"

Lizzie shook her head. "I don't think she could have. She loved you, Will. But when she saw how you lived . . . and Minty told her you were just after a meal ticket."

"*Minty*," said Will. "That crazy bitch pursued me for months and wouldn't take no for an answer."

"So you never slept with her."

"Well. Just a couple of times, you know. But then she really got the knives out for me. Practically stalked me. She called me 'Daddy.'" He shook his head in horror and looked at his empty plate again. "There never was a baby."

Lizzie shook her head gently. She really thought he ought to know.

"So I messed it up all on my own?"

Just then, the door tinged, and Georges and Maria-Elena stepped in. Maria-Elena sniffed loudly.

"I see," she said. "This place . . . it smells very much like something in your country I have heard of that is called a transportation café, no?"

Georges shook his head. "No, we do good food and . . ."

He looked at Will, then Lizzie, who shot him a warning look, whereupon Georges changed his tone and said, "We do whatever is the best for the customer. Is that not right, my friend?"

Will stared at him. "You're Penny's new boyf—"

"Nothing," said Lizzie. "That's what you were about to say, wasn't it? Nothing at all. Ha ha!"

"I do not understand," said Georges. "But here, this is my beautiful fiancée, Maria-Elena."

"You know," said Maria-Elena to Will. "If you are to keep eating those English breakfasts you will get fat and die."

"Good," said Will.

"Shh, shh," said Georges. "We will have none of this talk."

"Would you like an omelette?" said Lizzie. If she couldn't make Georges love her, she could at least make him an omelette.

"Yes, please," said Georges, smiling at her.

"No!" said Maria-Elena. "At least this man is thin. You are fat. Too fat. No more eggs before the wedding. You should be thin for a wedding."

"I cannot do that," said Georges as Lizzie stood undecided over the frying pan. "I was a fat baby. Then I was a fat child. Then I was a tubby young man. Then I was a plump grown-up man. And now I am Georges! Thin and I are two things which will never be friends!"

Maria-Elena's brows knitted together and she muttered something in Portuguese.

"And if we have children they shall be fat little babies and podgy children and plump teenagers . . ."

Lizzie thought of having little plump babies with big dark eyes like Georges's and bit her lip a tad wistfully.

"No, we will not," said Maria-Elena. "You." She was talking

to Lizzie, who was staring into space and not noticing. "You. I would like orange juice, and make a fruit salad."

Lizzie stared at her. Maria-Elena said something to Georges, and it wasn't necessary to have a word of Portuguese to know that she'd just said something along the lines of, "Is your employee a retard?"

Georges looked cross, then his face cleared as he remembered something.

"Aha," he said, pointing at Will. "For you, a man suffering a broken heart."

"I'm not suffering a broken heart," said Will. "Oh, yes, I am. I forgot. Can I have that omelette?"

"Of course," said Lizzie. "You'll have to be quick, though. I have to go and pick oranges or something."

Georges dashed out and returned in moments with a parcel covered in bubble wrap.

"You're going to try and cheer me up with bubble wrap?" said Will.

"Ooh, I love bubble wrap," said Lizzie.

"No," said Georges. "But I forgot it had arrived!" and he pulled apart the badly wrapped parcel to reveal Will's painting.

It was the avenue of trees, and the painting looked very delicate and beautiful in the brightly painted café.

"I am going to put it up here," said Georges. "So all my customers will see it and say, Georges, where did you get this fantastic painting as everybody knows you have the taste of a mountain goat. And I will say, you must NOT go to Sloan's terrible art shop, you must call my friend Will, and everybody will call you and make you a *milliadaire*. What do you think?"

Will merely shrugged his shoulders.

"It looks terrible," said Maria-Elena. "All the colors are wrong."

"It's great," said Lizzie. "Put it up here by the clock over the door. People always look at the clock."

"That is very true!" said Georges. "Here. And now, we must open the shop."

"What about the fruit salad?" said Maria-Elena.

"Ah, my bride, I am so sorry, no fruit salad today."

"I'm making Georges a quick omelette aux fines herbes, though," said Lizzie. She knew it was a little mean, but at the moment, she just didn't care. "Are you sure you don't want one?"

"My dear," said Sloan to Penny. He cleared his throat and tried again. He had somehow mysteriously woken up on the floor of the gallery again and, all things considered, had found it least painful if he didn't try to move. "My dear, I sense you are sad. Or angry."

"How did you guess that?" said Penny, who was marching loudly over him when she needed to get anything out of the back.

"Call it my feminine intuition," said Sloan, who was trying to think of a polite way to tell her to stop stomping up and down like a baby elephant that wouldn't involve her redoubling her efforts and getting louder.

"How about making your old Auntie Sloan a bit of an eye-opener, eh?"

"You really are a hopeless soak," said Penny, who wasn't exactly in the mood to do anything for anyone. "Don't you think you should get help or something?"

"I think," said Sloan, propping himself up on his elbow with some difficulty in order to extract his cigarette holder from his smoking-jacket pocket, "help is for people who have difficult lives. Whereas my existence, a state, if you like, of near constant lunch, I find extremely pleasant. Now, if you look in the fridge I believe you will find some tomato juice, some Worcestershire sauce, one egg, and a bottle of Gray Goose vodka. I wish you to mix these ingredients in the order your heart tells you to."

Cigarette successfully lit, he returned to lying on the ground.

"Say what you like about that Will fellow," he said. Penny snorted loudly. "But at least you knew which way up to hang his paintings. Whereas with *these* . . ."

He indicated the new oil paintings hanging on the gallery walls. They were vast abstract canvases, covered with mustard-colored geometric shapes spattered with blobs of gray and mush-room. In short, perfect for any office lobby in the developed world. Sloan was fully expecting to make a killing.

"Ah, thank you," he said, as Penny returned with his drink. "No straw . . . no . . . ?" He huffed himself into a sitting position. "Ah. Worcestershire sauce as the primary ingredient. Interesting concept. Now, what did you say the matter with you was again?"

"My life is not going well," said Penny.

"Indeed?" said Sloan.

"The only millionaire I know is getting married and the man I love is a penniless conniver who hates me. I need you to intro-duce me to some millionaires. Nice ones."

"Funny you should say that," said Sloan. "Because I have just the job for you. We need to arrange a launch for the new pictures."

"Uh-huh?" said Penny.

"The artist supposedly lives in the cloud forests of South America and never comes down to taint her life with civilization, although she may make a special exception for cut-price champagne. Personally I think that's humbug and it's two blokes in a lock-up garage in Edmonton. But that doesn't matter now. Go through my Rolodex and invite everyone with a postcode starting W or SW, numbers up to eleven."

He fixed her with a slightly rheumy eye.

"If you don't find a pushover banking millionaire in that lot, Penelope, there is frankly no hope for you."

Penny smiled for the first time in three days.

"Thanks, Sloan!"

"Don't thank me," said Sloan. "You could get me a pillow, though."

# Chapter Twelve

Lizzie had meant to tell Penny she'd seen Will, but they still weren't speaking. Fine, she could lump it then.

Penny was in whirlwind mode in any case. For the first time in living memory, she was working incredibly hard, dashing around to put the opening together. She'd designed the invitations—"That's original," Sloan had said, looking at the red devil-shaped card, most unlike the plain Smythson stiffy he usually sent out—that said, *Be a devil. Come see our most dangerous collection yet . . .*

"It's not very dangerous," said Sloan.

"You have to know," said Penny, "that the concept of buying art is very scary to most people. So I'm playing on their fear."

Sloan raised his eyebrows. "What's scary about buying art? Oh, Christ," he indicated a student walking past the window. "Would you look at the shoes on that? Great legs and shoes like a carthorse."

Jenny Colgan

"Actually, that's what's scary," said Penny. "People like you checking out your shoes."

Sloan pouted. "People are terribly oversensitive."

"So, I'm convincing all these business people to take a risk," said Penny happily. "We've had loads of yeses already."

Sloan didn't tell her that few people were as likely to travel a great distance for a free glass of champagne as people who were already rich; it was one of the ways they'd gotten rich in the first place.

"Excellent work," said Sloan. "Now, what about the artist?"

"She's coming in today," said Penny. "To check the plassmong."

"The what?"

"I don't know. She said plassmong."

"Place-*ment*, my dear," said Sloan, chucking her on the cheek. "You are so adorable."

"Stop that," said Penny. "Just because I don't know your stupid posh German or whatever it is."

"Quite right, too," said Sloan, vowing to keep Penny and the artist as far apart as possible.

Unfortunately, as with so many of Sloan's vows, some old chums at the Reform Club and an excellent claret got in the way, and Penny was on her own, tweezing her eyebrows in the reflection of a particularly ugly steel sculpture that was supposed to represent womanhood but in fact represented something on the floor to bark your shins on, when the woman walked in.

At first Penny smiled politely, assuming a customer had just entered, and one of their more eccentric Chelsea types at that.

"Hello," she said.

The figure stood stock-still, framed in the doorway with the light behind her, and stared at Penny.

"Oh," said Penny jumping up. "Do you need some help getting up the step?"

There came a loud imperious sniff from the doorway.

"Sloan Williams-Forsythe, please!" boomed a voice loudly.

"Er, he's not here," said Penny. "I'm sure he won't be long, though." She always said this, hoping against hope that they wouldn't decide to wait for him. Most people, however, were aware of his lunching habits.

"I am Tabitha Angelbrain Dawson," said the woman, moving into the full arena of the shop. Without the light behind her, Penny took a closer look. She was a heavy woman, draped rather than dressed in shades of violet and purple, including heavy eye makeup and a mouth that was lipsticked so dark it looked like a place cherries went to die. Her hair was stiff, and a very peculiar aubergine color Penny couldn't have described, which gave her some respect for her artistic abilities.

"Hello!" said Penny. "You're the artist! I'm organizing your party."

Slightly regretfully she remembered the last artist she'd met in here. Somehow she didn't think this one would put up with quite as much cheek. Mind you, she wasn't quite so desperate to get in this one's knickers either.

"I've just got you down as Ms. Dawson, though," said Penny, looking at the sheet. "Sorry, I can change it."

"Tabitha Angelbrain Dawson is my full name," said Tabitha Angelbrain Dawson. "Tabitha from my beloved daddy, God rest his soul, and Angelbrain came as a gift from heaven when no less than Sir Flinty Fortescue himself said, 'Tabitha, dear, you have the brain of an angel.'"

And the body of a brickie, thought Penny, but didn't let it show on her face.

"Dawson, well, what can one do?" Tabitha continued, looking slightly glum for a moment. "It sounds like I run a pottery shop in rural Yorkshire. Anyway, no matter. Let me take a look at *le hanging*."

She started pacing around the shop. In fact, she was loping, so deliberately Penny couldn't help thinking she wanted it noticed.

"You have a very graceful stride," she said winningly. This party was very important, and it would be helpful to get Tabitha on her side, if at all possible, especially, as a general rule, she'd found fat women tended not to like her that much.

"Thank you," said Tabitha, straightening up and beaming. This had obviously been very much the correct thing to say. "My yoga teacher says that my spirit guide is almost certainly a big cat."

"Perhaps a panther," said Penny.

Tabitha nodded gravely, as if some huge secret had passed between them. "And all cats, you know, they find me irresistible."

Penny hoped that they hadn't hung any of the pictures upside down, but Sloan hadn't been in business for thirty years for nothing. Tabitha slowly completed her tour of the room, nodding occasionally in a cougar-like manner to show that she approved.

She stood in the middle of the room, finally, and closed her eyes. Painfully slowly, she lifted both hands out to the side, raising her fingers up until her arms were fully outstretched, her purple robes fluttering behind her, like a priest.

"I feel it!" she said. "I feel the vibrations! I feel for my art, for my creation, from the angels, from the mother spirit, I declare this . . . uh, this is the correct place and everything shall be good. And. Er. Let it be."

She kept her eyes closed for another twenty seconds or so and Penny squeezed hers shut too in sympathy, hoping nobody popped in and nicked the computer while she did so.

"Fantastic," said Tabitha Angelbrain finally, when she opened her eyes again. "I feel very strongly everything is going to go just fine. Got any tea?"

"Absolutely," said Penny. "But just normal tea, not chamomile or anything like that."

"Really? OK, then. Although I try not to pollute my body with caffeine. Ooh"—she had spied Penny's secret stash of chocolate digestives—"are those digestives? Can I have one? Absolutely starved. Can you think of anywhere good for us to lunch?"

"I'm not really allowed to take lunch," said Penny. "We have a strict one-employee, one-lunch policy."

"Nonsense," said Tabitha. "You just tell Sloan the artist ordered you. Plus, I have some very funny stories about my cats that I think you'll absolutely love. You strike me as someone who's very in touch with their inner spiritual core. Am I right?"

Penny was firmly of the belief that people's inner spiritual cores only ever made an appearance when they didn't have to worry about paying the council tax, but considered it wise not to say so.

"Well, there is this one place . . ." she said.

Penny stopped just before the window of the café, as Tabitha paused to smell the cooking on the air in the manner of a tiger.

Through the glass she could see Lizzie and Georges behind the counter. Lizzie was doling out food into containers which she was seasoning with parsley and tossing to Georges, who then, with a chat and a smile, handed them to hungry customers. They weren't even looking at one another, but working entirely on instinct, Lizzie passing the salt or finding extra change; Georges handing her another tomato or reaching for the toaster without her having to ask him. They were a perfect ballet of complementary motion, and engrossing to watch.

Tabitha looked ready to head in, but Penny couldn't move. They looked so perfect, so absolutely right together. How could she not have noticed it before? Was she really that self-absorbed? OK, yes, so she was incredibly self-absorbed, what else was new? But she hadn't really been trying to be cruel to Lizzie when she tried to seduce Georges. She really hadn't appreciated how Lizzie felt about him.

Now it seemed unbelievable that she could have missed it.

At the side of the counter stood a dark-looking woman, scowling at the customers. It wasn't hard to work out who that was.

"My inner leonine element of femininity," announced Tabitha, "is saying that it is experiencing a primal hunger for the misty plains. That means lunch," she added hopefully.

Swallowing quickly, Penny pushed open the door and marched in.

Lizzie wasn't in the slightest bit happy to see Penny. In fact, she was furious.

Here she is, thought Lizzie angrily, clop, clop, clop, on her little shoes, in to get the guy with the money. Make it even worse, the *engaged* guy with the money. Stupid cow. She ignored her, even when Georges looked up and smiled at the two women. Daft old Georges, she thought affectionately. You could probably kill his mother and he'd still want to give you a welcoming hug.

"Two beautiful ladies!" said Georges happily, "who look in need of a tasty aubergine Parmigiana!"

Tabitha bestowed on him a wide toothy smile.

"I like a man who sees inner beauty," she said. "And can cook."

Lizzie sniffed. She hadn't noticed Georges's amazing ability to discern inner beauty when she was chunky and looked like a frump.

"Hi, Lizzie," said Penny pointedly, but Lizzie just gave her a look.

"What's the matter?" Penny asked, just to be annoying.

"Nothing," said Lizzie.

The woman who was obviously Georges's fiancée let loose a torrent of another language, that equally obviously said, "Who are *these* women?"

Georges looked a bit haunted.

"Maria-Elena, this is Penny, Lizzie's twin."

Maria-Elena's eyebrows shot up so fast she might as well have had "I am a very rude lady" tattooed on her forehead.

"Hello," she said. "Georges, he has many female friends, yes? And you . . . ah, I see you dress in the 'London' style. Interesting."

This kind of talk didn't phase Penny at all, who'd been the victim of many a ladies' toilets backstab in her time. She stared Maria-Elena down until she took a step back.

Penny looked at Georges again as he flipped his tongs to get the nice corner piece of the Parmigiana for them. There was a wide sweat stain under the arm of his slightly grubby chef's whites, and sweat glistened on his low heavy brow. How on earth . . . I mean, obviously he looked a little better in his sharp suit, stepping out of a car someone else was driving, but you'd have to be really, really desperate . . .

"Who are you?" said Georges in a friendly fashion to Tabitha.

"I am Tabitha Angelbrain Dawson. I am . . . an artiste," said Tabitha.

Georges nodded. "Excellent. Me too. I am an artiste of Parmigiana. Here, try it."

And he passed over two warm plates.

Wow, thought Penny, looking over at Maria-Elena, that woman really is evil. She suddenly had a flash of inspiration. She saw it clearly. Georges was a good bloke and Lizzie really liked him. But he had an evil fiancée standing in her way. She could handle her, make out that her and Georges were a big thing, piss the fiancée off all the way back to Portugal, and then Lizzie would be free to settle down with Georges. And they would be so grateful they would buy Penny lots and lots of pairs of shoes, and Penny wouldn't mind a bit that she didn't have any boyfriends at all and Lizzie had a rich one. Penny felt so noble at her potential self-sacrifice she sniffed into her aubergine Parmigiana.

Tabitha reached out and placed a manicured hand, festooned with large rings, gently on Penny's arm.

"I see you too become emotional over a beautiful meal, breaking bread with kindred spirits," she said. Penny noticed she'd nearly cleared her plate already.

"I really think we are kindred spirits, you know," Tabitha continued, picking up some bread to wipe up the leftovers. "Me and the spirit world . . . we're very entwined." Penny picked at some lettuce—Georges placed salad on the side of everyone's plate as a garnish, but usually ended up throwing it out.

"Me, too," said Penny.

Tabitha took a huge intake of breath, then looked dramatically around the room to make sure they were not being overheard.

"Penny, my dear," she said in a near whisper. "Can I trust you?"

"Of course," said Penny, looking as serious as she could.

"Very well. Then I shall share with you . . . I have certain . . . certain gifts."

Penny waited for her to continue.

"They are a burden," said Tabitha, looking very sincere and sad. "They bring great power and yet great responsibility."

Penny was sure someone had said this in a movie, but didn't want to mention it.

"I have been told often by famous psychics and those who know of the spirit world that I must be very careful how I use my skills."

Penny nodded respectfully.

"So, my dear, do you have a problem? Is it a matter of the heart? A love spell? Or revenge?"

Tabitha was so excited at talking about her magic powers that a little bit of spittle came out and landed on her plate.

Penny rolled her eyes. "Do you know how to make a potion to see off a love rival?" she asked, glancing at Lizzie, who was watching her sourly while pretending to dry up.

"All love is beautiful," said Tabitha gravely.

Penny sashayed up to the counter, feeling strangely calm and in control. Georges was still passing over Parmigiana to grateful customers. Maria-Elena was watching her with a beady eye, as was

Lizzie (while manfully pretending not to). Penny knew what she had to do. She stroked down her eyebrows and slipped behind the display of sandwiches and cakes.

"Georges," she purred, staring straight into his eyes—and, on the periphery, noticing Maria-Elena's eyebrows drawing together in a suspicious frown.

She placed a hand on his large forearm. "That was the most *delicious* lunch I think I've ever had in my life."

Georges looked at her hand with a slightly puzzled expression on his face. "I make good food for everyone," he said.

Penny gave a little flirtatious giggle, and gently touched the side of his face.

"I think you make it specially for me," she said. She could swear she could feel the steam coming off Lizzie behind her. Ah, Lizzie. She didn't realize the self-sacrifice involved here. This was about Maria-Elena, not her. Once the Portuguese monstrosity was out of the way, she'd quietly withdraw. After all, all was fair in love and war.

Slowly, aware that the whole café was watching her, she leaned over and carefully placed an extremely deliberate kiss on Georges's slightly sweaty cheek. There was a *tchok* as Lizzie sliced her knife hard into the chopping board. Maria-Elena was looking absolutely furious. Georges couldn't have looked more surprised if she'd slapped him in the face with a wet halibut.

"I'll see you," Penny murmured suggestively, "later . . ."

She turned to go, then suddenly stopped in her tracks. For the first time, above the clock on the wall, she noticed Will's picture. She stared at it, open-mouthed.

"You . . . you're . . ."

This wasn't right. This wasn't right at all. What the hell was Georges doing putting that up?

"You've hung Will's painting."

She could sense Lizzie behind her, concentrating intensely.

"Well, yes," said Georges. "I like it."

"But I didn't think . . . I didn't think you . . . I mean, I assumed you would *burn* it."

Georges looked slightly discomfited. "But I thought . . ."

"You thought what? That I wouldn't mind? That I would like having to look at the fucking thing every time I came in here?"

"You do not often come in here," said Georges, shrugging. "And . . . well . . ."

A horrifying thought struck Penny.

"Does he?"

She spun around to look at Lizzie, whose face instantly gave her away.

"Oh, he does, does he? What, pops in from time to time, so all of you are lovely friends having a smashing time?"

"It's not like that," said Lizzie. "He just came in . . ."

"Really? What's it like then? Do you all just sit around having a good laugh at me?"

To Penny's horror, Maria-Elena had sensed the tide had turned, and had a mild smile playing about her lips.

"No," said Lizzie.

"So, what? Is this some kind of crazy revenge thing? You're trying to seduce him?"

"No!"

"Just to make me miserable, is it?" Appallingly, Penny couldn't help but feel the tears well up. "You've all ganged up on me," she said. Then, blinded, she pushed past Georges and Tabitha and headed out of the door.

Lizzie looked around. What the hell had just happened? One moment her sister had been playing some mad game of "Who's the biggest bitch on the block?" and all but unzipping Georges's trousers, then next she was dribbling and mewling like a *Big Brother* contestant deprived of cake.

Georges shook his head.

"Ah, your sister. She suffers terribly in love." He looked at Lizzie, with a sad expression on his face. "You are running to her, yes?"

Oh, crap. Five seconds after Lizzie decides to let Penny stand on her own two feet, she immediately has a public nervous breakdown. How very convenient for her.

"Uh, yes," she said.

Maria-Elena was looking disapproving as Lizzie undid her apron. "You will have to look at your staff," she said to Georges, very deliberately in English. "They are hysterical girls in England, no?"

Lizzie rolled her eyes as she headed for the door.

Penny was half walking, half running toward home when Lizzie caught up with her. She glanced at Lizzie but didn't speak to her.

"So what was that little scene about?" Lizzie said finally.

"I don't know what you mean," said Penny, trying to keep the wobble out of her voice.

"Well, let's see. First you try to have sex with Georges behind the counter and the next you have a complete shit fit because of a picture of some trees."

"I didn't . . ."

Penny searched desperately for a way of denying this version of events, but couldn't think of one.

"Oh, what's it got to do with you, anyway?"

"Quite a lot actually," said Lizzie. "Seeing as Georges is my friend and is getting married and doesn't exactly need to be mixed up with the likes of you."

"The likes of me?" said Penny, sounding furious. "What the fuck do you mean, 'the likes of me?'"

"Nothing," said Lizzie, worried that she might have gone too far.

"And what the fuck do you mean, *Georges is my friend*. Georges isn't your friend. He's the guy you'd like to get it on with. Don't pretend you wish him well with his wedding, you hypocrite."

"I'm a hypocrite. That's fucking rich given that you rubbed yourself up against him like a dog in heat, then caved like a fucking paper bag because of your ex-boyfriend's little drawing."

"It's not a 'little drawing,'" said Penny. "Like you know anything about art. Like you know anything about anything, you complete mouse."

"I'm not a mouse."

"You're a pathetic cowardly mouse that can't even chat up a bloke she stands next to for like nine hours a day."

"And you're a gold-digging slut."

"Mouse!"

"Slut!"

"Mouse!"

Without realizing, they'd arrived in front of their building. Sitting on the step was a man. He was middle-aged and shabbily dressed, reclining against one of the white pillars reading a tabloid. He watched them with some interest, but for a short time Penny and Lizzie were too engrossed in shouting at each other to notice.

Finally, his attention made them turn around. He had a keen eye on both of them.

"Who the hell are you?" said Penny, who was in no mood for tramps, salesmen, Jehovah's Witnesses, or anything else except getting upstairs and slamming the door on her fucking annoying sister.

The man smiled enigmatically and rather annoyingly.

"Well, well, well," he said. "The little twins."

Lizzie drew in a breath and stepped forward. The last time she'd heard them called that... "Who are you?" she asked, echoing Penny, but with a strange beating of her heart and a funny dry feeling in her mouth.

The man stood up, folded his paper carefully, and put it in his pocket.

"Little twins," he said, straightening and opening his arms wide. "Don't you recognize your old dad?"

# Chapter Thirteen

They found a third chair buried under some newspapers and drew it up to the old kitchen table. They managed this without speaking to each other at all, except when Lizzie went to put the kettle on.

The man took off his coat, which was old and worn. While Lizzie waited for the kettle to boil she studied his face. He was clearly attempting to look relaxed and unconcerned, stretching out in his chair, but he couldn't help his eyes flicking around nervously, taking the whole place in. This was, Lizzie supposed, where he'd grown up. He had fair hair, like Penny, now turned mostly to gray, and his eyes were blue like hers. But the wide mouth was Lizzie's, undoubtedly. She could see he'd probably been handsome once, but now he looked slight and nervous and pushed down by life.

They knew so little about him. Yes, a few stories they'd pestered out of their mum and grandmother, but mostly Lizzie remembered her mother saying, "Girls, if you get pregnant in your teens, I will cut my throat with this knife here. Now, who wants cake?"

And Lizzie would say yes, and Penny would say no.

Lizzie dished up tea, along with some grapes she'd bought.

"So," said the man finally. Lizzie wondered what to call him. Dad was . . . unlikely. Out of the question. His name was Stephen, but that seemed peculiar too. Mr. Willis? Maybe she'd stick to not calling him anything at all.

He looked very happy to be given a cup of tea. Maybe he'd been maligned, she allowed herself to think for a moment. Maybe despite everything it was her mother who'd caused all the trouble, made things impossible for him to stay so he'd had to go out and fend for himself, but he'd loved them all along . . .

Then she got a sudden mental image of her mother's dishwater hands, her swollen ankles as she rolled in from yet another day serving mush to ungrateful brats who gave her backchat and lip, and felt terrible. Her mother had held the whole thing together and she hadn't had a word of thanks nor an iota of help from this man.

Penny had already reached this conclusion and was eyeing him unfavorably. Why, she wondered, would he have come to find them now—a few months after they'd moved into his mother's flat? She folded her arms and waited to hear what he had to say.

"Girls," said the man finally, after taking a long gulp of tea and looking suspiciously at the grapes. "I never thought you'd grow up to be so beautiful."

Penny rolled her eyes. "I'm amazed you know we grew up at

all," she said. "We could have been thrown into the river in a bag without you noticing."

The man laughed in a forced kind of a way.

"Not at all," he said. Then he put his hands on his knees, as if he was about to come clean with them.

"Look," he said. "I've been a terrible father."

Penny made a snorting noise. Lizzie shot her a look. Please, please, could Penny just hear him out? Of course he'd been a terrible father, but he was the only one she was ever going to get and, maybe, just maybe, he was here to make amends.

"But I've learned my lesson," he said, looking at his hands. The nails were bitten almost down to the quick. It seemed a strange habit in a grown man.

"I've messed up so badly," he said. "You know, when me and your mother were together, I was so young . . . twins, you know. It was a lot to take on."

"Which is why you didn't," said Penny. "Thanks for the birthday cards, by the way. Oh, no, hang on, we never got one."

The man shifted uncomfortably. Lizzie noticed, though, that Penny hadn't asked him to leave or shoved him out. Penny wanted to hear what he had to say as much as she did.

"I had to move away," said Stephen, looking bitter. "My mother was crazy, I was trying to make it as an artist . . ."

"You were *what?*" said Penny quickly. Her face looked shocked. Neither of them had known that.

"Well, that doesn't matter," said Stephen. "Thought I'd make it, didn't I? Be the biggest thing since Andy Warhol. But life doesn't always work out like that."

Penny's eyes were wide. Lizzie could see exactly what she was thinking. Her face was stricken and, without being able to help herself, all her rancor gone, Lizzie reached out and gently put her hand on Penny's shoulder.

"What kind of work did you do?" asked Penny.

"Conceptual," said Stephen, still with the last dregs of arrogance in his voice. "Installations, you know? Birds, shouting, and broken glass everywhere."

He paused for a bit.

"Not enough people really want to buy an experience like that. Fucking cretins."

"I work for an art gallery now," said Penny.

Stephen smiled. "Really? See, there you go. Runs in the family. Whereabouts?"

"Sloan's," said Penny.

Stephen's face darkened immediately.

"That bastard," he said. "He would never exhibit me." Nervously, he tapped his jacket until he found a crumpled packet of cheap cigarettes. Without asking their permission, he lit one up and drew on it deeply, screwing up his eyes.

"You don't smoke, do you, kids?" he said. "Good," he said as they shook their heads. "Your mum didn't half do a good job. Much better than I'd have managed."

"Sloan is a bastard," said Penny, eyeing Stephen with distaste. "But *he'd* probably have made a better job bringing us up than you."

"No need to get nasty, sweetheart," said Stephen, and there was an awkward silence.

"So, uh, what else have you been up to?" said Lizzie, trying to lighten matters up. Penny and her dad were glaring at each other, and looked ridiculously alike all of a sudden. Stephen broke his gaze first.

"Oh, this and that," he said. "Worked in, er, retail for a bit. Went to America. Tough place, America." His short-stubbed nails rubbed the back of his neck thoughtfully. "Then I worked on a few ventures with, uh, an acquaintance. Selling personalized plates for weddings. Door to door. Should have been a great hit, but, you know . . . people let us down and the, uh, production lines didn't function correctly. Anyway, after a short period of time as company director I've, er, recently resigned to look into other options. Back here, you know. Good old London town. City of my birth and all that."

Penny and Lizzie watched him, waiting to hear what he was going to say. Lizzie just wished it would be something like, "And I came in to say I love you. And would you like me to take you out for ice cream?" But somehow, she knew that wasn't about to be forthcoming.

Penny, though, was beginning to guess where this was heading.

"So, anyway, I thought, Wow, I have to look up my gorgeous girls. I wonder if they're as beautiful as I'd always dreamed. And you are."

Penny still didn't say anything.

"And I called in on me old mum, you know. Still bonkers, of course."

"She's not that bonkers," said Lizzie. "She's just eccentric. I like her."

"So do I, of course, of course," said Stephen. "So I got talking to her, and I was saying, well, here I am, back in London for the first time in, ooh, twenty years or so." He didn't sound like his

263

mum. His voice was more aggressive mockney, like he thought he was in an old British gangster movie.

"Uh-huh," said Penny.

"And, my Christ, hasn't the old town got expensive? Eh? Eh? Can you believe the cost of things in old London town these days?"

A line of sweat had popped out on Stephen's brow, and he looked around for something to stub his cigarette out on. As neither girl moved, he used his saucer.

"So, of course, she says, 'Stephen, you're my only boy and I love you . . .'"

That didn't sound like Gran, thought Lizzie.

"Course you've got to go and stay in the flat, haven't you? After all, it's practically yours."

He rubbed his eyebrow and attempted a grin that didn't succeed particularly well.

"I mean, she's not long for this world, is she?"

"I think she is," said Lizzie. "She just likes having a bit of a lie-down, that's all."

She was aware how feeble this sounded.

"So . . ." said Stephen. He sat back in his chair as if what came next was obvious.

"So what?" said Penny immediately. Her cheeks were very pink. "You want to move in with us?"

Stephen looked uncomfortable.

"I suppose there's the boxroom," said Lizzie, trying to pour oil on the troubled waters. After all, he wasn't coming across so well, but he was her dad. Maybe he was just nervous; maybe underneath it all there was a good man, and they could all live together and get to know each other again and they'd all get on really well and she could reintroduce him to their mother and they'd fall in love again and . . . Lizzie sighed.

"It's got all the most obvious crap in it, though," argued Penny, realizing what Lizzie was thinking. "If we take stuff out of there we won't be able to move around. Especially with three people here."

"We'd find somewhere for it," said Lizzie. "Of course we would. This is a big flat, there's plenty of room for everyone."

"I suppose," said Penny, looking mutinous. "How long would it be for?"

Nobody spoke for a moment. Then Stephen cleared his throat.

"The thing is, girls, you know, it's lovely to see you and everything, it really is. You're my gorgeous girls and I can't wait to get to know you again. But I'm a grown man, you know? I'm a grown man, with, you know, various business arrangements to set up, and there'd be various comings and goings, know what I mean? And a man needs a bit of privacy. Bit of, you know, space to get his head together. And, anyway, so I spoke to Mum, and she said—well, she said she'd only seen one of you by the way, wanted to know if you're identical and she'd just forgotten . . ." Penny rolled her eyes, to cover up how guilty she felt suddenly. "So, anyway, I think she wants me to live here now. Her son. On my own."

And he stretched out his legs, revealing a stretch of slightly grubby-looking white calf and a pair of cheap brown shoes.

"No fucking way," said Penny. They were in her bedroom, holding a council of war. Stephen was still in the sitting room; they could smell his revolting cigarettes. "I'm not going anywhere. I'm squatting."

"But what about when we go to work?" said Lizzie. Their argument was completely forgotten. It was them against the world.

They'd tried phoning their mother—although what she could do, apart from march around with a rolling pin and pound the crap out of him, which Penny couldn't see an earthly reason against at the moment—but there was a message on her phone about her being out at the zoo impersonating an antelope for drama class, and they were only to leave a message if they could bray it.

Lizzie was just miserable. For a second, a tiny second, her heart had inflated with the possibilities of having a daddy. And then—well, he'd turned out to be just the shit her mother had told them he was. Hardly surprising, given their mother had never lied to them about anything in their lives. Which was why Lizzie's expectations had been so low. Whereas Penny's had been so much higher—had she taken after their father much more, with dreams of breaking free, becoming famous, being successful, which was why she seemed to be crashing to the ground so much harder?

"Well, our father's a prick then," said Penny, sitting back against the wall. "Do you think social services would do anything?"

"What, like take us into care?"

Penny winced. "What about the police? What if we say he's not really our dad but an imposter that's trying to break into our house?"

"That would work brilliantly, until they lined you up and looked at you side by side."

"Oh, for *fuck's* sake," said Penny. "When am I ever going to catch a break?"

Lizzie shrugged. "When I do, I suppose."

There came the sound of the television being turned on followed by the noise of the horse racing.

"Oh, good," said Penny. "John McCririck is exactly the person to make all this better right now."

Lizzie sighed. "Well, listen. We're not going to sort this out sitting in here."

"We're not, eh? Oh God, I need to phone Sloan."

"Sloan will understand it's a family crisis."

"No, he won't. He believes in severing all ties with your family at eighteen and never speaking to them again."

"Apart from taking money out of his trust fund," said Lizzie. "I suppose using your cashcard can be an act of love."

"We wouldn't know," said Penny, scowling.

"Well, what I was thinking was, we could go and see Gran," said Lizzie. "Just, you know, to make sure that having *him* around is what she meant."

"She doesn't know what she means," said Penny. "Can't we just lock him in and run away? It's not like there's any food in the house. He'd die in about two days."

"There is food in the house," said Lizzie, peeved. She'd started to build up the basics of a cook's cupboard, and had been selecting olive oils, balsamic vinegars, and various staples on Georges's advice, and was annoyed Penny hadn't noticed. "You just don't eat any of it."

Penny weighed things up. Going to see their grandmother was probably the most sensible idea. But what if—and she probably would—she told them that it was OK, her only son was looking after the house now, and thanks for the help?

She didn't want to go back, she really didn't. The commute, if she were to keep her job at Sloan's—and she really wanted to—would be about four hours a day. To go anywhere with Minty and Brooke would either cost her her entire wages in taxi fees or set her back on the night bus to hell. Her chances of life looking up would go. Maybe they should just sit tight. On the other hand, he was a man they didn't know anything about. Who knew what he was capable of?

Penny looked at Lizzie. "I've never even met her," said Penny. "She's going to be really fond of me, isn't she?"

"Well, I did tell you when I was going," said Lizzie.

"Yes, yes, all right, Saint Elizabeth. No need to point it out." Penny shrugged. "What about if you go alone and I go and try and save my job?"

"I don't think that will work," said Lizzie. Penny heaved a sigh.

"OK. Are you absolutely positively sure we can't just kill him and dispose of the body?"

"*Penny!*" Lizzie was genuinely shocked.

"Oh, come on, we didn't even know for sure he still existed till ten minutes ago. And now he's clearly an idiot. Let's just kill him."

"Shh."

The girls tried to look insouciant as they walked back into the sitting room.

"Is that you off then, girls?" said Stephen who was trying to look relaxed on the sofa, though not making a very good job of it. "Great. Well, see you later, maybe Christmas, yeah?"

"We are *not* off," said Lizzie. "We're going to visit Gran, actually."

Stephen looked a bit uncomfortable.

"Oh, yeah? Great. Tell her I said hi, yeah? And I'll be off to see her soon."

Penny and Lizzie stared at him.

"So I guess you'll need a couple of days to move," said Stephen. "So maybe I'll leave the locks till then."

"That's it," said Penny. "I'm not going anywhere, you fucker."

"Shh," said Lizzie, trying to push her out the door.

"I'm sure Mum wouldn't like to hear you talk to your father like that," said Stephen, an unpleasant smile playing on his lips. "Would she, now?"

"You're not my dad," spat Penny viciously. "You're absolutely bloody no one."

"And who are you?" shot back Stephen. "I mean, you look like a tart, but it's so hard to tell these days."

Penny finally stopped shaking after they'd waited for the bus for twenty-five minutes. Lizzie knew well enough just to let her be. It was the one benefit of being pessimistic, Lizzie thought to herself. You weren't quite so open to disappointment.

They traveled in silence, Penny staring out of the window. She wanted to vow that she would never travel by bus again; she had sworn it, she remembered, when they'd first moved there. And she was getting so tired of it all.

"Come on," said Lizzie, getting up.

"Are we there?"

"No. We have another bus to get."

"Of course we do."

It was getting dark as they alighted at the end of the street. Penny found it just as spooky as Lizzie had the first time she'd come.

"I want you," said Penny, "to shoot me before I ever have to come to one of these places."

"OK," said Lizzie.

"You're not meant to say that!" said Penny in despair. "You're meant to say, 'Don't be daft, how would you ever end up in one of these places? You'll be surrounded by family and friends and grandchildren before you painlessly slip off in your sleep one night like that old lady in *Titanic*.'"

"Sorry," said Lizzie. "That's what I meant."

"You don't say, 'OK, I will take the gun and shoot you dead when you are lonely and mental, which you definitely will be because you'll have inherited the mental genes from your gran and the evil genes from your dad.'"

Lizzie patted her on the arm. "Come on," she said.

"There you are again!" said Penny. "You could have at least suggested I wasn't evil."

"You just tried to get me to help you to murder our father."

"Yes, well . . ."

Lizzie said hello to the usual staff, who were getting to know her well enough that she occasionally almost got a grunt in return, and headed toward her grandmother's open door.

"Hey, Gran," she said, knowing the old lady's closed eyes didn't necessarily mean she was sleeping, merely that she was unable to find anything of interest around her. "I didn't have time to get any flowers, I'm sorry."

"Little twin," said their gran with a smile on her face. "I get so many visitors these days! I think downstairs they think I'm the Queen."

She glanced up and took in Penny, then looked at Lizzie inquiringly, waiting to be introduced.

"And this is Penny," said Lizzie. "The other little twin."

Penny had the curious feeling of being looked up and down. She had no sense that this woman had lost her marbles at all.

"Hello, Gran," she said. "It's . . . uh, nice to see you again after all these years."

"You look like Stephen," said their gran almost instantly. "So like him."

"I'm not like him!" said Penny. "Not at all. Well, you know," she added, remembering he was Gran's only child, "a bit."

"So you've met him?" said their gran. "Is that why you're here?"

"Well, and to see you," said Lizzie.

"I know," said Gran. "How's that man you're in love with?"

Oh, great, thought Penny, bring that up. Even a senile old woman in bed knew more about Lizzie's life than her twin had noticed.

"He's engaged," said Lizzie, going pink. "To somebody else. But it's OK."

"Well," said Gran kindly, "you tried your best. You look very lovely, little twin."

"Thank you," said Lizzie, biting her lip. "I didn't try my best. But maybe next time . . . you know. If there's a next time. I could maybe try a bit harder."

"There'll be a next time," said their gran. Penny waited for her to ask a question about her, but she didn't.

"And my Stephen is back," she said. "I told you he would be, didn't I?"

"Yes," said Lizzie. "Well done you. Was it nice to see him?"

Her gran rubbed her eyes. "You love your children, Lizzie. So much. One day you'll find that out."

Lizzie doubted whether she'd ever get the chance, but she nodded and patted her gran on the hand.

"So. Did it feel strange to meet your father again?"

"Strange?" said Penny. "Well, he tried to throw us out on the street."

"What do you mean?" said their gran.

"He wants to live in your house and he doesn't want us to live there." Penny's voice sounded accusatory.

Their gran pushed herself farther up on her pillows. When she spoke again, her voice was much stronger.

"And you think . . . you, by the way, who I have only just met, who has only just come to see me . . . you think you have a right to my house?"

Penny swallowed hard. "Well," said Penny, "I thought . . ."

"What did you think? Did you think, I don't care two bits for what that old lady tried to do for me, I don't ever have to see her, but I deserve her flat?"

"No," said Penny. She looked down. "I've been busy."

"I haven't," said their gran.

"We've loved staying there," said Lizzie. "Thank you."

"That's all right, little twin," said their gran. "But, you know. Your sister . . ." She looked harshly again at Penny.

Penny didn't say anything. Lizzie nodded.

"Thank you for looking after the flat for me. But now Stephen is back . . ."

She let her voice trail off, but it was obvious what she meant. Penny slowly nodded. It was all her fault.

"Will you still come and see me, little twin?"

Lizzie nodded. "Of course," she said. "It's an easier bus ride here from Mum's anyway."

*

" 'It's an easier bus ride from Mum's anyway,' " mimicked Penny as they stood at the bus stop. She was feeling enormously guilty, and it was making her aggressive. "You are such a complete dish-cloth. She's just made us homeless!"

"She's an old woman. It's her house. And, by the way, she might not have been quite so happy to get us out if you had ever bothered . . ."

"I know, I know, I know," said Penny. "And you're perfect. What do you care? Grainne's waiting for you at home, you can get a job in any old caff—there's six thousand around the corner—and everything will be fine for you. It's just my life that's ruined."

Penny looked at her sister, wanting a reaction, but Lizzie turned away and, in the rain-spattered light from outside the home, Penny noticed for the first time that she was crying. Great big tears were running down her cheeks, collecting in a puddle with the rain.

# Chapter Fourteen

"I'm not clearing my stuff out when he's there," whispered Penny as they mounted the stairs.

"I'm sure you could leave it," said Lizzie. "It could just blend in and become part of the mess. I don't think Stephen's much tidier than his mother is."

"Oh God," said Penny. They were mounting the stairs to the apartment, possibly for the last time. Lizzie tried to take in the polished mirrors, the immaculate parquet, the works of art on the wall. Best not to think about that. "Are you absolutely *sure* we can't kill him? Surely the world would be better off without him. I'm sure I didn't notice when he wasn't around."

"Really?" said Lizzie. "I always did."

Penny stopped outside Brooke and Minty's apartment.

"Oh, no," said Lizzie.

"Come on," said Penny. "I need to see some friendly faces."

"Well, we should go somewhere else."

"No," said Penny severely. "I need to find someone who'll make us a cocktail and talk nonsense about two-hundred-and-fifty-pound boots. And I think this is the best place for it."

Lizzie, unwilling to head upstairs on her own, lingered behind her sister.

Brooke came to the door, fastening her earrings, obviously heading out.

"Darlings! How are you doing!"

"Great!" said Penny immediately. "Fabulous, in fact. Where are you off to, you gorgeous creature?"

"Oh, some boring old hunt ball. Grosvenor House again."

"Again," said Penny, trying to sound sympathetic and keep the disappointment out of her voice. "That sounds tedious."

"Alarmingly so," agreed Brooke.

"Great," said Penny. "Why don't you blow it out and we'll go and get drunk on Tanqueray and pomegranate?"

"That sounds good," said Brooke. "But I have literally hundreds of people waiting for me to be there."

Lizzie rolled her eyes.

"All tedious, of course."

"Of course."

Brooke eyed herself up approvingly in the huge hall mirror.

"I wouldn't want to keep you from your public," said Penny. "Is Minty about?"

Brooke's gaze lowered and she moved toward them into the hall.

"Ah," she said, "rather a delicate matter."

"What?"

Brooke looked around, but there was no sign of Minty behind them in the large room.

"Well," she said, "it's nothing really. Minty's just having one of her *turns*."

"What kind of turn?" asked Penny suspiciously.

"Oh, usual stuff. When a man breaks up with her. She tends to go a bit . . . hmm, what's the word?"

"Psycho?" suggested Lizzie from behind Penny.

"Yes, that's it. A bit psycho. Wanders around in a daze, trails them to their house, phones them up a million times an hour, that kind of thing."

For a moment Penny couldn't speak. Was that how it had been with . . . Then she found her voice.

"Does that . . . does that happen often?"

"Only all the fucking time," said Brooke. "It's all right, I'm quite used to it. We just say she's fragile, poor girl."

Just then Minty wandered into view. She was dressed in a hideously stained dressing gown, which didn't conceal holey pajamas that weren't buttoned properly. Her hair was a huge pile of straw, and her eyes tiny and red. She was carrying the telephone.

"Hello, Minty," said Lizzie. She knew it was wrong, but she couldn't help it. "You look tired."

Minty grunted in their general direction. "Men suck." She sniffed.

"Of course they do," said Brooke kindly.

"They do," agreed Penny, nodding vigorously.

"I don't know enough to do a statistical sample," said Lizzie. "But I've heard . . ."

"I've been phoning him nonstop for forty-eight hours," said Minty. "There's no way he can't be in for forty-eight hours! And now it's saying that that phone has been disconnected from the network! So he's not going to know I've called!"

"I'm sure he'll know you've called," said Brooke. "Now, hey, the trick is to play it cool and let him come running."

"They never do, though," said Minty, looking confused. "They start running and then they go all funny. Why is that?"

"I've told you before," said Brooke. "You've got to stop buying them pets and calling them Daddy."

Minty stuck out her bottom lip. "I love my daddy."

Penny and Lizzie looked at each other.

"Actually, we should get going," said Penny. "Call us if you need us, Minty."

"I can't call you," said Minty, as if explaining something really obvious. "I'm calling Kieran. I love him, you see."

"You don't think . . ." said Lizzie as they mounted the next flight of stairs.

"Don't say it," ordered Penny. "You weren't there. Will's a gold-digger and having a run-in with Minty the nutcase doesn't change a thing. Oh, Christ."

They had reached the top of the stairs. Outside the door were two old, stained suitcases, full to overflowing with their clothes.

Lizzie swallowed hard. "You know what? I think I'd rather be the nutcase with the daddy who loves her."

Penny banged hard on the door, then opened it with her key, which still worked.

"Hello, little twins," said Stephen. He was sitting on the patched armchair, a cigarette flickering in his fingers. "I thought I'd help you get a move on with packing. But you can leave a few things here, of course. In case you ever want to come and visit your old dad. How's the old girl, then?"

Lizzie's voice quivered as she spoke. "You'd better keep going to visit her and be really nice to her."

"Yeah, whatever," said Stephen. "Off back to your mum's, then? That's nice. Everyone lives with their mum and it all works out nice and tidy. Course Brandford's not quite so handy, is it, but then, I think it suits you two better anyway. You're more local girls than Chelsea types, don't you think?"

Penny looked at him. "You're unspeakable."

"Course I'm not, darling. I only want what's mine, don't I? We've all got our lives to lead."

Lizzie had telephoned Georges, reasoning that if there was ever a reason to ask for a favor from a friend who had a car service, it was now, but she'd got Maria-Elena on the telephone. She'd tried to explain the situation, but Maria-Elena affected not to understand a word she was saying, so it hadn't got across. It had ended up with Lizzie hanging up in despair.

"That woman is—"

"Is probably going to turn Georges into a billionaire," finished Penny, who was throwing tiny pieces of underwear into an ancient carpetbag with a fierce right hand.

Parkend Close had never looked quite as bleak as it did that night. They'd planned to spend a little bit more time in Chelsea while they figured out what to do, but it simply wasn't possible; Penny said she couldn't trust herself to spend a night in the same house as that man and not stab him with the bread knife, using the sleepwalking defense to help her get off.

It was getting on for midnight when the grimy, stinking bus deposited them, with their luggage, at the end of the road to the estate. It had been the journey from hell. Neither of them mentioned, or could bear to think of, their triumphant departure on that sunny spring morning, in the shiny black cab.

And now they were "home." They'd finally gotten through to their mother, who was sad but, she said, not entirely surprised. Stephen had had a nasty streak then, and it didn't seem to have mellowed with the years. She didn't even show much interest in how he looked or what he'd been doing, which Lizzie found astonishing.

Oh, and she was going out tonight—an unmissable rehearsal, apparently. And the lodgers were still there and she wasn't going to be able to get rid of them for a week or two. Sorry, darlings, but not to worry, she'd cook them up a huge stew the next day and everything would be much better.

Neither of them was convinced.

"I can't believe we've both got to sleep on the living-room floor," moaned Penny. "You realize this means we really are officially homeless? If I had been pregnant we could have thrown ourselves on the mercy of the council."

"Christ," said Lizzie. And she heaved her bags up the stairs.

Has the house shrunk while we were away? wondered Lizzie, lying on the patterned carpet between the ancient worsted three-piece suite.

Penny was snoring quietly beside her in an old sleeping bag that smelled of mold, but there was a banging coming from the loud rap music one of the pale weedy student lodgers was playing upstairs, and their mother wasn't even back yet. Not to mention she was going to have to get up at five in order to reach the café in time. She could probably forget about sleep altogether. But she couldn't get up and do anything either. There was nowhere to go. Nowhere at all.

Things seemed slightly better in the morning. But not much. At least the acned lodgers didn't show their faces first thing, and the sun was peering, ever so weakly, through the dirty downstairs windows, and their mother was up, at the crack of dawn as always, making white bread toast and instant coffee.

"Hello, my girls!" said their mum, and at the sight of her face—still worn, but looking a lot less tired than the last time they'd seen her—kind and concerned, Lizzie felt like tucking herself inside her mum's strong arms and never coming out again.

Their mother put some eggs on to fry. "Would you like some breakfast?"

"Uh, no thank you, Mum," said Penny and Lizzie at the same time. Their mother looked up.

"So, changed with your new London ways?" she said pleasantly. "I knew it would get you."

She put another couple of slices of bread in the toaster, and sat down with her arms folded.

"So," she said. "Did you enjoy your experiment?"

The girls looked at each other and nodded.

"I didn't expect it to end so soon," their mother said. "But I'm glad you're back."

She was, it was so wonderful to see them, especially with Lizzie looking so well. But she'd hoped that this would be their chance to fly the nest.

"It's good to see you again. Have you adopted lots of fancy ways?"

"I already had lots of fancy ways," said Penny grumpily. "I haven't changed at all."

"Hmm," said their mother. "You look different to me. What about you, Lizzie? You look different to me too."

Lizzie shrugged. "Oh, it's nothing," she said.

"It doesn't look like nothing," said their mother. "You're definitely different. Slimmer . . . more grown up."

Lizzie swallowed. Well, she supposed she had learned a few things. "Not really, Mum," she said, giving her a hug.

"You're not in love are you?" said their mother suddenly. "My little Lizzie?"

"No!" said Lizzie. "Of course not, Mum."

Penny jumped in quickly. "So," she said, "you never told us our father was such a prick . . ."

Their mother quickly turned back to the oven.

"I should have known something like this might happen," she said. "I should have . . . never trusted your gran really. But she's so old now, and he's been gone for so long . . . I didn't think it would matter. But when there's some money, Stephen will be around for a sniff. Leopards don't change their spots."

She sighed and glanced out the dirty window.

"It's the only reason you haven't seen him, you know. Because I never had any money. Sometimes I think it's almost what's kept me down. On purpose, you know. If I'd won the lottery, well, your dad would have been around like a shot." She turned to face them. "And I'm not sure it would have done you any good."

"No," said Lizzie.

"He was a bad lot," said their mother. "I'm sorry, but it's true. You two, however, are my wonderful, gorgeous girls. And I couldn't be more proud of you."

Even Penny sniffed.

"Sloan," said Penny in what she hoped was a winning tone. She had just managed to sell one of Tabitha's paintings to someone who looked so suspiciously similar to Tabitha—and had swooned so extraordinarily over them, particularly when someone else had popped into the shop—that she could only be a relative or some kind of a plant. She hoped Sloan hadn't noticed: he didn't see so well in the mornings.

"Yes?" said Sloan. He was looking at his unrequested cup of tea and Penguin biscuit as if Penny were trying to poison him. She never made him anything without being asked, begged, then finally shouted at, and even then she usually disappeared into the back of the gallery and read *Heat* for half an hour while pretending to wait for the kettle to boil.

"What's *this*?" He held up the biscuit.

"It's a chocolate biscuit. I bought it for you myself. Well, out of petty cash."

Sloan continued to look at it dubiously.

"I don't understand," said Sloan. "Has it got fish in it?"

"Oh, for goodness' sake," said Penny. "Ordinary people eat chocolate biscuits all the time, you know. Just because you're a big snob who only eats, I don't know, swan."

"You can only eat swan if you're eating with the Queen," said Sloan. "So, of course I have."

"When did you last have chips?" asked Penny.

"Game chips?"

"What are they? Like, chips with gravy?"

"Oh, my little Penelope. I do love you so."

"Good," said Penny. "Because there's something I need to ask you. You live just around the corner, don't you?"

"Well, I just can't wait to see where this is heading," said Sloan. "Book me a cab to the Ivy, will you, darling, I feel the sudden urge to leave immediately and eat fishcakes."

"I was just wondering," Penny plowed on regardless, "if you'd be interested in a lodger."

Sloan guffawed. "You?"

"What's wrong with me?" said Penny, affronted. "I'm tidy."

"And I know how much you can afford to pay me," said Sloan. "Anyway, darling, of course I already have lodgers."

"You do? Really?"

Sloan looked careless. "Well, yes. I call them lodgers. Helping out the young men in the vicinity. Builders, brickies, plumbers, that kind of thing."

"Sloan," said Penny, genuinely shocked. "You like a bit of rough!"

"Why do you think I hired you, my sweetness?"

"Bugger," said Penny. The doorbell pinged and Tabitha glided in.

"Hello," said Penny. "Where do you live?"

"I am a citizen of the sun and the moon, my dear," said Tabitha. "I have no earthly shape nor form, and I sleep with the wild wind and the high seas."

"Really?" said Sloan. "Because I've got your VAT address down as Watford."

"And Watford," said Tabitha.

"How's that meant to help me?" grumbled Penny. "Would you like a Penguin?"

"I believe so," said Tabitha gravely. "Now, tell me, my darlings. How is my party coming along?"

Sloan raised his eyes to the heavens. "I *so* have to be somewhere else." And he picked up his cane.

"If you're looking for a new lodger they're putting up scaffolding at the corner of Sloane Square," said Penny as he left.

"What a terrible loss not to have you living with me," said Sloan, sweeping out.

"So," said Tabitha, "do we have lots of people coming?"

"Loads," said Penny. The party was only two days away and she'd been extremely busy, organizing drinks and snacks—she'd gone for bright cocktails and sausages on sticks, with pineapple and cheese, also on sticks, pushed into oranges to look like hedgehogs, which she'd thought would be a nice touch, what with Tabitha being a nature lover and so on. Sloan had laughed his head off and told her it was delightfully retro.

"Excellent," said Tabitha, clapping her hands together so the rings rang out and made a noise. "According to my spirit guide it's a most auspicious day."

She cast a look around the shop. "But where is *The Daily Unfolding Meridian of the Sublime Abyss, II*?"

"That orange one?" said Penny. "Oh, we sold it this morning."

Tabitha looked cross. "To a woman? Wearing a jeweled turban?"

"Do you know, I can't remember what she was wearing," said Penny. "Uh, yes, that was her."

"Bugger," said Tabitha. "She was meant to buy it at the party. No matter. Anyway, I have something for you."

She looked mysteriously to the left and right, then drew something out from under the voluminous folds of the cloak she was wearing. It was a small burlap bag, which smelled strongly of herbs.

"Here," she said.

"What's this?" said Penny.

"It is a potion. To see off a love rival."

"A *what*?"

"Did you forget our little magic chat?"

"Uh, no. But I didn't realize you . . . you meant it."

"You must slip it in the glass of the love rival, who will then appear spotted and horrible in the eyes of the beloved."

"You are kidding?"

"Are you questioning the power of the spirits? Because, you know, they hate that."

"No," said Penny. "No, really, no. Thank you very much."

And she took the sachet and slipped it into her pocket. Of course it was completely ridiculous.

"You are so sad this morning, Lizzie," said Georges eventually. He hadn't wanted to mention it. He felt slightly uncomfortable about why she might look this way, without quite admitting to himself why.

Lizzie had assumed he knew everything about it already from Maria-Elena, and hadn't mentioned it for fear of being insensitive.

"I'm all right," she said. "Well, you know."

"I do not know," said Georges. "I know that frittata is not made better with tears, huh?"

"Well, you know about my dad . . . coming back and taking the flat . . ."

When she saw Georges's look of incomprehension, Lizzie realized he didn't know at all, he didn't have the faintest idea what she was talking about.

"I called you yesterday . . . when we had to move at short notice . . . I was wondering if we could have borrowed a car."

"I did not get a call."

"No, I spoke to Maria-Elena . . . but you didn't call back, so I presumed you were too busy or it was too rude a thing to ask you . . ."

Georges was still staring at her, so, seeing as they were quiet, he made them two cups of tea and they sat down while she told him everything. By the end, she realized her eyes were once more full of tears.

"Oh, Lizzie," Georges said many times. "Oh, Lizzie."

He didn't try and tell her what to do, or give her advice, or suggest that she be angry or indignant at her father or her grandmother. He just sat and listened thoughtfully. At the end he patted her gently on the arm. It was like being stroked by a friendly bear. Lizzie wanted to collapse onto him and stay there forever.

"This is a very sad story," he said. "And you had to take the bus all the way to Brandford with all your things?"

"It wasn't so bad," mumbled Lizzie. She felt like she was telling tales now.

"Why didn't Maria-Elena tell me?" wondered Georges.

"Well, you know . . . I thought, maybe she just didn't understand me . . . her English, you know . . ."

"Her English is perfect," said Georges. The door opened as some customers came in, and he stood up, looking annoyed.

"You know, I have some places . . . some homes around. I will be able to sort you out, I'm sure. Somewhere not so inconvenient as Brandford."

"No . . . No, Georges, it's all right. We really couldn't . . . I mean. We couldn't afford to rent a flat. At the moment. We'll be OK."

"Ah, but I'm sure we could sort something out . . ."

The idea of living in one of Georges's properties for free as some kind of a favor was so awful and embarrassing, Lizzie couldn't countenance the idea. Imagine having to work for the person who was putting you up for free.

"No, thanks," said Lizzie, a bit stiffly. "We'll be able to manage perfectly fine on our own, thank you."

Georges had to turn to serve a customer, and Lizzie headed through into the back to wash her face. She let the cool water run over her brow and into her hair, completely unaware of Georges who, having said goodbye to the customer, had turned to watch her.

## Chapter Fifteen

"So, you know. It was an interesting experience, I suppose," said Lizzie. "Like a holiday, really. But I suppose it's better to be back where we belong."

Grainne stared into her glass of cider and chewed speculatively on a McCoys crisp. Lizzie remembered turning her nose up at the restaurant opening—really. And now, here they were back in Coasters. At least in the new restaurant her feet hadn't stuck to the floor, and there wasn't a bunch of feral thirteen-year-olds messing about with the darts. There weren't any darts.

"Miss Friss says hello," said Grainne. She was being kind, Lizzie noticed, and sympathizing rather than gloating that they'd been brought back down a peg or two.

"That's nice," said Lizzie. "Say meow from me."

"She's sulking," said Grainne. "Doesn't like her new kilt."

Penny arrived. She'd never usually come out with them, but

that hadn't seemed to matter so much recently. She was wearing a smart, sober, Victorian-style blouse, which looked completely out of place among the muffin tops and pink tank tops of the bar.

"I need to plan the party," said Penny. "There's too much acne cream in the house and nowhere to sit."

"Where's Mum?"

"She's at some play in an old match factory. It's about worker exploitation. Why can't she be the kind of actress that gets friendly with Sienna Miller and gets us invited to West End openings?"

"Because we're Berrys," said Lizzie. "Nothing good can happen to us, remember?"

"So how are you, Grainne?" said Penny after she got back from the bar.

"Good," said Grainne. "I slept with an Australian at the Walkabout bar."

"Well done," said Penny. "I've heard that's really difficult to do."

Grainne looked pleased.

"So, how's the party going?" said Lizzie.

"A party?" said Grainne. "Can I come? Will there be Australians there?"

"Not just Australians," said Penny. "We're also having crisps."

Grainne looked even more pleased. Lizzie couldn't believe Penny was inviting Grainne. Six months ago she pretended she could never remember her name, even though Lizzie had known her for years.

"It's a shame," Grainne said finally. "About you having to lose your big London flat and your dad turning out to be a bastard and that," she said.

Lizzie nodded in agreement. "I know." She looked around. Maybe she could work here. No, she couldn't do that. But she knew, now, for absolutely certain, that she couldn't carry on working for Georges. It wasn't just the commute, although that was impossible; it cost her about ten percent of her wages as it was, and they put the bloody fares up once a fortnight. It was the thought of seeing Chelsea, and everyone they'd met there, drift further and further away from her. Georges and Maria-Elena would get married, and either move back to Portugal or stay away from the shop and have beautiful, chubby, dark-eyed babies and laugh a lot and things, and Penny . . .

Lizzie regarded her sister with a wry smile, watching Penny as she tried to be polite and listen to a confusing story Grainne was telling her about a dog taking a poo in her communal hallway. Penny would make it out of here. Not this time, but one of these days, with one bound she'd be free. Parkend Close was just too small for her. Lizzie had no doubt she'd keep working for Sloan, and she'd meet someone, or one of Minty's crazy friends would turn up, or . . . well, something would happen. But for her, well. Maybe not.

Lizzie smiled at Grainne when Penny went to the bathroom.

"Penny's changed a lot, hasn't she?" she said.

Grainne shrugged. "Hmm. A bit maybe. She's still the same underneath."

Lizzie wondered if this was true, watching Penny catching the eyes of several men lined up against the bar. Oh well. And she was back to being dependable old Lizzie.

"Actually," said Grainne suddenly, "the one who's really changed is you."

*

Later, when they were getting ready for bed, Lizzie told Penny that she thought Penny would escape, that she would still be a Chelsea girl.

Penny stopped brushing her teeth for a moment.

"Do you really think so?" she asked.

"I don't think it's possible that you won't," said Lizzie. "You'll probably meet someone at the party and you'll be away."

Penny grimaced and put the toothbrush down. "I'm sorry," she said. "I'm really sorry. About Georges, I mean. You know, it was . . ."

"Don't worry about it," said Lizzie. "I was kidding myself anyway."

"No, you weren't," said Penny, fiercely. "Stop underestimating yourself. You look brilliant, you're, you know, great. I know I cock things up but I just never want to . . . you know, get chucked out of my house again. I want security. Do you understand?"

"Yes," said Lizzie. "But it still seems high risk to me. Money over love and all that."

"I had love, though," said Penny. "And look where that got me."

"You had it once," said Lizzie. "You'll get it again. And it made you so happy."

"A car service would make me happy," said Penny, spitting. "Liz, you were great to me all through my . . . well, my little difficulties. And you looked after Gran and everything, even though she's a vindictive old bitch."

"Who's looking after her family," pointed out Lizzie.

"Yeah, the evil bit of it anyway," snarled Penny. "Stop bloody underestimating yourself. I bet Georges is kicking himself. With his big, hairy podgy feet."

"Stop it," said Lizzie, but without rancor.

"You've changed, Liz. You really have. For the better, with or without Ape Face."

They headed into the lounge and turned in. Lizzie was so knackered she was about to fall asleep despite the pounding Snoop Dogg coming from upstairs and the musty smell of the carpets. Just as she was nodding off, she heard Penny say, very quietly, "When he came into the café . . ."

Lizzie didn't have to ask who she meant.

"Did he . . . I mean, how was he, Liz?"

"Shocking," said Lizzie.

There was a silence.

"Good," said Penny. "He deserves to be. Doesn't he?" She didn't sound entirely convinced.

But Lizzie had already fallen asleep.


"You would never think I was from Brandford, would you, Sloan?" said Penny, at four-thirty on the day of the party. She had been bouncing about on nervous energy all day, fiddling with the tiger lilies that had been delivered, on Tabitha's instructions, at eleven on the dot so they would be opening perfectly by seven.

Revved up by Lizzie's belief that she'd have another chance, Penny had gone to town with her outfit. She was wearing a gray tweed dress she'd found in a charity shop, which fitted her like a dream, and looked like something out of the forties. She'd applied bright red lipstick and, as a finishing touch, the beret. She looked marvelous.

Sloan regarded her through half-closed eyes. He'd tutted over the wine Penny had ordered in ("Well, you did set me a budget of two ninety-nine," she'd pointed out. "And when I asked you if Chateau Loup was OK you snored at me"), and popped out to get his own, just to get them in the mood.

Penny had one glass but no more. She'd learned her lesson. Plus the last thing she needed was to do something really atrocious and lose this job. Mind you, she wondered what she could do that was so awful Sloan would sack her. It would really have to be pretty bad.

"*Crisps?*" said Sloan suddenly, noticing a pile of garishly colored packets piled up in the back room. "What on earth are they doing there?"

"Well, you said we couldn't have any food," said Penny.

"Yes."

"But I thought, if people can have a little snack they're more likely to stay longer."

"*Crisps*, though."

"Well."

"Penelope, having crisps in this shop is a sackable offense. Get rid of them, you guttersnipe."

"*Sloan*," said Penny. "What am I meant to do with two hundred packets of crisps?"

"Feed some of your illegitimate children by different fathers, I shouldn't wonder," said Sloan.

Penny tutted and threw a bag of Skips at him. They hit his wig and knocked it slightly askew.

"Can*not* get the staff these days," said Sloan. "Now, pour me another glass and get the music sorted out. The music has to be loud. Then people lean over to shout in each other's ears and sometimes they end up accidentally snogging, which is always good for a party. And also, if some fartypants critic turns up and starts bellowing about how shit they think the artwork is, no one can hear them."

"Can do," said Penny. "I've put together a compilation. Of cat-themed songs."

"Oh, yeah?" Sloan raised a skeptical eyebrow as Penny brought out the CD.

"Here we go . . . 'Lion Sleeps Tonight,' 'Lovecats,' 'Tiger Feet' . . ."

Sloan snatched the plastic box out of her hands.

"*I'll* handle the music," he said. "God, I really do have to do everything myself around here."

By seven, people were already gathering outside the doors, and by five past, the place was filling up, buzzing merrily.

"That was fast," said Sloan. "Even for Rentamob."

Penny was standing next to the door, greeting people with a big smile. She looked fabulous, she knew, partly because people kept telling her so, and partly because she was standing next to Tabitha, who was wearing a lime green muumuu with a yellow feather in her hair.

"*Namaste*," Tabitha was saying to everyone as they walked in the door. Most people said "bless you," thinking she'd sneezed.

Lizzie arrived at seven-thirty, nervous but excited. She was wearing a simple, belted dress she'd found in the Jigsaw sale, which she knew looked good on her, and she'd used Penny's lipstick. It was far bolder than she was used to, but as soon as she'd put it on she'd realized it suited her perfectly.

"Hey, look at you two," said Rob and Sven, who'd just arrived. "You look like twins."

"We are twins," said Penny. "We've met before, remember?"

"I'm sure I'd remember you," said Sven to Lizzie's breasts. Lizzie and Penny looked at each other and grinned.

Grainne sidled in looking nervous. She was wearing a black skirt and a white shirt, out of which her breasts spilled alarmingly.

"Hey, there," said Lizzie. "How are you?"

"Terrible," said Grainne. "I wore this just in case I'd misheard you and you actually wanted me to be a waitress."

"No," said Lizzie patiently. "And here. These two men are desperate to meet charming young ladies."

"They don't really have to be charming," said Rob. "Just handy."

"Are you Australian?" asked Grainne.

"Nope."

Grainne thought for a moment. "Ah, that doesn't matter. Do you like crisps?"

"Who doesn't?"

By eight the party was really starting to move. Tabitha was standing in the center, letting people come to her and allowing copious amounts of raw red wine to be poured into her glass. Sloan was sitting behind the desk, deep in conversation with several young men who appeared to be models of some sort. Penny had been grabbed by a bunch of enthusiastic young money men from a Mayfair office who were asking her to explain the history of art while attempting to pinch her bum. Normally this would have been a perfect state of affairs, Penny was thinking. Why did it feel so hollow?

Lizzie was nursing a glass of wine, happy to survey the clearly successful party—there were already red stickers on the smaller pieces, and Tabitha was gaily instructing people to buy immediately, otherwise she would do a large tiger roar at them.

Minty and Brooke had arrived with some of their louche friends, and despite spending at least twenty minutes explaining how they couldn't possibly stay long, they had much more exciting plans elsewhere, they were still here, listening to the ridiculous pop music Penny had finally managed to get on the stereo, and clearly enjoying themselves. Minty was in a corner with Sven, tossing her shiny blond hair meaningfully and giving him a slightly unhinged wide-eyed smile. Lizzie wondered how on earth she could ever have been scared of her. Even Krystanza had turned up, with a photographer in tow so he could get pictures showing how cultured she was. Unfortunately her bosoms were obscuring the view for the other punters, but it couldn't be helped.

Then a sleek black car drew up. Of course. Lizzie nodded her head. If it was up to her, Georges would walk everywhere, not sit in the back of a big car, getting podgy.

But it wasn't, of course.

The doors of the car opened and Georges and Maria-Elena got out from opposite sides. It was odd, mused Lizzie, eyeing them from her vantage point at the window, that they didn't talk to each other at all. Their body language was extremely frosty. Maybe they'd had a row about something. She didn't think it would be difficult for Maria-Elena to pick a fight with someone. Probably didn't want to come to evil Penny's party, and she supposed she couldn't blame her, after the terrible display Penny had put on.

Nonetheless, Georges, courteous as ever, stood on the outside edge of the pavement, and made sure he opened the gallery door for his future bride. Of course he would, thought Lizzie, going forward to say hello. She was going to have to tell him she was leaving. In fact, she should tell him sooner rather than later. The faster she stopped having to pay these ridiculous bus fares the better, and he had plenty to do with organizing the wedding and whatnot.

"Lizzie," he said, his face, as always, bursting with warmth. "You get more . . . well." He stopped himself. "What a lovely party."

"Hello, Maria-Elena," said Lizzie. Maria-Elena raised her eyebrows and handed her coat to Georges without looking at him. She grabbed a glass of wine and went off to look at the paintings.

"Actually, I have to talk to you," said Lizzie.

"Oh, yes?" said Georges.

"It's about . . . well, I have to . . ."

Just then, Tabitha Angelbrain Dawson rang her fork sharply against her glass and made a loud "huhhummm."

Sloan, who'd looked to be dropping off to sleep, raised his head. "Oh, Christ," he said. "What is this, a fucking Cheshire wedding?"

"I just wanted to say, thank you all so much for coming to my party," began Tabitha in very loud, imperious tones.

"Who's that?" Sven could be heard asking plaintively over the crowd.

"Well, of course, I say my party, but I like to think it's really the spirits' party. They have guided me—I am merely the vessel. A toast. To the gods of creativity, of animalistic spirit, and of course, to the inner-leonine passion that has guided us all here today."

She raised her glass impressively.

"To the gods of creativity . . . animal blah blah, spirit, blah

blah, mmm mmm," said the rest of the crowd, raising their glasses too.

"And buy lots of the damn things," said Tabitha. "There's a free packet of crisps with each one."

There was a huge round of applause at this, then everyone went back to quaffing their wine, throwing it back quickly before it peeled the enamel off their teeth. The chat level increased commensurately.

"What?" said Georges urgently.

"Sorry?" said Lizzie, who'd got slightly sidetracked by trying to work out what exactly Tabitha had stenciled in gold on her fingernails. They looked like claws. Also, the woman with the Nicole Kidman nose from her first day at the gallery had just walked in, and had bypassed Lizzie without a second glance. Lizzie wasn't certain whether to be pleased or slightly annoyed by this. Even Sloan hadn't insulted her or anything. She supposed she was fitting in around these parts, just as she was about to head on the long way home. And there, she reflected, wherever she ended up, she was going to be completely out of place again. God, life was annoying. She sighed.

"Lizzie," said Georges, snapping his fingers. "You are in a dream."

"Oh, sorry," said Lizzie. She swallowed hard. She wasn't looking forward to doing this, but there was no way around it. She had to be brave, and upfront, and all the things Georges and her gran kept telling her to be. Get it over with.

"Georges," she said. "I have to . . . I mean. I resign."

There. She'd said it now. It was out of her mouth and out of her hands.

"No," said Georges. "No, you cannot! I need you, Lizzie."

"Of course you don't," spluttered Lizzie. "I think you're doing OK, don't you?"

She looked meaningfully at his expensive watch.

Georges blinked rapidly.

"But . . . you know, I say already, I can help find you somewhere to live and . . ."

"Georges, I'm not an abandoned dog. I can look after myself."

"I know that, Lizzie, but . . ."

His face was stricken. "But . . ." He seemed to be searching for the words.

Penny had been listening to a monopolies manager trying to explain to her what his job entailed. He'd lost her about ten minutes ago, but she was nodding politely and trying to look alert and interested. She glanced sideways; Lizzie and Georges seemed deep in conversation.

"Excuse me," she said with her most professional smile. "I have to go and look after all my clients."

"Of course," said the man charmingly. "I'm sorry to have monopolized you. Ha, ha, get it?"

Penny composed her features into a look of surprise. "Oh! Aha! You're so funny! Now, excuse me."

And she sidled up to Maria-Elena to size her up.

"Hello," she said coolly. "Having a good time?"

"What do you expect?" said Maria-Elena. "This town is no good for Georges. Is full of whores who want his money."

"You think?" said Penny.

"The women here . . . they are tarts, they drink, they cannot dress. I heard Chelsea was a smart part of town. Hah! It is disgusting. How anyone could live here I cannot imagine."

Penny felt down into her handbag. Goddamn it, if all Tabitha's potion did was give someone a nasty stomach, this witch was getting it right now.

"Here, give me your glass. I'll refill it," said Penny with her smoothest smile. "Maybe you can forget for a few hours your life of terribly upsetting luxury."

"No!" said Maria-Elena. "What, you think I want to drink more of that gut rot and get staggering and vomit like the English girls?"

"Just a bit," said Penny desperately, seizing the glass. "Who knows, it might melt your iron knickers."

She poured some wine from a nearby table, then turned away slightly to get the herbs in.

"What are you doing?" screeched Maria-Elena, loud enough to be heard above the hubbub. "What are you doing with my glass?"

"Nothing!" said Penny, jerking suddenly and spilling the contents all over the floor.

"What is this? Georges! Georges! She is trying to poison me!"

"I'm not trying to poison you," said Penny, desperately trying to force the herbs back into her bag. OK, as whims went, this one was really dumb. "Stop being stupid."

Georges came over. "What is it?"

"Nothing," said Penny, putting her hands behind her back.

"Show me that glass!" ordered Maria-Elena. "Georges, she is trying to poison me. Phone the police immediately."

"Of course she is not trying to poison you," said Georges, adding something sharp in Portuguese. In response, Maria-Elena merely pointed at Penny, who still had her hands defiantly behind her back.

Georges looked apologetic. "Penny, please, can you show us the glass? So we can sort this out."

"No," said Penny. "Uh, I mean, what glass?"

"Don't be silly, please," said Georges. His face was imploring. "You know Maria-Elena is a little . . . how should I say, highly strung."

The entire room now (except for Sloan, who had vanished) was watching the scene in silence. Penny looked around feeling cornered, and slowly brought the glass around. Sure enough, traces of the herbs were very clear on the rim.

"See!" shouted Maria-Elena. "See!"

Penny rolled her eyes. "I'm not trying to poison her."

"But what is this, Penny?" asked Georges, looking grave.

Tabitha swooped in on them like a vast purple eagle.

"Ah, my dears. You tinker in the dark arts at your peril."

"What?" said Georges.

"This is a little potion I made up for Penny . . . you are very naughty, by the way."

"It was only a joke," said Penny sulkily.

"What kind of a potion?" demanded Maria-Elena.

"I am gifted by the spirits in many ways," said Tabitha, "and Penny asked me to do a love potion. It is to see off a rival."

"Yes. *Poison!*" screamed Maria-Elena.

"It's not poison," said Penny. "Plus it could hardly make you any uglier," she added, not quite quietly enough.

"I *knew* you are after him!" Maria-Elena's face had gone completely puce. Georges just looked bamboozled. Penny looked embarrassedly at Lizzie, who was also looking completely disbelieving.

"So did I," said Lizzie. "For Christ's sake." And she turned away.

"But I did it for you, Lizzie," shouted Penny. "You know I did. I mean, if it really worked. Plus it would only have been a few boils or something. Enough to postpone a wedding, anyway."

"You don't do anything for anyone else," said Lizzie. "Just yourself."

"You've got to believe me," said Penny.

"You've got to get over here while Georges calls the police," said Maria-Elena. "Call the police, Georges. Now. *Now!*"

"Do not speak like that, please," said Georges. "I will not call the police. This is all very silly."

"Call the police, you *grande cabrao*!"

Georges looked shocked, and Penny bounded for the door. Bugger them, she thought. Bugger Lizzie, bugger Georges, bugger Chelsea, bugger London, bugger the world. She was getting out.

She reached the door and pulled it open, not noticing the trembling figure on the other side of the glass.

Standing there panting, damp, agitated, filthy, and emaciated, with a desperate look in his eye, stood Will.

# Chapter Sixteen

"Penny!" shouted Will. "You have to come with me."

He stepped up into the doorway of the gallery.

"To live with a gold-digger under a bridge?" said Penny. "No I fucking don't."

She tried to push past him, conscious that it absolutely was not beyond Maria-Elena to follow her and grab her by the hair, in preparation for a good slapping.

"You do. You have to come. It's your house."

"What do you mean, my house?"

"Your house. In Chelsea."

"That's not my house," said Penny. "Oh, you haven't been keeping up, have you?"

"Shut up!" said Will. "There's no time for that. It's on fire!"

For a second nobody spoke. Then there was a yelp from the back, as Brooke realized that if the twins' place was going up in smoke, theirs would be too.

"My Birkin bag!" she yelped. And immediately everyone started to move.

Lizzie and Penny tore down the streets with Will, who was exhausted, falling behind them. The rest of the gallery stood watching, Maria-Elena spitting blood oaths as Georges immediately shouted that he was phoning for a fire engine.

"I can explain," puffed Penny as they rounded Redmond Street.

"Don't," said Lizzie, her face clouded in pain.

Sure enough, smoke was billowing from the second-floor windows. They halted, inhaling the unfamiliar burning smell.

"Oh God," said Penny. "It must have been Stephen."

"Those bloody cigarettes," said Lizzie. "You don't think . . ."

They turned to each other, the same thought in their minds. Was he still in there?

Just as they thought this, Lizzie caught sight of it. At the kitchen window. A white smudge, banging hard. Their father's hand.

"Look!" she screamed. "Look! He's up there!"

They looked around. The fire engine hadn't arrived yet. There was nothing else for it.

"Have you still got the keys?" yelled Lizzie, rushing to the door.

"Oh God," said Penny again. "Well, yes. I like to look at them sometimes. Not for sentimental reasons or anything."

"Quick, then," said Lizzie. Penny would rather have waited for the fire engines, but couldn't help being impressed by Lizzie's all-action stance.

Even from outside the front door they could feel the oppressive heat; cautiously they went in.

"We've got to put something over our mouths," said Lizzie as they inched upward holding the banister, which felt warm to the touch.

"Why?" said Penny, who was trembling with adrenaline.

"I don't know, do I? Saw it in a bloody film."

With no small heartbreak, knowing this was likely to be the last of her nice dresses for quite some time, Penny pulled at the neckline of the antique frock until most of the top came away, and tore the paper-thin material in two.

"Here you go."

"Thanks. We're meant to wet it or something."

They were outside the door to their flat now. Although the big thick door was holding the flames back, they immediately had a sense of the terrifying force of the heat that was behind it.

"Oh God," said Lizzie. "Oh God, Oh God."

"Are you sure you saw him?" said Penny. "Why hasn't he broken the window?"

"I don't know, do I? OK. We should probably push open the door, then run backward."

"I like the running backward."

"In case the flames jump out or something. Why did I spend the whole of *Backdraft* thinking about William Baldwin naked?"

Penny shrugged. "I dunno, I spent it snogging Fingall Mc-Stankie because he had a motorbike."

"OK," said Lizzie, fitting the key in the lock. "One, two, three . . ." She turned the lock and they both pushed the door, then jumped back into the stairwell. Immediately the flames burst out with a roar.

"Shit," said Penny. There was a sound of sirens, but it was very far away in the distance. Now they could hear, "Help! Help!" very faintly from inside.

"Bollocks," said Lizzie. She peered in. Everywhere in the huge apartment, crap was burning: timetables, newspapers. and macramé. The entire place had always been a fire hazard waiting to happen.

"OK," she said to Penny.

Penny looked at her. "We're going in, aren't we?" she said, her teeth chattering.

"We have to," said Lizzie. "Unless, you know, you still want to kill him and everything?"

Penny, the choking smoke already getting to her eyes, shook her head.

"OK," said Lizzie. "Down low. He's by the kitchen window. We'll take an arm each."

Penny nodded.

"Shall we do it on three again?"

"Yup."

They looked into the burning apartment.

"OK," said Lizzie.

"I just want to say . . ." Penny started.

Lizzie looked at her. "Don't be stupid. One . . ." said Lizzie.

"I know," said Penny. "But I love you."

"I love you, too, you idiot. OK. Two . . . THREE."

They burst into the flat on all fours. Lizzie half shut her eyes and relied on her memory to locate the sink, Penny followed on her heels.

"*Dad!*" shouted Lizzie. "*Dad!*"

"I'm over here," came the voice, followed by a lot of coughing and choking. Peering upward Lizzie saw him. The kitchen cabinets had caught now, and he was crouching down, underneath the sink. The tap was running, and he'd drenched himself and the ground around him.

"I'm burned!" he shouted.

"Follow us!" said Lizzie.

"I can't move," he said. "I can't. I just can't."

"Of course you can," said Lizzie, looking around worriedly. There came a roar from the far side of the room as the old dusty curtains went up.

"I can't," said Stephen. "I'm not brave like you two."

"Yes, you are," said Lizzie, starting to panic. If he didn't move, they'd all get stuck here and they'd all die.

"I can't!"

"*Please!*"

As Lizzie shouted, choking on the smoke, she realized that this was something she'd been screaming to her dad since the day he left, and great heaving sobs threatened to overtake her in the burning room.

"I can't," Stephen repeated.

Penny scrabbled up next to Lizzie, giving her a push on the knee.

"Of course you can," said Penny. "You're just a complete old prick. Come on. We have to go. We *really* have to go," she said, as the smaller panes of glass on the windows started to shatter. She linked her arm under his and Lizzie grabbed the other one, and in a strange, crab-like maneuver, they scrabbled their way out to the door, chests heaving with the effort.

They cascaded directly into Georges and Will, who'd just reached the top of the stairs.

"Lizzie!" screeched Georges.

"Penny!" yelled Will, as Penny went crashing straight into him. Unbalanced, all five of them collapsed down the stairwell. They rolled over, cushioning each other, until they landed with a bump outside Brooke and Minty's door, where Brooke and Minty had formed a human chain with willing bankers from the gallery and were passing out a line of expensive shoeboxes.

Penny disentangled herself and leapt to her feet, the adrenaline causing her to ignore the bumps and bruises all over her body, and screamed to be heard over the deafening sirens.

"Is it just me, or is this building on fire!" she hollered. "Get out of here."

Minty looked at her. "You know water damage is the worst, don't you?"

As if on cue, the sirens ceased, and the first, huge, tumbling deluge of water came piling through the windows, dripping down on top of their heads.

"Out! Everyone out!" bellowed Georges, and those who could, ran, and those who couldn't were helped out of the building and onto the street below, which was now filled with rubberneckers and hundreds of hunky-looking firemen. Minty's face brightened immediately.

Lizzie couldn't quite piece together what happened next. She had a vague impression of her dad being whisked to hospital, of lots of people talking to her—but she couldn't hear what they were saying. Or, they were saying something, but she didn't understand what they were talking about, or what language it was in. She had no idea how much time had passed, as the water was trained on the building, which took on the appearance of a bedraggled and ruined wedding cake left out in the rain. It wasn't falling down, though. The firemen were smiling, and kept giving her thumbs-up, so she guessed that maybe it wasn't going to burn down to the ground. In fact, there weren't even any flames anymore. A friendly policeman gave her a cup of tea, and a neighbor came up with a small tot of brandy and a foil blanket to go around her shoulders.

"There, there," they seemed to be saying, but their voices didn't quite match their words. Suddenly she noticed Georges was kneeling beside her, holding her hand, which seemed nice enough, so she didn't move a muscle, just watched Penny and Will, who seemed to be silently yelling at one another.

"I'm not yelling," said Penny, who was still coasting on adrenaline and felt massively, hugely invigorated by what had just happened.

"That's good," said Will. "Could you whisper with a little less volume, then? And really, please, will you sit down, have a drink of something."

"No," said Penny. "And I don't want a silver blanket either, thank you."

"It's very you," opined someone from the crowd.

"And your bra is showing," said Will. Penny remembered she'd had to rip up her dress, and accepted the blanket—and, while she was at it, the brandy.

"I just want to know . . . what were you doing lurking outside my house?"

"I wasn't lurking," said Will. "I didn't know you'd moved."

"So what were you doing? Stalking?"

"No," said Will. He looked around, then, from behind one of the trees, picked up his art materials.

"Actually," he said, "I was doing this. It was for you. To say sorry."

He pulled out the canvas. It showed a beautiful, exquisite watercolor of their building. Every elegant window, every curlicue of the builder's art was there, every shade of the trees on the road. At the front door was a figure, small, but recognizable. With the blond hair and the combative stance, it was Penny, clearly, slipping out of the building and into the autumn light, a huge bunch of cornflowers in her arms. She wasn't naked, or on a sinking ship. But it was beautiful.

"I was going to give it to you. But not in a stalking kind of way. Just to say I was sorry. I knew you wanted to pose for me. Then I was going to be a very good, tortured-artist type and disappear forever, I promise."

"But, instead, you set my house on fire."

"No!" said Will, looking shocked. "That wasn't me."

"Looks like a cigarette, love," said a passing policeman. "Usually is. Did anyone in the house smoke?"

"Uh, just a bit," said Penny.

"Just as well you two were here, eh?"

"Do you know," said Penny, "I think that's the first time that would ever have occurred to him. Is he going to be OK?"

"Should be," said the ambulance man. "Bit of smoke inhalation, third-degree burn to the leg. Made a hell of a fuss. I'm a bit worried about your sister, though. I think she might be in shock."

Penny looked over to where Georges was kneeling on the

ground, oblivious of the water cascading over his expensive trousers and shoes.

"She's in good hands," she said.


"Oh, my *gawd*," Minty was saying. "Look at this painting! It's our house! It's fab. I want one! I'll buy it with the insurance money! Quick, Brooke, hide those shoes! Insurance! Is that me, Will?"

"No," said Will.

"Are you sure?" Minty's bottom lip was pushed out in time-honored fashion.

"I can do you one, if you like," said Will. "With you in it."

"It'll be very, *very* expensive, though," said Penny.

Will looked at her. "What are you talking about?"

"You know. When I become your business manager."

"What do you mean?"

Penny rolled her eyes. "Well, you may want to live in that garret forever, but I certainly don't."

She watched him carefully, gauging his reaction.

"Do you . . . uh, what do you mean?" said Will, trying to disguise the wobble in his voice.

"Look," said Penny. "There wasn't any baby. It was a mistake. Not a trick, or blackmail, or a test. Just a mistake."

"I know," said Will. "Lizzie told me."

Penny's eyes went wide. "You *knew*? And you still didn't bother coming to see me or anything?"

"I thought it was too late," said Will. "Even though there wasn't a baby, I'd still behaved so badly . . . You looked so angry at me at the damn restaurant."

"I was . . . I was confused," said Penny. "Then you started yelling and . . ."

Will was gazing at her. "Could you bear it?" he said. "Never being rich, I mean?"

Penny stared at him, her heart in her throat.

"You know, about twenty minutes ago," she said, "I wasn't entirely sure I was even going to be alive. So I don't know how bothered I am really. As long as I'm with you, I mean."

"Are you sure, Penny? Are you sure?"

Penny looked at Will's gorgeous open, honest face and thought of the stupid ideas she was leaving behind, the scheming, and the jostling and maneuvering into position. Life could go up in a puff of smoke.

"God, yes," she said, and rushed into his arms, kissing him passionately, even though they both tasted of charcoal.

Lizzie stirred. Someone was speaking to her, she could hear it now. It was a lovely voice, a kind, sweet, gentle voice, one she loved very much. Was it her mother? No, it was a man, definitely. She let it tinkle on, like a wandering stream, and felt herself come back into herself, back together. She remembered why she was here, and what had happened, and that everyone was all right, and that the person talking to her was—Georges.

". . . and so," finished Georges, an intense look on his face. "After all that, that is why I am asking you, will you marry me?"

Lizzie shook her head and blinked hard. "Sorry?" she said. Georges was kneeling on the wet road in front of her. "*What* did you just say?"

"Ah, well, it was a long speech, you know, Lizzie. I do not

think I can repeat it again. Especially, you know, now, with all this weight on my knees."

He looked at her face. "But for you, of course, I will repeat. To say, this: I do not love Maria-Elena. That was a mistake to please my family. Sometimes you cannot always please your parents, huh, Lizzie? Well, what would you know about this?"

"Uh-huh," said Lizzie. Her heart was going pitter-patter. Fortunately she could not see the dirt and soot covering her face. Even though he was facing her, and gazing deeply into her eyes, Georges couldn't see it either.

"It was a mistake. She told me so, too. She will go. She thinks we are all disgraceful."

Lizzie nodded.

"And, you know, when you said you would not move into one of my houses, my heart was broken. And when you said you were leaving, I thought, this cannot be. I spoke to your sister, OK, I think maybe she is crazy."

"She is crazy."

"But she says that you maybe have feelings for me too and she was pretending to like me to get rid of Maria-Elena. Although this I do not believe. Who could not like me? And also that I am a big idiot elephant."

Penny and Will had come dashing over, hand in hand, full of the joys. Eyes sparkling, Penny came up behind him.

"You are," she said. "You're a big idiot elephant."

"Lizzie," said Georges. "You know me. I am not a man of half measures. I am not a man who says what he does not mean, or wastes time. All I have, is yours. My heart, my soul."

"His car service," muttered Penny, as Will took the executive decision to take her away to the side of the road and quietly snog her up a bit.

"So, Lizzie, I ask. Would you like to be my wife?"

Lizzie squinted at him. "I think I must be concussed."

"That is why I choose my moment now. You know. Take advantage of you while you are in a weak state."

Lizzie looked at him. "Oh, Georges. Oh, yes. Oh, yes, please."

And she jumped up, shrugged off the silver blanket, and threw her arms around his big strong shoulders.

# Chapter Seventeen

They moved slowly and carefully, one twin on either side as their gran was taken out of Georges's car and into the waiting wheelchair. Only two people per bed were allowed at visiting time, but the hospital was making an exception for the twins and their gran. It had been a long process picking her up from the old people's home. Lizzie had managed with ease to persuade Georges to give her the day off—in fact, they were both taking far too much time off, seeing as they had spent most of the last two weeks staring at each other—and Penny had left Sloan hanging Will's new exhibition—a collection of Chelsea town house paintings, which seemed likely to sell out as fast as he could finish them, both to the residents and the aspirationals.

The hospital smelled just like Gran's room. "Ah, home," she said, as the double doors opened automatically.

"Which ward?" said Penny.

"Honeysuckle," said Lizzie. "Down here."

Lizzie had expected to feel more nervous about going to visit her dad, but she wasn't. Partly because he didn't scare her anymore—he was just a man, a weak man—and partly because she was wrapped in such a cloak of happiness, very little could penetrate it. She had moved into Georges's flat right away—it was very tidy and practical, and she had set about trying to make it a little more homely and comfortable. Maria-Elena had left no traces at all, except an invoice that had arrived for her first-class flight home and other expenses. Georges had laughed, and paid it straightaway, apologizing fulsomely to Maria-Elena for wasting her time.

Since then it had been a blur of food and sex so unlike anything Lizzie had associated with the words before it made her go pink even thinking about it.

Only once had she asked timidly, in bed one morning, "Georges . . . when I started working with you and I was, you know, fat and a bit spotty and stuff . . . did you like me then?"

"Ah, *cara*. Of course I like you. I think you are very nice girl. But when you become beautiful, when I come back from Portoogal. That is when I fall in love with you. I cannot help myself, I am a man, and I love beautiful things. You want an Englishman, huh, who does not care and wears sports pants with lager on them and goes on television on *Trisha* to shout in the mornings?"

"No," said Lizzie, but still felt oddly insecure all of a sudden.

"Of course, now I love you forever," said Georges, turning over to face her. "So you can grow fat, grow moustache, I don't care."

"I don't want to grow a moustache!"

"Fine, grow goatee. Maybe some sideburns, huh? And an ear, here, on top your head. And a tail."

"Georges!"

"A tail, very useful for many things. You can pick fruit, peel bananas."

"Come here."

Penny had almost the opposite conversation, lying naked on the ancient couch she'd covered with a new throw, watery sun coming through the windows, showing up the motes of dust in the room as Will sketched.

"Of course I fell in love with you when I saw you," said Will. "Well, I thought you were a fox. Then I filled the rest in about six hours later."

Penny grinned ruefully. "And my postcode. You loved my postcode."

"Oh, shush. You were at it, too."

She smiled at him. "I don't think I even knew what love was. Till you went away."

Will, very carefully, put the paintbrush down.

Penny couldn't care less about visiting the hospital. But that was good. It meant she didn't hate him anymore. She didn't hate anyone. It was done, and she was through with it.

In fact, Penny was privately full of the not unpleasant—but unfamiliar—sense of self-sacrifice that came with pretending not to mind that Lizzie was living in a duplex in Eaton Square while she was commuting back to a bin liner in Clapton every night. But every time she got on that daft old bus, her heart leapt with joy. She couldn't help it. Knowing Will would be waiting at home with a dirty brush stuck behind his ear, ready to tease her and make her laugh—and, if they didn't learn to be a little bit more careful, probably make a real baby one of these days, and then what kind of a pickle would they be in?

They turned into the ward and asked the Sister which bed he was in. She indicated the fourth one down, which had the curtains drawn around it.

"OK," said Lizzie. "Deep breath."

Penny pulled back the curtain, patting her grandmother on the shoulder at the same time.

"Hello," she said. But the bed was empty.

"Well, the doctors didn't sign him out," said the Sister, after the ward staff and security had been alerted. "But you know, we're not a prison. We can't keep anyone here who doesn't want to be here."

"I know that," said Penny. "Was he OK?"

"Perfectly recovered, yes."

"And he didn't leave a forwarding address?"

The ward clerk shook his head. "Sorry, miss. I think he's just gone."

"Oh, Gran," said Lizzie, reaching down to give her a hug. "I'm so sorry."

"That's all right," said their gran. "I'm . . . I'm used to it."

She looked up at the two girls.

"I backed the wrong horse, didn't I, my dears? With you two lovely girls. But families . . . you know how it is. You love them and hate them all at once."

Lizzie and Penny traded a glance. Yes, they knew how it was.

"Take me back to the Larches," said their gran. "I'm so tired. Everything tires me so."

"I know," said Lizzie, "shall we stop for tea first?"

Their gran put up her hand to touch Lizzie's face. "You saved his life," she said.

"I helped!" yelped Penny.

"You're such good girls, little twins," said their gran. "Even you, the slutty one. I want . . . I've made up my mind. I want to turn the flat over to you two. It's for you. I hope you have more luck there than I did. Or Stephen, for that matter. I'm giving it to you. I've got my solicitor's number back at the Larches."

She looked wistful for a moment, then snapped out of it.

"That's my home now. And do you know why I like it? Because it's so *tidy*."

And she let out an old-lady cackle as they wheeled her back toward the automatic doors.

They walked with trepidation toward the front door. What if Stephen was back? What would it look like inside? The insurance money would turn up, but most of that would go to restoring the plasterwork and exterior of the building, there was so much to do.

The hallways had just about dried out, but there were big patches of damp here and there, with strips hanging off the wall. They mounted the stairs carefully.

On the landing, the door opened. It was Brooke.

"Thank *God*," she said. "You're coming back, aren't you?"

The twins shrugged.

"It's boring as *anything* without you. Same old, same old premieres, yah? Bloody red carpet, I am just so *fed up* with it. Plus Minty's in love with a fireman and driving him absolutely bloody crackers as usual."

"I'm glad to hear it," said Penny.

319

Brooke eyed her. "There's something different about you," she said.

"Just being myself." Penny smiled, as they continued up the once-beautiful stairwell to the front door. Now it was blackened, peeling.

"Here goes," said Lizzie. They pushed open the door together and stared into the room.

The entire floor was knee-deep in ash, rubble, and water-stained debris. Everything small and flammable—all the papers, all the pictures, all the collections, all the bric-a-brac, all the baskets, all the macramé. It was all gone. There was none of it left, just ash upon the floor.

The table was still there, but the nasty mismatched chairs were a pile of charred sticks on the floor; the horrid filthy curtains mere scraps of material at the tops of the windows. Apart from the smaller kitchen panes, which had been blown out, the huge sitting-room window was intact, and, thanks to several thousand liters of water, blasted clean. It let huge swathes of light into the room, now huge, open, and practically empty. The girls stood and stared.

"It's . . . it's beautiful," said Lizzie. Penny just nodded, overcome by emotion. Will could have a studio here . . . it would be so perfect for him. And her. They would be back. And everything would work . . . if Lizzie still wanted to live with Georges, of course. They were planning a wedding already. Penny couldn't have imagined her safe, dull, quiet sister doing anything quite so crazy as agreeing to marry a man she'd never even kissed. But somehow, two weeks later, she couldn't have imagined her *not* doing it.

"So . . ." said Lizzie.

"So," said Penny. "Once this place is done up it's going to be . . ."

"Yeah," said Lizzie.

"So, do you . . ."

They were both being incredibly polite to each other.

"Penny," said Lizzie. "I . . . I'm going to live with Georges. I love this place, but I think you should live here. If you want. You know, it's yours."

Penny nodded, her brow furrowing. It definitely sounded like there was a "but" on the end of that sentence. And, looking around she realized what it was. Of course. The person who'd done everything for them. Who'd never complained. Who'd always looked out for them.

"Yeah, yeah," she said. "It's not all that. You know, Clapton's a really up-and-coming place. I wouldn't move from there for anything, really. I think Will and I are making it fashionable all on our own."

"Really?" said Lizzie. "I mean, it's OK for me, I'm sorted, but . . ."

"No, don't be an idiot," said Penny. "What do you take me for, some kind of spoiled, shallow princess?"

"Never," said Lizzie. "Never in a million years."

Penny picked up her phone. "Mum? We've got a surprise for you. How do you feel about launching your West End career from . . . well, the West End?"

# Acknowledgments

Thanks to Ali Gunn of Gunn Media, Jo Dickinson, Ursula Mackenzie, Tamsin Barrack, Louise Davies, Kerry Chapple, and all the reps at Little, Brown.

Tally Gardiner, Lynne Drew, Rachel Hore, and Deborah Schneider; Debra Sweeney for saving my copywriting bacon; Chris Manby for plotting help; Joaquim Caetano, whose English is *much* better than Georges's, and the Board, by far the most fun office I've ever worked in.

Special thanks to Marina and Galina, without whom—no book; Andrew Mueller, Roni Dutta, Theo Burrow, and Roseline Beaton for friendship and emergency babysitting; my family; and all my love to Mr. and Baby B.

# ALSO BY JENNY COLGAN

WEST END GIRLS

CHRISTMAS AT THE ISLAND HOTEL

500 MILES FROM YOU

WHERE HAVE ALL THE BOYS GONE?

DIAMONDS ARE A GIRL'S BEST FRIEND

AMANDA'S WEDDING

MY VERY '90S ROMANCE

THE BOOKSHOP ON THE SHORE

CHRISTMAS ON THE ISLAND

THE ENDLESS BEACH

CHRISTMAS AT LITTLE
BEACH STREET BAKERY

THE CAFÉ BY THE SEA

THE BOOKSHOP ON THE CORNER

SUMMER AT LITTLE BEACH
STREET BAKERY

LITTLE BEACH STREET BAKERY

THE CHRISTMAS SURPRISE

CHRISTMAS AT ROSIE HOPKINS'
SWEETSHOP

CHRISTMAS AT THE CUPCAKE CAFÉ

WWW.JENNYCOLGAN.COM